# Scopophilia

by

## Selby Parker

WIPF & STOCK · Eugene, Oregon

Wipf and Stock Publishers
199 W 8th Ave, Suite 3
Eugene, OR 97401

Scopophilia
By Parker, Selby
Copyright©2006 by Parker, Selby
ISBN 13: 978-1-5326-4841-0
Publication date 1/23/2018
Previously published by PublishAmerica, LLLP, 2006

# Dedication

To my wife Fay for her love and strong support for making the difference in guiding this novel to completion during hard times with three hungry children to feed and another on the way. Three-fourths of the manuscript was written while I was a counseling psychologist with the U.S. Department of Veterans Affairs in New Orleans, Louisiana.

# Chapter 1

The headlights of the forest-green Mercedes played along the curve of the thick hedge bordering South Lakeshore Drive on Lake Serene. Lake Serene in South Mississippi was nestled among hundreds of wooded acres with dogwood and pines trees in abundance. Feeling particularly lonely, Collier had been on the move so much lately—New York, Miami, London, and Switzerland. It also looked like rain tonight, further adding to his mood.

The headlights reflected on the drive leading up to his lakeside home, shelter and delight, his wife used to say. Easing the Mercedes into the garage. he noted the vapor lights were on for protection. The house had a security alarm system, plus Karris and Heidi, but Osmond housed them on his Saturdays off.

A gentle zephyr blew through the pines as Collier paused to reflect on the stillness of the night. No moon was in sight, no creatures stirring about. He gazed into the interior of the den through the translucent glass doorway off the portico in front of the house, and was curious why the den light was not on, since this was standing orders for Osmond.

Easing his key into the lock of the large redwood door, Collier quietly stepped inside. He felt an odd feeling in the pit of his stomach. A feeling he had long since repressed, so he thought. He imagined a peculiar odor, but he could not associate it with anything in particular. Nervous perspiration broke out like beads on his forehead as he stood in the darkness.

Was he overreacting? he asked himself in the darken hallway.

Slipping off his loafers, he listened intently before padding across the den and up the short flight of steps to the upper bedroom landing. He paused to peer along the darkened hallway. The darkness could be a friend, his training had taught him in the Marines. But in the darkness, there was death as his thoughts turned to Viet Nam.

Soft, pale light reflected below the closed master bedroom door as the rain began to patter lightly on the cedar shake roof. He was trembling, a reaction to the tension and adrenalin coursing through his body. In the absolute silence, he began to feel the rhythm of his pulse, with his back against the board-on-batten redwood paneling in the hallway.

Unmindful of the threat, he threaded on tiptoe closer and closer to the bedroom door. Collier had killed in the war. He knew he had the capacity to kill again if necessary. As a student of the martial arts and a member of the Black Belt Hall of Fame, he could choke a man to death using *Nami Juji Jime*. Instinctively, he readied himself for the automatic impulse of attack and defense. Collier emptied his mind, as in Eastern philosophy, for total commitment of one facing death. So intense was his concentration that he could feel the redness on his face, the body heat, the taste of salt on his mouth where the perspiration had evaporated.

Assuming the Judo positions know as *Schizentai,* he eased closer to the bedroom that now seemed miles away. With his hand on the door jamb, he turned the brass knob ever so slowly, as he eased the bedroom door open silently across the soft pile surface of the carpet. Sound and smell overwhelmed Collier, as

6

he protectively leaned his head into the room. An old blues tune, "It's Raining in My Heart," by Slim Harpole was playing on the stereo record player. The figure in the room rejected the record player and turned towards him.

"Oh, God, Raymond, you nearly scared me to death standing there, looking so fierce," she cried out on seeing his menacing figure.

Naomi Selber reacted instinctively, a startled look on her beautiful face. Eau de cologne invaded Collier's nostrils as he entered the bedroom to confront her. He now realized that it was the scent of her perfume that he had smelled earlier.

"Dammit, Naomi, How did you get here?" Collier snorted angrily as Naomi took one step backwards fearfully…

"Why didn't you stay downstairs and turn the lights on?" Collier said, as his stomach contracted and the muscles knotted in his neck.

"I'm terribly sorry." Her voice sound genuinely apologetic.

She sat down on the Victorian sofa and said, "But I only wanted to surprise you, Raymond."

"You didn't surprise me, you scared the hell out of me," he said as he loomed over her, his face reddened in a scowl.

She lay back on the sofa, trembling with tension and fear. Collier realized that his own fears and anxieties were being misdirected and that a load had been lifted off his mind on his finding that it was she in the bedroom.

"Naomi," he said softly, as he sat down on the sofa beside her and put his arm around her.

"Yes?" she whispered softly as the tears begin to swell and her eyes redden.

"I am sorry," he said with all the tenderness he could muster, for his callous remark.

She was trembling; tears were rolling down her pretty face. He ran his fingers through her thick black hair to bring it off her tear-stained face.

"I love you," he said hoping she would understand as the thunder rolled overhead.

Her head was tilted back, resting against his chest. She had a beautiful face, ebony eyes, full sensual lips, high cheekbones, long jet black hair parted in the middle. The slightly curved nose betrayed her Sephardim Jewish origin

"I love you, too, Raymond," she said, tenderly touching his cheek.

Relieved, he felt all the unpleasant emotions melting away, replaced by other feelings of need. He was not one to let women get too close to him in the past. His relationship with Naomi was special however.

"What are you thinking?" she asked, trying to read his mood now.

"About how happy I am that you are here. By the way, how did you locate where I was? I didn't even tell my secretary in New York where I was going. To my knowledge, she doesn't even know about this place," Collier admitted on reflection.

Naomi went on to explain how she begged Marie, his secretary, to tell her where he was, but she swore she did not know. "Marie said she telephoned you to review the mail and other matters, but she never asked where you were, and that you never offered to tell her from where you were calling. I remembered you told me before I left to visit relatives in Israel that you planned to take a vacation and visit some old friends. It was a simple matter of detective work," she offered with pride in her voice.

Naomi went on to explain how she recalled seeing the picture of an elder Negro man and two German shepherds overlooking a lake in his office. While Marie reportedly did not know where it was exactly, she offered that it was in Mississippi and called Lake Serene. A few telephone calls established a Lake Serene in Lamar County, Mississippi, but no Dr. Collier was listed in the telephone directory, Naomi offered.

"So I made a few calls to veterinarians in the Hattiesburg

area, and one remembered two German shepherds, by the name of Karras and Heidi, that were brought in for shots regularly by a Negro man named Osmond. They were even willing to give me the address when I explained that we needed it for their registration papers," she recalled smiling at her own deception.

"I asked you about the names of the two German shepherds in our first counseling session we had together, don't you remember?" Naomi offered with wide-eyed enthusiasm.

"Who said Jewish girls weren't smart?" Collier smiled.

"Did Osmond let you in this morning before he left for the day off?" he asked with more than passing interest as she ran her hand through the curly hair at the nape of his neck.

"Very reluctantly, but I knew the names of the German shepherds and explained that we were very good friends and it would be allright. He asked if I was Jewish. I told him yes," Naomi explained without any feeling of bias as to the question.

"What did he say to that?" Collier asked, arching his eyebrow.

"He kind of smiled to himself," Naomi replied.

"I bet he did," Collier laughed as he held her close to his chest and enjoyed the strong aroma of her perfume. Jewish women could always be counted on to smell good, he recalled from his counseling sessions in New York.

"But Naomi, you can't stay," Collier said emphatically as hard reality set in now. He held her away from him to look her in the face to garner her consent.

"But, Raymond," she pleaded, "why?" She did not understanding after she had made every effort to be with him.

"No buts. I want you to take the Mercedes and drive back to New York City Monday morning. I will meet you there later," he demanded firmly.

"It will take three to four days to drive to New York City, Raymond," Naomi pleaded weakly for she knew how headstrong he could be at times.

"I'm actively working on a project and will not be free until

9

the end of the week," Collier asserted regretfully. But it had to be in his mind.

"But, Raymond, I hate to leave you," she said tearfully bringing her lips to his.

"I know. We have until Monday then," he said. His arm circled her neck as he ground his lips on hers as if to seal the deal between them.

Her long hair brushed his shoulder as he kissed her roughly. Naomi seemed to exude a musky aroma, he noted, a perfume that was peculiarly her own. The rain was now pelting at the windows and the glass doors leading to the balcony that faced the lake.

Later after donning a dark green cotton robe, Collier pulled the drapes back to view the lightning effect on the lake.

"Naomi, come here," he called out to her.

She quickly eased to his side and instinctively clutched the robe around her as she stood facing the lake.

"Don't worry," he assured her, "you can't be seen from here." Affectionately, he put his arm around her, as they both stood enjoying the light show. The wind bent the tall pines and caused the large oaks to billow from the strength of the thunderstorm. Collier had forgotten how tall she was as he put his lips to her long black hair. *Why would a tall woman prefer a shorter man? Especially one so beautiful*, he thought to himself. Strange that he had never developed that particular psychology, he mused to himself.

"Oh! Raymond, take me to bed, darling," she crooned wickedly, realizing that they would only have a short time together before she would have to return to home.

His arms slid around Naomi's back and knees, as he lifted her gently and carried her to the king-size bed. His beard nuzzled the underside of one breast as he gently placed her down on the bed with its satin sheets. Turning off the bedside lamp, Collier shed his robe and stood for a moment nude in the dark bedroom as the thunder and lightning continued to roll overhead.

Illumination from the light that bathed the room from the open windows, he was a big man with shoulders of an athlete resting on thick, muscled legs. She could feel the strength of him and wanted his strength now.

"Raymond," she called, pleading, as she held her arms out to him.

"Yes, my love," he said, as he moved to join her in bed.

Both were unmindful now of the raging thunderstorm outside on the lake. The storm lit up the bedroom at times with lightning flashes overhead. Rolling thunder could be heard as it played noisily on the rippling waters of the lake, while the tall Southern pines swung to and fro from the fury of the storm.

# Chapter 2

The next morning Naomi was awaken by the soft breeze that blew like a whisper to bring life to the shimmering lake. The windchimes tinkled merrily on the deck outside. The lake was spring-fed, and the house was perfectly situated on concrete piers to overlook the glistening blue water winking in the sunlight. The fresh clean air in the bedroom provided a wonderful ambiance in the morning. Sitting up, Naomi pulled the sheets around her full breasts, while recalling the events of the previous evening.

Wonderfully happy and content now, she watched the moving curtains at the open lattice door leading to the deck outside. The treetop leaves and the canopy of white dogwood trees were visible from her bed. Just as she was about to rise and seek out Collier, he presented himself at the doorway with a breakfast tray of coffee, juice, toast, eggs and grits.

"Stay where you are, my sweetness, you've done your night's work," he said with a broad grin, while observing the virginal pose symbolized by the satin sheets over her breasts.

"Raymond, not Southern grits?" she said.

"Yes, grits for my pagan high priestess," he said as he set the tray down on the bedside table. Collier was one who believed in grits, no hash browns for him.

Naomi sat up and with a long, drawn-out sigh, she swung her legs over the side of the bed, looking at Collier. Experiencing a delicious soreness, she donned her light blue robe and ate breakfast in bed as commanded.

Marveling at her dancer's legs, darkly golden body and large full breasts, he resisted a powerful urge to bed her again, but settled for a warm affectionate hug.

"Gather yourself and have breakfast, for in ten minutes we chase the big ones," he called out to her gleefully, like a schoolboy at his first summer camp. "I will wait for you downstairs and don't tarry," he admonished her.

Fishing was not what she had in mind this early in the morning, but she wanted to please Raymond. Thank goodness she had the presence of mind to pack appropriately for every occasion, she thought. She pulled back her long black hair in a chignon, after donning a cotton shirt and khaki slacks that women in the South like to wear. Later, in a shady nook under the protection of huge cypress trees, Naomi snaked out her crank bait lure that Raymond had said stood little danger of snagging.

Naomi felt Raymond was totally obsessed with the business of catching fish. She surmised this from the electronic gear on the bass boat. The fish stood little chance since Raymond had every electronic device known to man to locate bass.

While the wind moved the trees to sound and the gentle breezes caused a lapping of the waters on the lake's shoreline, Collier paddled her to a shady nook beneath huge cypress trees. The shore line was matted with soft pine cones and rotten leaves. Deep humus beds were created for small ferns to emerge in the dappled sunlight under the cypress trees along the shoreline.

Large pine trees were darkly silhouetted against the sky and threw deep shadows across the lake. Two squirrels were chasing one another around a large oak tree in the distance. Lake Serene was aptly named, Naomi thought to herself as the boat rocked gently on the placid waters, making every reflection clear while filtering the summer landscape.

"Look out for the snakes, Naomi," Collier jested as he used the paddle to control the boat's movement away from the cypress trees along the shore line.

"Snakes, Raymond, are we in danger of being attacked by snakes?" Naomi cried out, looking back at him horrified.

"Not really, but they have been known to fall out of trees into fishermen's boats," he said calmly.

Naomi was moved to reflect on her relationship with Raymond as she sat comfortably in the shade on padded seats, which one would not expect to find in a bass boat. She recalled being advised three years ago to consult with a Dr. Raymond Collier, psychiatrist, by her Jewish family physician for relief from psychogenic complaints.

Her husband had died a year earlier and the relationship was not a satisfactory one for either of them. Their marriage had been pre-arranged by their parents for economic and social reasons. Her mother, while a gentle soul, did not perceive marriage in the traditional manner—for her it was a necessary evil. Marriage was considered a form of legalized torture for Naomi's mother, to which a woman was required to submit by God's law.

As a consequence, her mother restricted all of her social activities, while her father was too preoccupied with his business ventures to take much interest in her development as a child. To make matters worse, she was an only child. A female at that, as far as her parent's were concerned. Naomi's husband was twenty years her senior. He later suffered a heart attack, leaving her heir to one of the largest department store chains in New York. At the time of her consult with Collier, she was acting as the chairman of the board, a self-imposed responsibility to permit her to develop a persona of her own in the business world.

"Psychic distress" was her major complaint related to her recent responsibilities on the death of her husband. While she had attractive features of face and figure, she presented herself as an ambitious, aggressive woman who preferred to reject the feminine role in favor of masculinity. She wore her hair in a tight bun, pulled close to the ears, set off by large Christian Dior rimed glasses. Her clothes, while expensive and tailored, were severe and not given to flattering her figure. She also preferred slacks in favor of dresses for both work and play.

She immediately detested Collier, with his Southern drawl, as she called it. She could not fathom why a Jewish physician would refer her to some Southern "redneck" when there were so many good Jewish psychiatrists in New York. Since his background was so different from Naomi's, it aroused her curiosity.

She felt superior to this Gentile and did not perceive him as a threat. Her demeanor openly challenged Collier's evasiveness and she reacted with sharp words when she became impatient to understand.

"Jews throw sharp words, while the Irish throw bricks," he told her on one occasion when she was given to acting out her frustration.

His humor, empathy and sensitivity were soon communicated in such a non-verbal way that Naomi accepted him in time. He was worldlier than she had thought, and her Jewish friends did not even raise an eyebrow when she mentioned his name socially.

She revealed more of herself than she ever dreamed. When she began to feel more at ease with Collier, she complained of sexual dysfunction and painful or difficult coitus when she was married. She admitted to an inability to experience sexual pleasure and satisfaction in her marriage.

15

Naomi's symptoms suggested psychogenic causes related to her aversion for her martial partner. She was found to have a puritanical aversion to intercourse and was given to faculty interaction with her husband, in large part because he shared some of her same attitudes towards sex in general. Collier recommended that she take a hiatus from her position as chairman of the board of her late husband's corporation and that she participate in a three-stage-sensate focus exercise recommended for couples. Since she was a widow, he agreed to participate in a limited fashion and supplement the sessions with videocassette tapes for her personal viewing at home.

After the tenth session, Naomi informed Collier that she planned to terminate further sessions. Naomi offered no reasons for her decision and declined to continue therapy in spite of his protestation. After several months had passed since she terminated counseling, Naomi mailed Collier a formal invitation to attend her "Coming Out Party," as it was stated in the engraved invitation.

Naomi's reflections were suddenly interrupted by a force that had unexpectedly taken her crank bait and was about to pull the rod from her hands. Instinctively she clutched the rod and forced the tip upward to snag a huge bass that broke the placid waters of the lake with a flurry and was now fighting for his life.

"Raymond," she squealed, "what do I do now?"

"Reel him in, love, reel him in," he said with real excitement in his voice as he saw the rod tip nearly bent to the side of the bass boat.

A four-minute battle ensued between a wily old bass and a neophyte angler from New York. The bass dove hard for deep water to escape, and the reel spun in Naomi's hand, but she held the rod tight with both hands. She clutched the rod with a death grip in one hand and the flywheel in the other, causing the line to become taut as the bass plunged for the safety of dark waters.

Naomi was sweating now, but from something else besides the sun. Small tiny droplets of sweat were forming on her forehead like white beads. With the line now taut, the bass veered to the right for the safety of the cypress stumps in the shallows. With her hand on the reel, Naomi turned the knobs slowly and the bass broke the water again with the force of his tail. He made a huge fountain-like spray as he cleared the lake's placid water.

Naomi saw the prize for the first time, a huge large-mouth bass, twisting and turning, with her bait lodge securely in his mouth. The challenge caused her to be unmindful of any criticism of the sport. She was as much hooked as the fish now. Like some prehistoric being that required food for survival, she was returning to a primitive way of life. Her state of mind made no accommodation for time or place; the focus was on the fish now and the feel of the rod in her hands and her ability to control the bass with the reel. It was as if she and the bass were one. What had been soft and delicate fingers were now like tensile strength steel as they gripped the rod and reel.

Collier offered no advice now, less she loose the fish and feel she had disappointed him in some way. He saw the raw determination in her face as she played the bass out on the other end of the taut line. Without a word, she saw the slant of the line and realized the bass was tiring and swimming at a higher depth. Holding the rod tight, she slowly reeled the bass in towards the boat until the rod was fully bent in her hands and she could clearly see the colorful stripes and the bass' huge mouth.

Naomi landed her first large-mouth bass without any assistance from Collier other than his netting the bass after she expertly played him to the side of the boat.

Beaming with joy and excitement over her accomplishment, she was not aware that her glands were working overtime. Her clothes were wringing wet from sweat and her pretty bosom moved up and down beneath her shirt because she was out of breath and gasping for air.

"How much do you think he will weigh, Raymond?" she asked excitedly when she was finally able to speak.

"Eight to ten pounds at least," he said with pride in her accomplishment.

"Oh! I want to have him mounted in the den along with your trophy bass," she pleaded.

"Let's go ashore now and show Osmond," he said proudly as he started the motor on the bass boat.

"Oh, I am so happy, Raymond," she squealed.

"So am I, love," he said genuinely, realizing that he had not been happy for some time now.

That evening, Collier and Naomi sat in the den sipping their after-dinner drinks and reflecting on the events of the day. Osmond shared in Naomi's excitement over her catching her first large-mouth bass. He assured her that he would personally see to it that her first catch was mounted. Later she watched him filet fish with a sharp pointed knife and make hush puppies.

"Why are they called hush puppies, Osmond?" she asked as she watched his delicate hands filet the fish and turn the hush puppies over in pan.

"In the South," Osmond told her, "we all have dogs and puppies, and they would be around smelling the cooking outside and getting in the way. The cooks would roll the corn meal with onions and throw it to the puppies to keep them quiet. Some of the men folk came along and started eating the cook's hush puppies and found it delicious."

"Osmond, is that really true?" she laughed.

"That's what my mama used to say," he replied with a broad grin on his face as he recalled better times as a youth.

All the while, Osmond filled Naomi's head with secret western African rituals of black dolls, conjure balls, and tales of Marie Laveau, the voodoo queen in New Orleans. He told of ceremonies where only virgins were permitted to cook and no one was allowed to enter the kitchen unless their head was covered by a cloth.

He described amulets for her that had their own unique powers such as the Figa, worn like a talisman to protect against evil and shaped like a clenched fist. He spoke of a lively dance called Juba, which was developed by Negroes on the plantation and later gave rise to words like juke joint, juke box, and juking in the South. Naomi was spellbound with Osmond's tales of life in the South in times past.

While Osmond fried fish in an outdoor cooker, Naomi romped with Karras and Heidi. Filled with love for Raymond and his little family, Naomi was regretting her decision to drive back to New York the next morning. It would do no good to argue with Raymond she knew. Determined to make him happy for the short time they would have together before she had to leave, Naomi had a gold Celtic cross and chain to give him as a present later that evening. For the first time in her life, Naomi felt maternal instincts and a sense of belonging and of being loved.

The next morning, with moist eyes, Naomi said her good-byes to Raymond, Osmond, and the two German shepherds. Collier assured her that it would only be a week at the most and then he planned to return to New York with the idea of closing out his practice. Naomi did not question Collier at the time, but she wondered why he was considering closing out his office and what that might mean as far their relationship was concerned. While he was sought after socially, being a handsome, eligible bachelor, she knew he was not really happy with the New York scene.

# Chapter 3

The hot summer wind stirred outside in the heat of the early morning as Steve Haralson tossed and turned. Still asleep and kicking off the hot sheets, Steve moans loudly. With a gentle nudge, his wife Barbara woke him, still sweating shivering and shaking. She assured him that he was just dreaming again. The same thing had occurred many times over the past three months. Steve felt imprisoned within his own brain. To him it was like an iron ring that was being slowly tightened around his forehead at some unconscious thought too terrible to be borne in the light of day. The feeling was intolerable and loathsome for Steve and seemed to dominate his whole being, a sense of terrible guilt.

Steve tried to deal with his anxious feelings by speculating on the symbolic meaning of his dreams. He had majored in psychology at the state university and was a student of Sigmund Freud's theories. Steve was familiar with writings of the English writer Thomas Dequincy who once wrote that *"it seemed he had transcended time, so to speak to have lived for 70 to 100 years in one night."*

Steve felt the same sense of foreboding, except his dreams were accompanied by a sense of deep-seated anxiety and melancholy. While he never seemed to attain a state of conscious awareness, he always felt himself to be in the role of the victim.

Trying to shake the feelings of anxiety by thinking of pleasurable thoughts, sexual thoughts, Steve leans over and kissed his wife Barbara on the cheek.

"Boy, you smell good," he whispered as his arm snaked across her stomach.

"Don't get any ideas, the boys might be in here any minute. It's Saturday, you know," she said, with some misgiving, "and you have an appointment with Dr. Collier about those headaches."

"You're right," Steve said as he leaped out of bed, forgetting about his psyche pain for the moment.

"I have to go by and see the folks first; you will have to take the boys to the football game in the Bronco, fix the Gatorade, and remember to pick up Tommy Price and Jesse Branch — and take their mouthpieces," he said as he hurried to the bathroom to dress.

"I know the routine, Steve," she called out to him.

"You just get yourself under control."

Barbara tried to hide her concern over her husband's recent "night terrors," as he called them. She had researched the literature on dreams in the library and found that night terrors represented a panic reaction emerging from the deepest stages of sleep. Barbara attributed Steve's problems to Viet Nam and the two tours of duty he served in the Marine Corps. Because he was in an intelligence unit in Viet Nam and spared from combat on the actual battlefield, she felt he suffered from painful survival guilt.

Other wives of Viet Nam veterans complained that their husbands suffered from intense anxiety, battle dreams, depression, and explosive aggressive behavior. Steve, on the other hand, was troubled with headaches, nausea, malaise, general aching, and chest pains of unknown origin. Barbara recalled adjustment problems in her relationship with Steve, but nothing problematical, just a sense of detachment and bitterness over his part in the war. A war fought by kids, according to Steve.

"Anybody home?" called Steve later as he opened the screen door to his parents' modest retirement cottage on Lake Serene.

"Is that you, boy?" said his father, a large, overbearing man who dominated ever social gathering.

Steve's father was a retired, Methodist minister who was converted by the tenting Mississippi evangelist, Gypsy Smith. Old-timers said it was a sight to behold to see Tom, yelling like a banshee, tearing down the sawdust aisle, out of control with tears streaming down his ruddy face, towards Gypsy Smith. It was said that Gypsy Smith's eyes got as big as china saucers when he saw Tom bearing down on him from the back of the tent. Gypsy later said that he received the largest donations that night of any night that they were tenting on the road.

Steve's father had been a submariner in the Navy in WWII, and no one ever believed he would become a Methodist preacher, and certainly not attain the rank of superintendent. Steve's mother, on the other hand, was a soft, gentle woman who offset her husband's crudeness and intolerant attitude.

Steve greeted his father with a hug and asked if the coffee was on.

"Sure, son, sit down, Mary will set you a cup."

"How do you feel, Steve?" asked his mother solicitously.

"I have a headache now; do you have any Extra-Strength Tylenol with cyanide?" he replied grimly.

"Steve, you shouldn't joke about things like that," his father said sternly.

"Why do you have to see a psychiatrist, Steve? There is nothing wrong with you mentally," his mother said.

"Aw! Mary, if Dr. Knox feels Steve needs to see a psychiatrist, then that's the right thing to do. You know he brought Steve into this world," his father said respectfully.

Steve noted that his mother smiled at that observation, probably because his father was not there when he was born.

"Mom, Dr. Knox said he could not find an organic basis for my symptoms," Steve explained. He wanted to assuage his mother's fears.

"Dr. Collier is home visiting now," Steve told his mother, "and would see me as a personal favor according to Dr. Knox Dr. Knox intimated that Dr. Collier called on him for a favor, and that the referral was tit for tat, so to speak. You know he has that summerhouse here on Lake Serene that everyone would like to see."

"I remember when he built that house, Steve," his father recalled, pouring himself and Steve another cup of coffee.

"As a matter of fact, his wife died shortly thereafter in a tragic airline crash in Dallas. She was an airline stewardess, as I recall," he said.

Steve's father went on to say that Collier never really lived there for any time, that an old black man and some wild German shepherds guarded the place. Steve laughed to himself, it was probably the only house on the lake where his father had never enjoyed a fried chicken dinner.

Steve was now reflecting on his relationship with his father. Being a preacher's son was a heavy burden for Steve in high school and college. When his classmates learned that he was a preacher's son, they just assumed he was a self-righteous moralist and not be much fun to socialize with on campus. Steve was active and popular on campus in spite of his religious orientation.

He personally took a dim view of the socialization process on campus that seem to support abandonment of one's moral views while encouraging the "intoxication of youth" to be free to make choices. Choices he felt that parents might not approve of, if their daughters were still living at home. Coeds in particular possessed vulnerability and were taken advantage of by older classmates.

Freshmen girls were particularly naive and subject to exploitation by football players. Since the football team was on campus twenty to thirty days before the start of school, players' hormones were raging for lack of feminine companionship. If a coed could survive until the end of her sophomore year without being victimized, she generally became worldlier and looked to establishing a meaningful relationship with the opposite sex.

A girlfriend of Barbara's was not so fortunate; she was involved in an abusive relationship and had three abortions before she left the university her senior year. While she was a beautiful girl and voted Homecoming Maid, Most Beautiful, and Who's Who among College Students, she was vulnerable as far as the party atmosphere on campus. Desperately she tried to avoid her unhappiness from childhood but became addicted to cocaine and the party lifestyle.

It was only after she signed a contract with Paramount Pictures and relocated to California that she was able to reestablish her self-esteem. Later she wrote that she met a wonderful man and was active in a church in Los Angeles. Because her girlfriend graduated on the honor roll with a double major in broadcast journalism and communications, Barbara could never understand the social dynamics, for she was so admired by her classmates and sorority sisters.

Steve later saw the effect of negative socialization on young sailors in boot camp. The need for membership—macho get drunk, screwed and tattooed—was the standing order of the day for neophyte recruits in boot camp. One young recruit recalled returning from a hardship leave to attend a family funeral in West Virginia and how he became the product of conditioning at boot camp. He described family members sitting on the front porch of the small family cabin on his arrival. They waved to him as he made his way up from the valley. When they hailed him in a welcoming gesture, he blurted out, "What the hell is this, holiday routine?"

Later at the dinner table with all the family members present, he again snapped, "Pass the fucking blood." That was a common expression in boot camp when a recruit wanted the catsup passed along in the mess hall. His father later asked him to check the outdoor toilets because the heavy rain and water seepage off the hillside caused the toilets to overflow with sewage. When he reached the outdoor toilets, his father was right behind him. Opening the door to inspect the toilet, his father shoved his head down in one of the toilet holes.

"You little bastard, if you are going to talk filth, you might as well eat the filth you're spewing," he said his father growled angrily.

"Mom, I really would like to have another cup of coffee," Steve said, as his thoughts turned to the present, "but I need to be on the road to make my appointment with Dr. Collier."

"Steve, your mom and I are going to the football game today to see the boys play," his father said as he walked him to the car.

"You call us later on tonight, and come over and watch the college football games on TV," the elder Haralson commanded, trying not to show his concern for his son outwardly.

"O.K., Dad," Steve replied.

Steve felt the uncertainty in his father's voice and admittedly was somewhat anxious himself over seeing a psychiatrist professionally for the first time. It was not something that one would want to readily advertise, especially where gossip was the fountainhead of news in Hattiesburg. Steve was reminded of a club member's comment about the pastor of his church who offered, "That Jesus could get around on his ass, but Brother Bryant had to have the latest Cadillac."

# Chapter 4

Two vicious looking German shepherds greeted Steve at the entrance of the grounds of Dr. Collier's summer home and created a Mexican standoff, until a voice commanded them, to sit.

"Who's there and what do you want?" implored an elderly black man.

The man had fine features, closely cropped white hair and moustache and was wearing green coveralls. His smooth, brown, well-veined hands looked more like an artisan, rather than one given to hard labor.

"I have an appointment with Dr. Collier, my name is Steve Haralson," he replied, while still eyeballing the two shepherds.

He was amazed at the old man's control over the German shepherds. Most Southerners thought that blacks hated German shepherds and that the feeling was mutual.

"Dr. Collier told me to expect you," the old man replied.

"Come on, the dogs will not harm you," he said with confidence.

Steve was wary as he was led down the brick walk to the house, sheltered among the tall pines, oaks and dogwood trees that nearly blocked a view of the house from the road that circled Lake Serene. Because Dr. Collier was somewhat of a mystery person in the community, Steve felt the need to make conversation with the old black man.

"You really have the dogs well trained. Did you train them yourself?" Steve asked with genuine interest in his voice.

"Raised them from puppies," the old man beamed, apparently taking pride in his work. "Missy, she showed me how to make them behave," he said.

"Missy, was that Dr. Collier's wife?" Steve inquired.

The man did not respond. He was silent to the question, as if he didn't hear Steve. A sense of sadness seemed to cross the old black man's face. Steve had seen that look many times before in Viet Nam. It caused Steve to feel uncomfortable. One of the dogs broke the spell of the moment by nipping at the old man's hand as they walked his path.

"Go on, Karras, I can't break him of that, or Heidi for that matter," he said affectionately.

"Karras, that's an unusual name," Steve said.

Karras was as an NFL football player for the Detroit Lions Steve recalled and Heidi was a children's story that was not shown timely, because the Jets game went into overtime.

"Dr. Collier named him after some football player, and Missy, she named the female, Heidi," he retorted, with a sigh.

As they paused at the bottom of the redwood landing, the old man said, "You will find Dr. Collier in the den, go on up those steps, he is expecting you."

So engrossed in conversation with the old man and his thoughts, Steve did not realize that they were standing at the footing near the deck of the house that overlooked the lake. *What a magnificent view*, Steve thought to himself, for he had never viewed the lake from this vantage point. The hillside house was perfectly situated to take advantage of the evening sun that often beamed a red fireball across the lake at dusk. The house was an architect's dream. The main floor of the house facing the lake was surrounded by a deck at treetop level. The buckskin color would turn a tan-gray over the years and give the house the appearance of always having been part of the wooded setting.

As Steve approached the glass panel doors to the den, he noted that redwood was selected for the exterior siding as well as fascia and sills, giving one the impression of leisurely luxury. The oversized den was definitely masculine with its rustic stone fireplace and earth tones. The adjacent enclosed atrium, lighted by narrow clerestory windows just below the ceiling, was obviously a feminine comprise. The den was an expression of warmth and comfort.

"Is that you, Steve?" said a voice from within. "Let me rig this Mister Twister and I will be right with you."

"Sorry to take you away from your football game this afternoon, Steve," Collier said, entering from a sunshade poolside recreational house off of the den.

"I read in this morning's paper where two boys by the name of Haralson were playing in a Pop Warner League football game today, and I recalled reading Dr. Knox's referral of your personal history that indicated you had two sons," Collier explained after seeing the puzzled look on Steve's face.

Steve was readily drawn to the man. He was a stocky, powerfully built man with the shoulders of an athlete. He was probably in his late forties, with a receding hairline and full red beard with a sprinkle of gray. He was dressed in a pair of brown, well worn, Hunter's Run corduroy trousers and a soft-looking tan sweatshirt set off by a pair of burgundy hand-sewn loafers. He appeared to be a man who was comfortable with himself and sensitive to the needs of others. He was not the cerebral, nerdy person Steve had imagined.

"You must like football, Dr. Collier, I noticed you named one of your German shepherds after Alex Karras of the old Detroit Lions," Steve said in an attempt to be collegial and control his own anxious feelings.

"I have always had a love for the game, Steve. Sometimes I think I missed my calling," Collier replied pleasantly.

"I appreciate your taking the time to see me. Dr. Knox said you were doing it as a personal favor for him," Steve acknowledged.

"I have been in the process of closing out my practice for a number of years now, Steve. For the past few years, I have been called, as an alienist, to testify before the court upon the subject of insanity," Collier said frankly.

"Is that why Dr. Knox referred me? He thinks I am insane?" Steve offered plaintively.

"No, not all. I think Dr. Knox referred you, out of respect for your father. Matters like these are best kept as private as possible. As a banker, I know you are aware how hard it is to keep financial matters private," Collier explained.

"I understand now and see Dr. Knox's point," Steve replied.

Steve took note of the African artifacts and the menacing look tiger pelt that hung on the wall behind a circular thatched hut on stilts. Coarsely woven and dyed African fabrics were used to complement the setting with stripes of brilliant earthy colors. The overall effect was startling. Steve found it incongruent with anything that he had ever seen in a home in the South.

"What do you think of my African rondavel, Steve?" Collier asked, while observing Steve's demeanor.

"Impressive. I don't think I ever expected to see one in a house as decorations," Steve said honestly.

"I have been a student of African culture for a long time, dating back to my boyhood days in Vicksburg, Mississippi. I delivered groceries for my dad to the Negroes who lived on nearby plantations, since he managed the Stave Mill Company Store. You've heard the tune, 'I Owe My Soul to the Company Store.' Well, my dad ran the company store and gave credit to the workers at the sawmill and the Negroes on the plantations. As a young boy, I enjoyed listening to the primitive blacks sing the blues, talk of their culture, witchcraft, voodoo and superstitions," Collier explained.

Discussing his visits to the Transvaal region of South Africa, Collier explained to Steve how impressed he was with the artistic ability of the natives to do interesting things with design and color, so much so that he combined the rondavel and the intriguing geometric designs of the Africans in decorating the den.

"It certainly creates an unusual effect," Steve replied, marveling at the complexity of the man.

"I know it's Saturday and you probably want to spend time with your family; maybe we should review your concerns," Collier said while glancing at his Girard-Perregaux watch.

Since he felt an immediate rapport with Dr. Collier, Steve settled into one of the big, overstuffed chairs and proceeded to detail his complaints almost clinically.

"Well, for the past three months, I have been experiencing tension, agitation, headaches and a sense of panic before going to sleep at night. And lately I have had disturbing dreams," Steve acknowledged openly without reservations.

"Do you recall your dreams?" Dr. Collier asked.

"I can't seem to remember my dreams, but I feel frightened on awakening, anxious and tense," he replied, wrinkling his brow.

"What basic emotion do you associate with your dreams?"

"A feeling of terror," Steve replied honestly, his eyes widening.

"Can you relate your dreams to your Viet Nam experience?"

"No. I served in an intelligence section in III Corps around Saigon and saw no direct combat," he openly admitted.

As a medical doctor with 12th Evacuation Hospital in Cu Chi in Viet Nam, Collier recalled survival guilt among corpsmen and medics because they often blamed themselves for their "incompetence" for the deaths of fellow comrades.

"I know that you probably think it's survival guilt from Viet

Nam and symptoms of post-traumatic stress disorder, but I worked through that when I was a volunteer counselor myself with the local Viet Nam outreach center for a number of years. It was nothing like this," Steve offered.

Impressed with Steve's self-disclosing attitude and his assertiveness, Collier felt he had a good psychological awareness and the capacity to integrating Sigmund Freud's dichotomies of conscious, preconscious and the unconscious.

Steve would be an excellent subject for hypnoanalysis, Collier reasoned from his experience as he analyzed Steve's responses to his questions. Furthermore, he owed Dr. Knox a favor and he liked Steve as well. Staying busy might help keep his mind off his own problems.

"Will you be available for five treatment sessions each day to undergo psychoanalysis?" Collier asked.

"Yes, sir, if you think it necessary," Steve replied, cooperatively.

"How about 3 in the afternoon, would that be too late for you, Steve?" Collier asked.

"No sir," Steve responded.

"Three p.m. it is, then," Collier said to confirm the appointment. "I will tell Osmond to expect you."

"Osmond, is that his name?" Steve asked with a sense of curiosity in his voice.

"The caretaker, he was given the Christian name Osmond, means 'protection of God,' Steve," Collier explained. "I want to caution you not to patronize Osmond because he is well-educated and has a college degree."

Steve was surprised at the comment that a black Osmond's age would have a college degree.

"How was Osmond able to attend college at his age?" he asked.

Collier realized that Steve's question was not a racist one, but one of interest. "Osmond's grandmother was born in Ellisville, Mississippi, the child of a quadroon and a white," Collier explained. "In other words, his mother was one-eighth black. Back then, they called them mustee, short for mustering, a half-caste. During the Civil War, Jones County seceded from the Confederacy and established the so called, Free State of Jones. Many whites and blacks congregated at that time in an area called Kelly's Settlement for their protection under the leadership of Newt Knight. He was a hardshell Baptist who refused to fight for the South. Osmond's grandfather became a black free man during this period and was a skilled craftsman. He passed along his skill to Osmond's father, who relocated and became very successful in the carriage trade, so the family was able to pay Osmond's way to college.

"Osmond grew up in Kentucky and graduated from a small college in liberal arts. The Collier family in Kentucky befriended Osmond as a youth and when he learned that a relative lived in Mississippi, he decided he wanted to return to soil his grandparents lived and worked. For some unknown reason, he enjoys my company and this place, so he has a place here as long as he desires to stay. Since he located family members in the area, he is content to act as my caretaker. Of course, he has the run of the place when I am not here, which has been most of the time lately," Collier confirmed.

Later that evening while enjoying the setting sun from the deck of the upper story master bedroom, Collier deliberated on the wisdom of taking the young man's case in view of current problems. He owed Dr. Knox, however, and Steve presented and interesting case. Clinical records from Dr. Knox revealed a negative blood Wasserman reaction to rule out a diagnosis of general paresis. The able Dr. Knox had the patient take the Kline test on a separate visit even thought there was no clinical evidence of syphilis of the blood or of the brain. Clinical evidence suggested a psycho-physiologic reaction. The apparent resistance to free association to dream content for one so psychologically open was puzzling to Collier, especially where strong emotions such as fear or terror were concerned.

Steve did not appear to have a conscious need to maintain control or to resist any revelation or significant material. Quite the contrary, Steve appeared to be an excellent candidate for hypnoanalysis as a shortcut to psychoanalysis, in Collier's opinion. All in all, Collier reasoned it would give him an opportunity to help a former Viet Nam veteran, especially since the U.S. Department of Veteran Affairs assisted him in becoming a medical doctor and psychiatrist.

# Chapter 5

As a psychiatrist, Collier was not one who believed in creating new theories or publishing, but one who believed in helping people to resolve their own problems. He reasoned that each patient was a unique human being with the potential for self-actualization. Collier knew from his experience that individuals have the capacity to make choices under the most difficult of circumstances. He saw that in Viet Nam, where many a Marine gave up his life to save the life of other men on the field of battle.

After his residency, Collier left the Department of Veterans Affairs Psychiatric Service because he could not abide the idea of financially compensating neuropsychiatry disabled veterans. Too many veterans were fixated on financial compensation, in his opinion, at the expense of higher order needs to enhance mental health.

While he understood the intent and purpose of the law governing compensation for psychiatric disabled veterans, he felt it was counter-productive in the long run. He noted that veterans' obsession with compensation served to hinder rather than facilitate psychiatric rehabilitation. He advocated a policy that would retain the psychiatric disabled in the military service for a period of at least three to six months for intensive psychiatric treatment, work evaluation and job readiness preparatory to the separation of the disabled veterans from military service. It was clear to him that the Department of Veterans Affairs had not learned anything from their experience with disabled veterans in World War II.

After relocating to New York City, Collier developed one of the most successful psychiatric practices in the country, catering to clients who were relatively more intelligent, spontaneous and expressive than the average person. His services were specifically sought after by the Jewish community, since he was familiar with Jewish culture from having grown up in Vicksburg, Mississippi.

It was common knowledge by the locals that Vicksburg was owned by the Jews and run by the Syrians. Collier learned early in his boyhood of the pain his Jewish classmates experienced. They suffered, due in part to their membership in a unique cultural group. Religious traditions and long held customs supported over-protectiveness and separate treatment for Jewish children in Vicksburg.

A number of his Jewish classmates voiced bitterness towards their parents for their role in maintaining long-held customs, ideology and social attitudes in a modern society. Since self-esteem was often impaired, many of his Jewish classmates compensated by "putting on airs" with fellow classmates. Because of his popularity in high school, a number of Collier's Jewish friends complained that they would rather live in his shotgun house with no indoor toilet facilities and furniture that rolled up from the humidity than their comfortable homes in town.

Not one to let a challenge go unattended, Collier admonished his Jewish classmates that their egos might not withstand the bias of the Jewish English teacher who required him to see her after class because she did not believe he read *For Whom the Bell*

*Tolls* for a book report. The incident was Collier's first experience with class discrimination and he felt the pain. Never again did he have respect for his English teacher.

Because he could joke with his Jewish clientele, Collier had good rapport that served him well in his practice. He would play point-counterpoint with his Jewish clients relative to stereotypical derogatory words associated with his Irish heritage. Many of Collier's clients were extremely wealthy and often experienced guilt over their status in society. Their ancestors were middle-class and well-educated German Jews who came to America in the late 1800s. Many German Jews settled along the Mississippi River. Collier recognized the names of his clients from his youth in Vicksburg.

The Kuner family, for example, was a well-known Jewish family in Vicksburg who lost everything during the Civil War because Mississippi was their home and they refused to leave. At the time of the Civil War, two-thirds of the population in Vicksburg were not native Mississippians. Vicksburg was a Unionist town as far as political thinking and interests were concerned.

Collier admired the Jews' acumen for business, but joked with his Jewish friends regarding their civic responsibilities. He liked to recount the story of his two Jewish friends who were playing dominos at Crowley's Smoke House in Vicksburg. He overheard the two merchants discussing the recent devastation caused by a tornado that came up the Mississippi River and destroyed a number of businesses downtown. One merchant asked the other if he had tornado insurance, and the other man replied, "Man, you can't set no tornado."

# Chapter 6

As the last rays of sunlight set at dusk on the lake, the silence was broken by the sound of a five-string banjo being strummed.

"Osmond, play my favorite," Collier pleaded as he savored his brandy.

"The dogs are liable to howl," Osmond laughed, as he began to sing and strum the banjo.

*I've got a chicken on my back, and dem hounds on my tracks,*
*I'll make it to my shanty, if I can, can, can, Lord, If I can, can, can,*
*I left a fox on the ground, to fool dem hounds,*
*I'll make it to my shanty, if I can, can, can, Lord, If, I can, can, can,*
*De Overseer, he decried, he's skin me alive,*
*But I got a woman, an hungry chill'in by her side,*
*I'll make to my shanty, if I can, can, can, Lord, If, I can, can, can.*

The song revived memories for Osmond that had been long forgotten. He recalled slave stories on the plantation—the hog killings and celebrations with dancing and singing. There were tales of the hard-drinking Irishmen hired as day laborers to perform hard and dangerous work because slaves were too valuable to their owners to get injured or killed. He also recalled stories of the bad times, of the so-called undesirable Negroes, who were sold down river, and the cruelty displayed against their own after the Civil War and the dark days of Reconstruction.

Osmond recalled his father describing Jones County as an almost classless society, inasmuch as slave conditions were almost equal with some of the dirt farmers in the heart of the Piney Woods. The Civil War in Jones County was seen by many as a rich man's war, and a poor man's fight when the call came for volunteers to bear arms. The majority of dirt farmers in Jones County just wanted to be left alone to cultivate their crops and raise their families, since they grew no cotton for the most part and had no slaves.

As a free Negro man, Osmond's grandfather was required to carry a certificate to prove his status in Jones County. Freedmen were generally not looked upon favorably in plantation society. Osmond's grandfather was given emancipation by his master and sent to Ellisville, Mississippi, to learn a mercantile trade with a planter friend of his master's.

Years later, he was given an opportunity to work on Andrew Durnford's plantation, Sainte Rosalie, in Louisiana. Durnford, a Negro planter, had slaves of his own. He was well-educated and accepted by the white planters in south Louisiana before the Civil War. Durnford was not a particularly good businessman and later fell on hard times.

"Good night, Osmond," Collier called out later as he walked up the landing to his bedroom.

Collier's voice broke Osmond's mood and recollections of the past. Heidi and Karras seemed to sense his mood as they wanted to put their paws on his knees, another habit he could not get them to break.

Retired to his bedroom, Collier wistfully thought about Naomi's visit while lounging in bed attired in green surgical pants. It was a habit acquired from medical school. He was the happiest at this moment than he had been for some time and regretted not inviting Naomi to stay. Sleep did not come easily for Collier and he reflected back to the first time he met Naomi.

She was a tall, aloof-appearing woman who informed him in no uncertain terms that she was referred to him by her own physician. The indication was that she was seeing him only out of professional courtesy and respect for her family physician. He understood her resentment and defensiveness and was prepared to cope with the initial resistance. Many clients resented the circumstances in which they find themselves and some were doubtful that psychotherapy could resolve their problems.

Naomi presented an interesting case in part because of her potential attractiveness and intelligence. She gave an outward appearance of being a very self-possessed person and spoke in a low, precise tone of voice. Her facial appearance could best be described as hard and tense or even pained on some occasions. In spite of Naomi's initial rejection of him, he was attracted to her as a woman, for some unexplained reason. There was a subtle magnetism, a force about her that intrigued him.

Collier had been criticized by his professional colleagues for getting too involved with his clients. His guard was up to some degree in his relationship with Naomi. Pygmalion was evident in every man, to some degree, Collier assured his colleagues and critics. Pygmalion was a sculptor and King of Cyprus who fell in love with one of his ivory statues that came to life in answer to his prayer.

The dynamics of Naomi's case was not too complex from an analytical standpoint. Frigidity and inability to achieve sexual orgasm were the primary causes of Naomi's symptoms, along with a strongly developed feeling of sexual inadequacy caused in part by dominating and unsympathetic parents. Frigidity and symptoms of vaginismus often represent physiological rejection of the feminine role in intercourse. Deep-seated hostility usually underlies the rejection of the feminine role and accompanying guilt. Naomi was punishing her own genital organs for her nagging sense of guilt while abjuring the appeal of feminine vanity and any trappings of seduction.

Naomi had committed herself in early adolescence to an ascetic life. Tall and gawky, she was not considered very attractive by her classmates. While she possessed artistic talent, most of her efforts were devoted to making good grades in school rather than any development of her artistic aptitude.

To develop her artistic interest would have been a commitment to her feminine impulses which she repressed. Unconsciously bitter over being a girl, Naomi tried to compensate by being competitive in math and science. She generally restrained herself from any emotional commitment and developed a conforming, compliant personality, thereby surrendering her own individual autonomy. As her achievement in school improved, the more depressed she became.

Resigned to her fate as a youth, Naomi was not willing to make a personal commitment to make choices on her own. Marriage to an older man seemed attractive to her because it would please her parents. Her husband had become a substitute father figure and the relationship was doomed from the beginning.

Naomi avoided anxiety-creating situations which simply caused an impoverishment of her own personality. She denied herself opportunities for psychological growth and individual autonomy to develop meaningful and emotional relationships with people. Collier felt it important for Naomi to deal with her anxiety and guilt if she was to actualize her potential.

As a psychiatrist, Collier preferred to share with his clients their unique predicaments in life and to analyze those circumstances for decision-making and choices. To that end, he exposed Naomi to long sessions on discussions of philosophy and the meaning of life. He believed as Socrates that *"the life unexamined is not worth living."* He had Naomi read Freud's

*Civilization and Its Discontents* because Freud felt that the progress of civilization has been made at the cost of erotic life of mankind. They reviewed together the works of Erich Fromm, Soren Kierkegaard, Vicktor Frankl, Abraham Maslow, and H.S. Sullivan.

When Naomi abruptly informed him that she planned to terminate therapy, he urged her to reconsider. His reservations were due in part to her seemingly noncommittal attitude on the appropriate biological role of the female. While he observed a slight softening of countenance and other physical manifestations of developing femininity in Naomi, he desired a conscious psychological connection on her part. Unfortunately, that was not to be the case since she prematurely terminated therapy, offering no specifics for her action other than to invite him to her coming out party.

# Chapter 7

Fingering Naomi's invitation in the coat pocket of his tuxedo with mixed emotions, Collier stood in the lobby of the upscale apartment complex and punched the elevator button for the penthouse. He felt compelled to respond to her invitation given his past association with Naomi, even thought she was a client. A musical chime rang on the penthouse floor announcing his arrival. He was ushered by the butler into a beautifully glassed walled room overlooking the New York skyline. The penthouse reflected an elegant eclectic decor and as he was to learn later, the obligatory marble gold and platinum fixtures in the bathrooms.

The butler announced that the hostess was predisposed at the moment. Surveying the familiar scene, Collier observed attractive, fashionably dressed men and women involved in light social banter, dancing, imbibing cocktails, and impressing each other with the latest gossip, the best spas, and the best tax shelters.

"Raymond, darling, is that really you?" a woman's voice called out over the din in the apartment.

"Jean, how did they manage to get you out of Washington?" Collier responded affectionately, hugging her in a light embrace.

Jean was an attractive widow and celebrated hostess in Washington who gave lavish parties for the rich and famous.

"Now that I've seen you again, it makes it all worthwhile," she said with sincerity.

"You look as lovely as a debutante at her first coming out party in that gown, Jean," Collier said, admiringly.

"Speaking of coming out, Raymond, have you met the hostess, Naomi Selber?" Before Collier could reply, he felt a light hand on his shoulder from behind and a voice say, "I am so glad that you could come, Dr. Collier."

He turned and stood in awe of the transformation. She was the most incredibly beautiful woman that he had ever seen. Her long, dark black hair was parted to one side and pulled over her ears to reveal perfect pearl drop earrings. The off-the-shoulder white silk jersey, toga-draped gown was perfectly fitted for her lush figure and dark golden complexion. Her ebony eyes sparkled and danced, and her full, sensuous mouth was perfectly rouged as she stood there in all her elegance. Collier felt flushed, that every eye in the room was on him. He had the feeling of being the hunted, rather than the hunter. His mind searched for words to respond appropriately, but his emotions were running rampant.

Naomi sensed his discomfort and took him by the arm.

"Jean, because you are and old acquaintance of Dr. Collier, let me introduce him to my friends," she said smiling.

"Why, certainly," replied Jean with a knowing smile.

"I should not have done that," Naomi said as she leaned against his arm and whispered in his ear.

"I need a drink," he groaned as they waded through the crowded room and the couples dancing to the bar.

"Brandy for Dr. Collier, Rudy," Naomi smiled to the bartender.

"Let us go into the study; it is more private," she whispered after Collier was served.

Led along to the large dark paneled study while still nursing his drink, Collier felt the warmth of her breast pressed against his arm. Almost wearily, he sat on the soft leather sofa and stretched his legs. Naomi reclined against the armrest next to him and smiled. *A vision of loveliness,* he thought to himself.

"Raymond, I terminated the sessions because I wanted to put an end to our professional relationship," she said in a very serious tone. "I knew that you would never violate your principles to establish a personal relationship with one of your clients so I had to terminate therapy. You would always have doubts that you took advantage of a client relationship if we developed a personal relationship while I was in therapy. The transference psychology that is operational between client and therapist would preclude you from ever entering into a personal relationship with a client and I did not want to risk that because of my love for you," Naomi explained.

Listening intently to her explanation, Collier sat sipping his brandy. She had apparently internalized more psychology than he had given her credit. Pressed to plead her case, Naomi went on.

"It became apparent to me after the third therapy session why Dr. Friedman referred me to you for consultation rather than a Jewish psychiatrist. After viewing your selected videocassette tapes, I reviewed a few of my own from a video club, that were less technical to say the least," she said, smiling wickedly.

"After termination of therapy, I flew to Lake Geneva and stayed at the Royal Hotel for a week and enjoyed the hedonistic pleasures of the thermal spa at the Erian-Les-Bains in France. The wonderful staff there advised me on diet counseling and physical therapy. I enjoyed a wonderfully relaxing massage on a waterproof table under three low-hanging warm showers. At the beauty institute, I learned about cellulite treatments, bronzing, and facials using Evian famous products. Raymond, I was literally intoxicated by it all, drunk with the promise of my newfound freedom, freed from the neurosis of society. In Ibiza, Spain, I walked almost au naturel on the beach at Playa Caballet and met some of Europe's most beautiful and wealthy people. One of the problems with becoming psychologically open is that you desire someone to share with you the luxury of freedom," she explained.

Overwhelmed, Collier sat quietly on the couch, his own emotions rampant now as he looked at her eyes that were beginning to tear up.

"Raymond, that is why I want you," she cried out, her voiced laden with emotion and her eyes now watery. Collier set his drink on the table and instinctively reached for her hand. Words were not necessary between them now. Taking her in his arms, he bent her head back on the couch and kissed her full lips.

Her full sensuous lips moved in response, her body communicated, her eyes were moist with tears and her cheeks tear-stained. "Raymond, I love you with all my heart," she said as she broke their embrace.

"I love you, too, Naomi," Collier said with tenderness and release from a terrible emotional strain. Collier hugged her to him and smelled the sweet fragrance of her perfume that was intoxicating in itself. He had been barren for true love for so long, a husk of a man as hollow as a locust shell attached to the bark of an elm tree.

"What does Naomi mean in Hebrew?" he muttered, regaining control of his senses.

"My sweetness," she replied, smiling; she could never remember anyone asking her what Naomi meant in Hebrew.

"What an appropriate name for you," he sighed, nuzzling her long slender neck that appeared so inviting to his lips.

"I have so much to learn about you," she whispered as she lightly brushed her lips against his while clasping his head in her two hands.

Women had been decorative sex for Collier for a long time since the death of his wife. He now felt an urgent need to give voice to his emotions and feeling that had been repressed for way too long.

"I felt like a fool tonight," Collier offered almost clinically, "because my highly sensitive autonomic nervous system gave me away."

"I know," she replied, knowingly.

"Naomi, my wife was an airline hostess and died in a plane on take-off from Dallas. She had telephoned earlier that she was pregnant and wanted me to know that it was her last flight. I was so emotionally wrought up after her death that I never gave consideration to establishing a serious relationship with another woman. For years I devoted myself to my work and wanting to help others but when I saw you tonight, I realized how personally involved I had allowed myself to become," he said, his voice shaky and chocked with emotion.

"Oh, Raymond, I love you," she said, caressing his full red beard with her fingertips and kissing him lovingly.

"Let me return to my guests while you relax and have another drink here in the study. There is a bar hidden there in the bookcase," she offered.

"That is my bedroom door," she smiled with wicked intent and dimmed the lights to one lamp.

He marveled at her extraordinarily supple back as she turned to leave. Collier located the hidden bar and discovered a full decanter of Chives Regal. Helping himself to a double scotch, he selected a book entitled *The Egyptians* and made himself comfortably in one of the large over-stuffed leather chairs. How sensitive Naomi was to his mood, he mused to himself. He was not interested in a party tonight. The effects of the Scotch whiskey, faint sound of music, and the earlier emotional rendering situation quickly induced sleep for Collier.

Aroused later by a light from under the bedroom door and the soft music that emanated from within, Collier blinked, adjusting his eyes to the light that played across from beneath the bedroom.

"Raymond, do you feel better after your little cat nap?" Naomi said teasingly.

She had changed into a black lace negligee that was loosely belted at the waist. The glow from the bedroom lamp accentuated her lush figure in the sheer gown, making it thin enough to see through. Her hands went to the hair piled high on top of her head. She withdrew the pins quickly to cause her long dark black hair to cascade like fine lace almost to her waist. Raven-black hair gleaned softly in the subdued light and strands of her dark hair framed her exquisite breasts, offering silken hospitality. He could see her full almost maternal breast and fleshy belly rise and fall from the irregular breathing caused by the atmosphere of sensuous expectation and gratification.

As he approached her, he could see the flesh shining through the black silk negligee and the long sweep of one perfect leg from thigh to ankle bent in a feminine pose. Naomi parted her gown to offer no impediment to give him full view of her thrusting full breasts, dimpled belly, well-developed mons pubis and ample hips. Opening her arms, she offered herself with a craving look of salacious pleasure. She was in any man's eyes a feast for the senses.

Collier took her in his arms and kissed her tenderly while she thrust her pelvis forward. Slipping his hands beneath the silken gown to enclose her golden buttocks, he drew her to him gently.

"God," she whispered, "I want you."

Sweeping her off her feet, Collier carried her purposefully to the bedroom. He lowered her gently onto the large bed, and he freed himself from her grasp. Her ebony eyes were erotic now as she watched him undress for she was intrigued by the man and his power over her. She now wanted most of all his love, having heard the summons deserting her past forever.

# Chapter 8

Less apprehensive the next day, Steve approached the iron gates to Dr. Collier's lakeside home. Heidi and Karras even greeted him more warmly, with only a sentinel bark to alert Osmond. The black man presented himself at the gate to permit his entrance with an air of dignity.

"Good evening, Osmond," Steve said, keeping in mind what Dr. Collier had indicated in confidence.

"Good evening. Dr. Collier is expecting you," he said in a friendly tone.

As they walked together, Steve could not restrain himself from learning more about Osmond.

"I guess you are going to watch the re-runs of Mohammed Ali's great fights on TV tonight, Osmond?" Steve asked to make conversation.

"Nope, I give Ali credit for being a great fighter and promoting boxing, but he was a poor role model for blacks," replied Osmond. "Ali acts like an overlord monkey in the ring and the name Cassius Clay was a name to be proud of. My father said Cassius Clay of Kentucky defended abolition in his day with a gun or knife if need be."

"Who were the fighters you admired, Osmond?"

"Joe Lewis and Archie Moore. I am only sorry they did not make the kind of money Ali has made in his lifetime," he offered without any hesitation.

"I do remember my dad talking about Joe Lewis and Archie Moore. I hope we will see re-runs of their fights in the future," Steve replied.

"Here we are, you had better go on up," Osmond said as he turned to walk the dogs on the lake.

Dr. Collier was there to greet him at the landing. "The sunset is so beautiful in the evening, Steve," he said. admiring the lake.

"It sure is. I love this time of day on the lake," Steve replied as he watched the shadows on the lake and the fish rippling the water with their tails as they looked for fallen insects from the overhanging cypress.

"Let's go in the study. It will be more private there and we want be distracted by the beauty of the lake," Collier reasoned.

They entered a room filled with professional books, journals, electronics equipment, a large desk and a long psychiatric couch. The psychiatric couch attracted Steve's attention. It was the first thing his wife bought him when he went into practice, Collier explained when he noted Steve's interest in the couch. While they are seldom used by psychiatrist today, he offered the couch was helpful to some degree in hypnoanalysis. Collier explained that he would record their conversation on a sound-activated microphone that would eliminate his having to take notes so as to not interfere with the flow of conversation.

"I have one question before we get started," Steve said. "It's regarding Osmond. I asked him if he was going to watch Mohammed Ali's re-run fights on TV tonight and he said no, and called Ali and overlord monkey."

"Osmond has been reading my medical journals again." Collier laughed. Collier explained to Steve that an overlord monkey uses a direct, uninhibited staring gaze to establish dominance over subordinate monkeys who will characteristically drop their gaze. "I think the analogy was well taken; Ali is a master at psyching out his adversaries, with George Foreman being a case in point. Steve, you mentioned in our last conversation that you worked as a volunteer at the local Viet Nam Veterans Outreach Center. How did that come about?"

Steve offered that he was a member of the Kiwanis Club that sponsored an outreach program to help counsel Viet Nam veterans. The counseling center found it essential to have veterans counseling veterans but he was not prepared to see grown men cry because of the exaggerated stereotypes of Marine Corps masculinity.

"There ain't no pity in the city," Steve recalled hearing a Marine's plaintive cry when the U.S. Post Office refused to provide handicapped parking or install a ramp for wheelchair access to the Federal Building in New Orleans.

While he served in Viet Nam, Steve was not prepared for the bitterness he found in returning veterans and the abuse the family structure suffered as a result.

"A woman's just a life support system for a pussy," was a veteran's response to Steve when confronted with his abusive relationship with women. Counseling Viet Nam veterans afforded Steve insight relative to his adjustment problems, which were minor in comparison with the veterans he counseled at the center.

"You are to be admired for your willingness to help your fellow comrade," Collier admitted.

Proceeding with the psychiatric interview, Collier found Steve to be a very intelligent young man with a great deal of insight who offered no resistance and was straightforward with his responses. Steve's history offered no clue as to etiologic factors that would contribute to the origin of his disturbing dreams or multiple somatic complaints. His history did not suggest a psychosomatic personality type to account for his complaints. On balance, he appeared to be a well-adjusted young man, a high achiever who was a vice-president of a local bank. While Steve was animated and spontaneous on personal interview, he admitted feelings of depression and anxiety on retiring in the evening, a reaction due in part to his anticipation of experiencing another night terror.

"Steve, I would like to recommend hypnosis and hypnoanalysis as a form of psychotherapy in your case," Collier said.

"I understand a little about hypnosis, but what is hypnoanalysis?" Steve inquired.

Collier explained that the technique consists of first placing the client in a deep hypnotic trance to permit the therapist to ask him to talk freely to recall his dreams and unconscious thoughts without any hesitation.

"I understand you cannot be made to do anything against your will, is that right, Dr. Collier?"

"Yes, a man cannot be made to commit murder or steal or perform any other antisocial act because his moral sense will censor his behavior. A woman would not expose herself or be made to have sexual relations against her will," Collier acknowledged.

"What would happen if you were to have a heart attack while I was in a hypnotic state? What would happen then?"

"You would simply go on sleeping for an hour or two, and then awaken by yourself, since the suggestion for you to sleep would have worn off," Collier explained.

"Is it necessary for me to recline on a couch for treatment?"

"While it is not required, I find it desirable for a client to recline on a couch to permit greater concentration of though processes by minimizing the influence of external stimuli in hypoanalysis in particular," Collier assured Steve.

"I would be willing to try anything to get rid of this feeling of apprehension before retiring at night," Steve said.

"Let me dim the lights and you recline on the couch and relax," Collier instructed.

Steve adjusted himself on the couch. He was told to fix his

gaze and concentrate his attention on a gold watch that Collier dangled about a foot above his eyes. Many clients expected and wanted the ritual of the gold watch because it helped reinforce the treatment process for hypnoanalysis.

Stroking Steve's forehead, Collier slowly and rhythmically repeated that he was comfortable and relaxed, that he would become drowsier and drowsier, and that he would go into a deep sleep. As predicted, Steve was an excellent subject and hypnosis was induced in a matter of minutes. Steve was highly suggestible to beneficial advice and treatment and his body language suggested to Collier that he was in a deep and relaxed state.

While under hypnosis, Steve was given the opportunity to recall his childhood, school and college experiences, marriage and military duty in Viet Nam. While he had painful memories and experiences related to Viet Nam, they were not found to be too disturbing or outside his ability to accept and cope. No significant anxiety was indicated.

Collier suggested that Steve recall certain experiences or memories that were painful for him, memories that he might not wish to recollect because they were too painful or traumatic. Steve's body language changed radically as Collier observed his reactions. He became agitated, his body contorted as he writhed on the couch, his facial countenance change and slackened. With droopy eyes he appeared almost childlike. Because of the strong physical reaction, Collier suggested that he was not to remember all of the events but to consider memories that gave him pleasure. Steve's body language suggested a noticeable relaxation. A subtle grin appeared as he described a vision while the tape recorder whirred silently.

"Compelled, I painfully strain my eye to the keyhole and wait. A cold shiver seems to run up and down my spine. There in an awe of silence, my heart is pounding because of the fear of being caught for my strange vigil. I have become a lover of keyholes and windows for peeping. I wait in the dark for something, with rapt attention. Things are coming into view as I flush with heightened anticipation of the suffused trappings of seduction before my eyes.

"I see a large, magnificently furnished boudoir with its delicate floral wall covering, fabrics and chaise lounge is in the corner of the room. While flowers, pillows, watercolors and fragile figurines all create a dreamy effect, the centerpiece is a huge sleigh bed with silk rosette tie backs and bed hangings, with a tent headboard with its floral silk lining.

"A man, my father, is clothed in a maroon silk embroidered robe with his initials A.E., as he lolls on the bed amid the floral cushions and ruffled pillows. He gives the appearance of one devoted to epicurean habits as he smokes an opium-tainted cigarette. His hooded blue eyes and the receding Hanoverian chin covered by a full brown beard and moustache give him the look of a butcher with his soft portly body and discreet tattoo. A small Florentine bedside table nearby affords him champagne and chocolates. Lazily, he strikes a match on a dainty gold case to smoke another cigarette with his dreamy languorous eyes that did little to hide his thinly veiled expectations. He calls out to someone in the bathroom, 'My dear', while sipping champagne from a sterling silver goblet. He reclines impatiently. An attractive woman emerges from the bathroom, apparently in good humor with herself. She is wearing a vivid blue military coat with wide flaring lapels with gold piping, gold buttons, epaulets and a high collar with embossed stars and braid that fail to hide her full thighs and breasts. Gracefully she comes to him, and strokes his pointed brown beard while sipping his champagne from the silver goblet. The champagne causes her lips to moisten and her under lip to seemingly swell with fullness. She insinuates her hand between the folds of his silk robe and she causes his hooded blue eyes to become warmly stirred with her lascivious touches. With her rouged, pouting-lipped mouth, she seems inclined to make the most of her opportunity to ply her artistry. Before she can become conveniently inclined and liberate him from his lustful desires, he causes the heavy, braided military coat to fall, revealing a statuesque woman, as broad in shoulders as in hips, and skin the color of cream. She is a seductive woman with chestnut hair, aquiline nose, and molded cheeks. She sits astride him, naked and glorious in all her beauty, tossing her head back in pleasure. She bounces about in rare style, as he takes her big breasts in either hand, for he is a generous lover skilled at infusing a lively brisk and vigorous bout sure to pleasure his lover in love and joy."

"The woman, is she your mother?" Collier inquires following a prolonged period of silence.

"No she is not my mother, my mother…" Another long pause elapses before Steve speaks again.

"I see a reflection in the mirror wall of my mother standing in the center of her bedroom, nude except for a blue ribbon around her slim throat to hide a tracheotomy scar. The pale moonlight streaming through the small leaded panes of the tall windows reveals a wonderfully attractive, vain woman with a look of passionate purity. The warm murky orange flame casts fantastic shadows against the wall and reveals the ripe enchanting breasts and the finest turned legs and thigh that one could imagine. A young man, enamored of his own beauty with his golden ringlets and heavy sensual mouth, reclines on her bed.

"He returns his book to the satin wood bed table bookcase and implores her to join him under the bedclothes. He gently draws her to him and unties the pale blue ribbon to kiss the curves of her throat and the faint crimson scar. The scene evokes such warm emotions that I find it hard to look, to breathe free. It is too much, I cannot bear it, even with my back now turned to door and the welcoming keyhole; I can still hear the bed noises, the faint creaking and finally gentle groaning of gratification.

"Oh yes. Oh yes…

"I pray to be free of her love that binds and envelopes me. I struggle like a newborn at birth with an imaginary cord. To cut the Gordian knot I cry feeling bound to that womb-like crypt of mother and child. Anxiety and guilt well up in me, as I have this tortured dream again. Memory of my past grandeur now only serves to cause me pain. I have become dissolute and faithless to everything except my self-indulgence in gluttonous, extravagant pleasures. Left now, I only have vain, empty dreams to pass on, if time permits, for others to profit from my experience."

Sensing the effect of the traumatic memories for Steve, Collier elects to terminate hypnosis.

"Now I am going to wake you. You will feel refreshed and in good spirits on awakening. I will count from one to five, at the count of five, open your eyes and wake up. One, two, three. Start waking up, four and five," Collier crooned softly.

"How do you feel, Steve?" Collier asked.

"I really feel revived, but I don't remember anything," Steve said.

"When you feel you understand the meaning of what we have been discussing, you will remember what is necessary. In the meantime, don't concern yourself with what you cannot recall," Collier explained.

"O.K., you are the doctor," Steve replied in high spirits.

Later that evening, while sitting in his bedroom, Collier reflected on the interpretation of Steve's dream. He played the cassette tape recorder over and over. While Freud called dreams the royal road to the unconscious, Collier was uncertain what road they were going down. Dreams, Collier knew, are condensed symbols which can be usually interpreted by an experienced therapist. This dream, however, was foreign to anything he had ever experienced as a psychiatrist in New York or in his training.

Clearly, Steve was describing the memory of traumatic incidents in the form of a primal scene. The reactions of the child were clearly that of an insecure child who had been rejected and felt overwhelmed by feelings of helplessness and frustration.

Incestuous desires and other unresolved Oedipal elements seemed apparent in the dream with associated voyeurism. The all-seeing eye references gratification rites of the scopophiliac and permits the viewer to become one with the characters themselves. The child's repressed libidinal striving seems to be the origin of his peeping and his innate desire to return to the womb to be reborn again.

Steve's dreams represented the mind's attempt to solve problems which disturbed him, but his personality was not one of an insecure child who had been rejected and denied legitimate demands for love and support. What then was the drama enacted in the dreams? Where is the locale and who are the characters in the dream? A most intriguing case to say the least, Collier thought, as he finished his brandy for the evening and snuffed out his cigar.

# Chapter 9

As he entered the kitchen, Steve could tell his wife was mad by the way she was slamming pots and pans around. He made an attempt to be cheerful to counter her mood.

"Are the boys in bed?" he asked as he ran his arms around her slim waist.

She looked very inviting in her cheerleader uniform. Barbara was coerced into taking the job of instructing the girl cheerleaders for the team because she was a former head cheerleader in college.

"No. I sent them upstairs to do their homework," she said angrily. "I am so damn mad at that new football coach; I wish you could have heard some of the things he said."

"You mean Jim Champion, the state trooper?" Steve asked.

"Yes, that fat, overgrown bastard thinks he is a warmed-over Vince Lombardi and that winning is everything," she said.

"Barbara..." Steve said. He was amused at her language which was really not like her.

"He was talking—not talking, yelling—at the boys about nutcracker drills, meat on meat, stink on stink, and that they have to play with pain. I think he has read too many stories about the National Football League and what coaches expect. Coach Walker never talked like that all the time; I was on the sidelines in college. This is the Pop Warner League not the NFL. You need to talk to Brad; he is all hyped up about what Champion said but Bruce and I think he is crazy," Barbara lamented.

"It does sound a little extreme," Steve replied. "I'll talk to Jimmy's dad across the street and get his impressions before I talk to the boys. In the meantime, let's talk about how cute you look in your cheerleader outfit," Steve said as he slipped his hands underneath her sweater to cup her full breasts.

Barbara held his hands for a moment and asked about his visit with Dr. Collier.

Steve explained how refreshed he felt but that he could not remember anything he said under hypnosis but Dr. Collier indicated that he was not to worry that he would recall in time what needed to remember. Steve told Barbara that all in all, it was a pleasant experience.

Disengaging herself, Barbara poured two tall glasses of red wine and gave one to Steve before settling herself in a chair opposite him at the kitchen table. Her cheerleader uniform did little to hide her long legs and buxom figure.

"What else did he say?" she asked.

"That's about all except I will see him every day this week in the evening so you will have to make do with the boys at football practice," Steve said.

She looked at him disapprovingly as he downed the remainder his wine and poured another. He felt he had a need to explain to Barbara his uncommon interest in the black man who worked for Dr. Collier. He told her of his discussion with Osmond.

"Osmond is a most interesting and intelligent person," Steve said; he returned the empty wine glass to the sink. "Tell the boys I will be up to see them after I talk with Mr. Price across the street."

Sam Price confirmed Barbara's observations regarding Jim Champion's behavior at football practice. Since Sam was not a football player himself in high school, he did not feel he could say much to the coach under the circumstances.

"But you played in high school and college, Steve," Price told him. "Champion will listen to you."

"I hope so because if any harm comes to those boys of mine while playing football, Barbara and my dad will settle the issue," Steve commented as he left the Price home.

While crossing the street later, Steve decided he would talk to Jim Champion.

He really disliked Jim Champion; Steve thought he was a bully in high school and a bully as a highway patrolman from the gossip around town.

Steve reassured Barbara he would have a talk with Champion, since Mr. Price confirmed Barbara's observations.

"You know I have an appointment with Dr. Collier every evening but I will call Jim after I get home to discuss your concerns," Steve told his wife to reassure her of his interest as they prepared to go to bed.

"You know, I haven't talked to your dad about this," Barbara said as she fluffed up her pillow.

"Thanks," Steve replied, smiling to himself.

Of course it was her way of threatening him to do something because he knew if his father got involved, there would be hell to pay for everyone involved where the boys were concerned. Steve knew his dad did not trust anyone when it came to care for his grandchildren. His father was pretty much that way with him growing up in that he never turned his responsibilities over to someone else as far as parenting went. He always wondered why but given the current abuses where children were involved, Steve could see his reasoning.

The smell of honeysuckles and gardenias invaded Steve's nostrils the next evening as he hurried towards the back gate at the Collier house for his appointment.

"You are early," Osmond, said meeting him at the gate.

"Yes, I know," Steve replied as their eyes met as to convey a common understanding.

"Can we sit and talk a few minutes before I have to meet with Dr. Collier?"

"Yes, I have penned Heidi and Karras for the evening," Osmond replied. "We can talk here in the gazebo."

"Osmond, the last time we talked I noticed that your behavior and speech are at variance from that observed earlier when I first met you," Steve muttered not feeling sure of himself.

"We call it going uptown," he replied through whirls of smoke from his cigar.

"Why the need, Osmond?" Steve asked, pointedly.

"Our station dictates it at times and at other times I think it is for convenience," he replied honestly.

"But it seems to make life a deception," Steve commented.

"An accommodation, to be more accurate," Osmond responded as he tapped off the gray ash of his cigar on the heel of his leather boot. "A reaction pattern borne as a consequence of our cultural paranoia to a perceived hostile environment."

"The behavior would seem justifiable," Steve replied sympathetically.

Osmond smiled, realizing that Steve had a real need to understand. "While it may seem justifiable, it still represents a negative adaptive response and retards growth for the individual blacks. Blacks who deny their African heritage will continue to suffer from psychological disorientation and experience negative adaptive behavior."

"But it seems to me that it would be difficult for blacks to accept a universal identification with an African ethos," Steve replied.

"No more difficult than your accepting your European ancestry," Osmond responded.

"But I don't think about it," Steve replied honestly.

"Therein lies the key. You have an acceptance and therefore are free to grow on the basis of your conception of self as an individual member of a broader society. Blacks, on the other hand, generally deny their African heritage and seek a group membership with collective values, attitudes, and behaviors for protection of self." Osmond explained. "We as blacks have to accept ourselves before we can accept others. If blacks are to cope with external reality, they cannot afford to segregate themselves under the guise of the black experience. This constant whining by some blacks that the white man led to the black man's decline in moral values is a myth. Blacks now have power of self-determination as evidenced by a number of elected officials around the country but they still have failed to gratify basic needs for safety, belonging, love, respect, and self-esteem, none of which requires the blessing of a white man," he offered in the manner of a college professor.

"That is a painful indictment, Osmond," Steve commented.

"The pain for the black man is the pathological fear of breaking the umbilical cord with the white man to become independent, separate and truly free. The black man fears knowledge and avoids the pain of knowing. A feminist activist once commented after a long history of her own failures that 'the truth will set you free after it scares the hell out of you.'"

Steve could not help but laugh at the joke. It was the first time that he had seen a black man be so brutally honest about his own race.

"I recall years ago my father and a black man were planting a tree to throw shade on the swing on the back porch. The black man asked my father why he was planting a tree so close to the house."

"'To throw shade on the porch,'" my father replied.

"'Mr. Haralson, it will be five years before that tree throws any shade,' the black man grumbled.

"'Cleve, that's the difference between a white man and a black man,' my father offered at the time.

"Delayed gratification is not a value commonly shared by blacks in general. After reviewing my own African ancestry and the primitive instincts required for survival, I understand why delayed gratification is not a cultural trait as you might find in European culture where the environment is less hostile and primitive for the most part." Osmond laughed at the analogy.

"What is you hope for the black man?" Steve asked.

"Given sufficient time and education the black man can, through acquired or learned behavior, cope with his environment, no matter how hostile, given a sense of freedom to make choices and a willingness to act on those choices," Osmond opined with wisdom of a savant.

The two rose together without another word between them and made their way up the walk together to the house. Steve was impressed with Osmond's insight. He had professors in college who became defensive over being asked questions on sensitive subject matters that students felt a need to understand. Osmond was so open and frank that it was an eye-opening experience for Steve. He hoped he could be that objective with his boys when they asked questions about life and relationships with people.

# Chapter 10

It was obvious to Collier that focusing on current interpersonal relationships would not prove beneficial in Steve's case. There was an apparent need to probe into the past as repressed by his dreams. Intense and traumatic experiences may have shocked his mind to create a state of repression. Veterans who suffer neuroses of war often blot traumatic experiences from their minds. What are the historical roots of Steve's disorder? That was the question in Collier's mind as he prepared for their second session.

Since Steve had accepted the mode of therapy, Collier decided to turn the recorder on prior to Steve entering the den in view of their working relationship.

Collier greeted Steve pleasantly and permitted opening remarks, but he intentionally discouraged small talk. To avoid any resistance, Collier's aimed to induce hypnosis timely to allow the opportunity for regression into significant periods of Steve's childhood.

Later on conclusion of the second session, Collier sat enjoying the soothing effects of his drink, in the quiet comfort of his den. He selected a Cuban cigar from the humidor as he critiqued the strange, emotive tale revealed to him by his new client while under hypnosis. The taped session stirred his intellectual curiosity with the startling revelations. Was he on the brink of a great discovery?

Collier depressed the play button on the tape recorder to reassure himself that his passion had not gone astray. He understood that psychology was not an absolute science, that the mind was capable of projecting monstrous fantasies and misshapen dreams to resolve conflicts. As the tape recorder whirred to divulge the dark contents of the second session, a steady pattern of rain began to fall, forming a mist on the glass paneled doors leading to the deck.

Steve's face was horribly imagined on Collier's brain. It held a strange expression, weak, sleepy eyes, that seemed to hide a hideous secret. It was a grotesque, unsightly mask of evil. With desolation and an elegiac intone to his voice, Steve spoke.

"The moment of my birth was a harbinger of things to come, borne of a father given to epicurean pleasures, and a mother fragile, sensitive, and partially deaf. That diabolical genetic connection destined me to become a tragic victim of my time. Born premature and cursed with a mild hearing loss, my education suffered. While I developed some artistic interest, I was still perceived as being slow, lethargic, and dull by my teachers and classmates. As a result, I was given to shyness and insecurity and resorted to fantasy to cope with my psychological state.

"My father has all but disowned me because I am not more like him. He has an enormous appetite for pleasure, enjoying music, dancing, and the theater. I learned later in life of his obsession for amorous adventures from Lord Charles Carrington, my father's companion, who shared his vices and interest in pornography. While he sought out the pleasure of Venus, I shopped elsewhere to prosper in vice.

"My mother, on the other hand, is a beautiful, sensitive woman given to false gaiety to compensate for her hearing loss.

She was not one to confront my father when his peccadilloes became public. Mother occupied herself with my younger brother, George, who was more athletic than I and my father's favorite.

"George and I developed a remarkable relationship and accommodated one another relative to our unique circumstances of birth. George progressed in school and his achievements were recognized by my father and mother. I, on the other hand, had problems with concentration and became bored with academia.

"As I grew older, my father decided that I needed a tutor. He proceeded to employ a personal tutor from a well-to-do literary family, who came highly recommended. Little did my father know that my tutor was to become a venal influence and leave his mark on history. Under his tutelage, I learned the art of gaming, swearing, drinking and other genteel vices like pederasty and the charm of birching. My tutor convinced my father that I was beyond hope as far as academia was concerned, but that he would try his best to educate me. Taking advantage of my lack of parental guidance, my inadequate constitution and strongly developing sensuality, he exposed me to the worst sorts. Of course, he wanted to do for me no less than what his first master teacher exposed him to at Cambridge.

"Many a man has had his power comprised by a dalliance into sodomy or for failure to resist a young man when his virility is in bloom. To slake one's appetite for the hedonistic pleasures is to dine not wisely, but too well he was prone to say. While he plentifully tasted the sweets of the world, never once did I hear him regret his insatiable cravings, seek sorrow or repent for his indiscretions no matter how vile, so strong was his appetite.

"My tutor's coarse streak showed through as we sneaked off to regale ourselves and become beastly drunk on occasions. Preferring to leave the moral burdens to the priggish clergymen and the working class, he took advantage of my idyllic innocence and introduced me to his convivial ways. His venality and cynicism were evident in regard to religion, and he abhorred and detested the pious, psalm-sing Christians. He developed a mordant wit about him and identified with John Wilkes, the famous essayist of the 17th century of whom it was said wrote of life:

*Life can little else supply,*
*But a few good fucks,*
*Then we die.*

"While he was a handsome, dashing, and articulate youth, he was also strong and athletic, and was noted for his skill in playing the wall game at Cambridge. Wall was a rough game, usually played alongside a wall near the river in most cases. While he was a man of letters, charming and entertaining on occasions, he could be vulgar and chauvinistic and his irreverence outraged people at times.

"My tutor was a misogynist and had an aversion to meddlesome whores, as he called them. To satiate his sexual needs, he preferred the male brothels. He had a coterie of famous, aristocratic friends, many of whom shared his bent, and they introduced me to the hells above Hanover Square and St. James.

"Mr. Sone, the porcine-appearing proprietor of the St. James Club, encouraged our patronage in particular. Given the fact that we were high-born gentlemen, he assumed it would afford him sanction against a police raid for our gambling along with the other bloated aristocrats insolent with wealth.

"Our favorite haunt, however, became the male brothel at 19 Cleveland Street, near the Tottenham Court Road. The owner, Charles Hammond, was a true, licentious Negrophile. He was known to court persons of quality who had a predilection for a wide range of tastes in human flesh and fetishes that would pay handsomely for a child's services.

"A leech-like toady, Hanson's driver was always at my tutor's beck and call. An unholy alliance, I thought at the time for high-born gentlemen. The driver was a seedy miscreant, but it was suggested by my tutor that he would help us get our jollies. A smart enough plunger, I will say, he had all the gossip bordering on blackmail. Blackmail was becoming an art form on Cleveland Street and in the East End of London. It would prove to be my undoing with the Royal family in the end."

Collier sat reflecting on the tape he just heard. Was it a case of reincarnation under hypnosis? How could Steve have such detailed knowledge of the East End in London, and who were the personalities he was describing under hypnosis? Scientific research has supported cases of prior life memory recollections, especially among the young. *The third session should be very informative,* Collier mused to himself finishing off his brandy.

# Chapter 11

"Steve, is that you?" Barbara called out from the den.

"Yes, are the boys in bed?" he replied going directly to the kitchen and opening a beer.

"They are dead tired from practice," she said as he entered the den and sprawled out on the couch.

"How did it go with Dr. Collier?" she asked with concern in her voice. "Was there anything unusual?"

"Don't know if it is unusual or not," Steve said. "Dr. Collier did seem more preoccupied this time than before as I recall."

"How do you feel?" Barbara inquired.

"My neck is really stiff," Steve replied. "I think I will take two aspirins and go to bed. By the way, I plan to be home early tomorrow to take the boys to football practice."

He did not feel it advisable to discuss his conversation with Mr. Price regarding her observations regarding Jim Champion. She was right enough on most issues as it was, he thought to himself.

The next afternoon, Steve was home early as planned. All four boys were excited over their win Saturday and eager to get to practice. Brad had the physical skills and the mentality, Steve knew to be good at football, while Bruce seemed more interested in eating. Bruce used football to justify his appetite. Because Bruce was always at the pantry door looking for something to eat, Steve called him "Rat." The discussion in the van among the four boys was all about winning and what they had to do in order to win. They acknowledged they were younger than the other clubs, since they were newly organized and some of the other teams had team members from the past year.

"We should win, based on how well we played last Saturday."

"No one should win, Brad," Steve said. "It is all about competing and doing your best."

"Winning is everything, Dad, that is what Coach Champion said."

"Competing is everything, Brad. Winning is sometimes more luck than skill or preparation in dictating the outcome of a football game. A competitor is always admired and people forget in time if a game was won or lost. Some of the best players in baseball have never played in the World Series."

"Why do they call it the World Series in baseball," Bruce asked, "if they only invite American?"

"No one but you could ever have thought of that," Brad replied at his brother's remark.

"Fellows, I am going to let you out while I run a few errands, but I will be back when football practice is over," Steve instructed the boys as they crawled out of the van with their gear.

"I hope you are going to be back in time to see us run some plays," Brad said.

"Don't worry, I will," Steve said as he watched a few other parents drop off their boys for practice.

Steve did not want the boys or the coach to know he was observing practice, so he decided to get a Coke and a candy bar at the Pic-A-Pac down the street from the high school. He was amused at Bruce's comment regarding the World Series. *Maybe we are a little too arrogant in this country? We may need to consider the perception of other countries in our decision making.* He would have to remember to tell Barbara of Bruce's comment regarding the World Series.

You could see the stone walls of the Smokey Harrington Baseball Field at the high school where the team practiced. The clerk at the Pic-A-Pac was a senior citizen who was apparently working to supplement his Social Security benefit. He was also a veteran apparently, based on the VFW baseball cap he was wearing. Since business was slow this time of day, Steve felt the need to make conversation as he drank his Coke and ate his candy bar.

"I wonder who built that baseball field." Steve nodded to the clerk, who was standing behind the counter.

"It looks like it was meant to be a prison, with that eight-foot high stone wall fence and single gate," the clerk observed.

"I wonder if it was not built back in the old Civilian Conservation Corps days," Steve responded.

"It would be too expensive to build today for sure," the clerk observed.

"I notice you are wearing a VFW cap, did you serve in WWII?" Steve asked, respecting his age.

"Yea, Dixie Division," he replied proudly.

"I worked at the Vet Center as a volunteer counselor," Steve said.

"You wet nursed those crybabies. Huh?" he said, as he frowned slightly.

Steve was not put off by his cynicism because working at the Vet Center had hardened him for negative reactions by Korean and Viet Nam veterans alike. Since he did not have experience in counseling WWII veterans, he was not inclined to pull out the old vet on his attitude.

"You think Viet Nam veterans are crybabies?"

"Yea, I see them at the VA Medical Center all the time. They whine and complain to increase their case for an increase in their degree of disablement, so the VA will pay them more money. For some of them, it is competition with their fellow vets, so they can brag at the American Legion or VFW clubs regarding their war injuries," he went on to say, reading Steve's face for a reaction.

Steve had learned from counseling at the Vet Center that negative self-statements are to be ignored. His role at the Vet Center was to reinforce positive behaviors and to ignore negative behavior. Steve had to admit to himself, that there were a lot of "want-a-bees" among Viet Nam veterans and some non-veterans for service in combat. Every man wondered how he would stand the test in combat when he saw films of combat or read horror stories about war.

"How do you feel about service organizations for veterans?" Steve asked, expecting a more positive response, since he wore a VFW cap.

"They have pretty much gone to hell," he replied caustically. He went on to say that WWII veterans got involved in the community and established baseball leagues and recreational parks for the youth. All the service organizations want to do now is to lobby to increase their membership rolls. The Disabled Veterans Organization has assisted veterans in lobbying Congress to get increased compensation for disabled veterans. They are also effective at leveraging VA Regional Offices to increase compensation, for individual veterans on the basis of worsening of condition.

"We had one guy who passed himself off as a Viet Nam veteran at the VFW Club. He was rated a 100% by the VA for war-related injuries. He misspoke one night at the bar, and a Viet Nam veteran who sat beside him reported him as being suspect. Turned out he was not even in Viet Nam. His injuries occurred in an off-duty car wreck while he was on military leave. Since he was technically still in the service, his injuries were considered service-connected," he growled indignantly.

Familiar with the old vet's concerns, Steve had heard similar criticisms from Viet Nam veterans themselves at the Vet Center. Too many of our institutions in and out of government were self-serving and deserved oversight and review based on current need, in Steve's opinion. Walking over to the counter, Steve threw his drink in the trash can.

"I will see you later, partner, I need to watch my two boys practice football at the park. Have a nice day," Steve offered.

The old vet limped from behind the counter as Steve started to walk out the door.

"Remember you can't buy happiness," he said, smiling at Steve.

*That could be the thought for the day,* Steve thought to himself as he waved to the vet on leaving.

A few parents' cars were inside the parking lot, Steve noted as he parked next to the big tin gate, which served as an entrance to the baseball field. A huge tin shed covered the park and protected fans from the weather. The field was huge as far as baseball fields go and seemed to have major league dimensions. The team was working out at the far end of the park. A number of women were chatting together in a small group as he made his way down the concrete walkway to observe practice. Two groups, one group was made up of older players who ran plays, while another group of younger players was in a circle, unattended, practiced blocking.

He recognized the drill known as the nutcracker drill Barbara was referencing in her complaint. He stood and watched the drill for a few minutes. It was obvious to him what was going on; the coach was using the drill to discourage younger and less talented players. Since the rules required you to play all the team members in a game, some coaches would attempt to run off the less talented players and players too young to contribute.

The drill required a small group of players to get in a circle with one player in the middle. The player in the middle was required to spin around like a top and individually block the other players who would take him on, one at a time. The drill was a difficult drill even for college players. Steve knew that some coaches in college used the drill to test a young player's toughness. It was a great drill for bullies who wanted to test themselves against younger, less seasoned players. Steve felt the drill had no placed in a youth league and certainly not the Pop Warner League, where young boys were just developing and maturing. He headed for the field not sure of what he should do or say. He always tried to keep his temper in check and just deal with issue and not let personalities get involved.

"Hey, Dad, come watch us run plays," Bruce said, as he saw his father striding across the field towards them.

"Hello, Steve, I am glad you could come and see us practice. I think Brad has the makings of a good quarterback," Jim Champion offered, looking up from his playbook.

"Thanks, I have some time on my hands, and thought I would watch for a while," Steve said, trying not to be too obvious.

Steve watched Brad run the offense and realized his son was athletic and ahead of some of the other players as far as his coordination and skills were concerned. Bruce was playing at the split end position and seemed to have good hands and ran pass patterns well during the passing drills.

Champion called an end to the passing drills and said the team needed to work on running the football between the tackles.

"You have to run inside if you want to win," he said.

The offense ran plays against the defense that was made up of less talented players, since the better athletes had to play both ways. Hardly any tackles were made by the defense against the offense, as you would expect. This caused Champion to get outdone with the defense, saying they at least could get in the way of the running backs.

"Coach, I think I see the problem. Why don't I get in the tackle position and I will play the role of the defensive end for demonstration purposes?" Steve suggested.

"That is a good idea," Champion said, and moved to replace the tackle at one of the positions on offensive line.

The defensive end stepped back and let Steve assume his position. Before he got down in his stance, Steve said to the defensive lineman, "The most important thing is to watch the ball. Don't listen to the snap count and don't look in the backfield. Your first step is the most important. After you make contact, fight through the offensive lineman's helmet, which will lead to the direction of the runner. You can use your hands to get the blocker off you as you pursue the runner."

Champion was struggling to get in an offensive lineman's position. He had to pull up his pants at the knees to squat. Steve called out to Brad to run the play. He though as he looked across the line, that Champion looked liked one of George Hallas' old Chicago Bear linemen in the early '50s. Steve exploded across the line on the snap of the ball and caught Champion under the face with a forearm shiver that sent him sprawling backwards on his butt. The kids all laughed at the coach when they saw him struggling to get to his feet. But it scared them when he turned to face them and his nose and lips were bleeding profusely.

"You bastard, you did that intentionally," Champion screamed in pain and embarrassment.

"You coach them from now on, I quit," he said, as he got to his feet.

"Come on, Rocky. We are going home."

"But, Dad, I want to play," Rocky cried out, pleading with his dad.

The boys were in a state of shock, they had never seen anything like that up close, and from two adults at that. Steve knew it was beyond their comprehension to understand at this point in time, so he did not apologize. He just told them to tell their parents that he would be coaching the team from now on.

"We will have a team meeting tomorrow to talk about what we need to do as a football team and to set goals for the team. Tell your parents that they are invited to sit in on our team meeting," Steve offered as the players stood silently in a small group as if for protection and support for each other.

No one said a word, not even Brad or Bruce; they just stood and looked at him, like deer caught in the headlights of a passing car.

"O.K., everybody, we are going to get down on one knee and pray. This will be our routine after every practice," Steve said as he gathered the team around him.

The players looked at each other and left quietly, without a word being spoken between them. The filed silently out of the park. In their minds they knew that things were going to be different from now own. One thing was for sure, no one was going to question Coach Haralson's authority. On the way home Steve was praying that Barbara would not kill him when she learned that he and Jim Champion were in an altercation on the practice field. The fact that some of the parents witnessed the incident made matters worse in his mind. What he had gotten himself in for, he speculated on the way home, now that he was going to have to coach a little league football team?

# Chapter 12

Since he was obligated to coach a football team in the Pop Warner League, Steve informed Collier the next morning to make arrangements to change his appointment schedule. Collier assured Steve he was happy to accommodate his schedule.

Collier appeared more congenial and direct in his manner in their third session it seemed to Steve.

"Have you found any connection between your headaches and your life situation?" Collier asked.

"No, not really, my headaches seem to have abated somewhat, now that I think about it."

"Let us talk about your life experiences. I know, of course, that you served in Viet Nam. Did you visit other foreign countries?" Collier asked.

"No, I have always wanted to visit South America, but that's about it."

"No interest in England or Europe?" Collier inquired.

"Not really, of course, I was a student of military history and WWII. I knew of the battles our country fought in Europe and the Pacific," Steve said.

"What about your interest in history? Have you any interest in biographies of famous or interesting people?" Collier asked.

"Being a Southerner, I have studied the history of the Civil War," Steve answered.

"What was France's role in the Civil War?" Collier inquired.

"The French thought little of the English influence. They felt they were in a position to influence the Civil War and have political leverage if the South won the war," Steve commented. He wondered at the time what that had to do with his dreams.

"What does the word 'Hanover' mean to you?" Dr. Collier asked.

"Not anything really, it sounds German or Russian, I would guess it is a city in Germany," he said.

Collier could find no basis for Steve's historical recollections, no prior brain imprints of any kind for the Victorian period. Under hypnosis, Steve presented the following dream in the third session:

"On the night of my downfall, James Stephen, my tutor, John Netley and myself sallied forth towards the East End of London for dinner and a night of entertainment. A specially designed hearse served to transport us discreetly and protect my Royal personage from prying eyes. No one would suspect that royalty would be riding in a hooded, specially designed hearse. James would later introduce me to his friends from Cambridge at the posh, opulent Marlborough Club. We were a noisy group of young voluptuaries, bellowing drunkards who regaled ourselves with expensive champagne and elegantly prepared food. A few of the club's members were seen having champagne on the veranda while mooning over the sensitive young boys who worked at the Marlborough Club.

"We visit 19 Cleveland Street to satisfy our vicarious pleasures for voyeurism as James called it and the charm of birching. Given my youth and strongly developing sensuality, I followed along, as we rode in a hearse through the narrow streets filled with raw sewage to 19 Cleveland Street in the East End of London. Netley, the whore monger, allowed us to mingle indiscriminately in the East End and to visit our favorite haunts. He knew every backstreet and back alley in the East End and knew how to deal with the lower order or meaner sort. James booked a table for the night's entertainment next to the orchestra stalls.

"The club was well appointed and posh, with dark red velvet drapes, erotic marble statues and dancing Pans on the walls. It was like an erotic garden. Men were handsome and fashionably dressed, and a few wore masks or costumes. They drank champagne and waited impatiently for the high advertised entertainment for the evening. James implied we need stronger stuff and ordered brandy to quench our thirst or remove any inhibitions we may have for the night's entertainment.

"The orchestra played a drum roll as the lights dimmed. A young, wooly headed Nubian was borne nude, flamboyantly aloft on the shoulders of four nude, Nubian bearers in a triumphal march through the crowd. The youth, grinning like a hebephrenic, was ceremoniously paraded to the stage where he was spotlighted nude for all eyes to feast upon. A distinguished looking gentleman wearing a fashionable tux moved from backstage to stand next to the Nubian to offer a foretaste of drama.

"'Gentlemen, the bidding will start now. Who will be the first to bid?' he announced with a flourish, while signaling for a drum roll from the band.

"'Five pounds,' a gentleman shouted in the crowd.

"'That's the standard charge,' another snorted with authority as he swaggered for the crowd's attention. Everyone in the crowded room roared with good humor at the bidder's spirit. The crowd's libido ran riot throughout the club at the degree of debauchery and sensual expectations in the offering.

"'Adoration for the divine,' one gentleman offered in jest as the men around him cackled. The gentlemen in the audience laughed with salacious pleasure of craving at the sheer indulgence that awaited them.

"The London police later arrested the owner of the club. The rent boys gave us away. I was later identified by Thomas Winslow, one of the post office boys, as having frequented 19 Cleveland Street along with two other members of the ruling class, Earl of Euston and Lord H. Arthur Somerset. Of course, no one had to go to the limbo. Government officials immediately informed the Queen and arrangements were made for the aristocrats to travel overseas and the owner of club fled to America to avoid the levying of criminal charges.

"When the Queen saw the name, Prince Albert Victor, in all the cables later she was outdone with me, of course at the time, the very idea that the eldest son of the Prince of Wales and heir presumptive to the throne of England would be involved in such a vile scandal was unthinkable for a woman of her status. She decried that I had inherited my father's vices without retaining many virtues, to say the least. Even the commoners were wont to express outrage at the behavior of the inbred crowd of royal stock that had become morally bankrupt."

Nursing his drink, Collier sat late into the night, pondering his client's third session. Playing the tape recorder over and over again, he felt his training and experience in psychiatry had never prepared him for a case like Steve's.

He preferred not to confront Steve with the content of his dreams until he had better understanding of the potential dynamics of his case. He ruled out confabulation, a symptom common in various psychoses, where the patient, upon suggestion, relates imaginary experiences as true. Steve, by all accounts, seemed to be a very stable person and had a good sense of feeling and personal identity. Multi-personality was also discounted as a factor in Collier's mind.

Steve was not subject to waking state memories; there was no evidence of any emotional catharsis. He was not given to fanciful thinking about telepathy, precognition, or mind-reading parlor games to contact the dead. He was not involved in any experiments with the military or CIA regarding extra-sensory perception. Collier was aware of ongoing research in out-of-body experiences while dreaming with subjects. Some researchers have postulated that we have a reality beyond this world and the potential within our minds to separate from the soul or physical being. Collier was too open-minded to discount any theory given man's limitation on knowledge.

Collier rang up his solicitor, Philip Collin, in London and asked him to make some inquiries in regards to the historical references made by Steve while under hypnoses. Philip was a longtime friend of Collier's who married a Navy veteran from Mississippi. Lisa was a civilian protocol officer for the U.S. Department of Defense in Italy when they first met. After they were married for a while Philip told Collier that Lisa was high maintenance.

"Collier, is that really you, I have been trying to reach you for weeks," Philip said.

Collier heard Lisa in the background wanting to know who was calling this time of the night.

"It's Collier, Lisa. I will take the call in the study."

"Collier, let me tell you first of off that I am taking care of your business affairs as you requested, but I got a call from Interpol and they want to interview you right away."

"Philip, I do not want them to know where I am until I conclude my psychotherapy sessions with a client," Collier requested.

"I don't think that is good enough, but I can hold them off on client-privilege for a while." Philip chastised Collier when he understood the nature of his inquiry. "Don't tell me you are going to roam through the slums of White Chapel like Cyril Burt to solve the mystery of Jack-the-Ripper?" Philip commented.

Sir Cyril Burt was knighted by the King of England and was a noted psychologist.

"The people and places you are referencing were considered suspects by Scotland Yard and other Ripperologists," Philip said, but he knew that a lot of information in Ripper murder case File has been lost or destroyed.

Collier gave Philip his e-mail address to download research data on the parties in question. He was aware of the fact that the Jack-the-Ripper murder case was never solved, with many case theories having been advanced in England and abroad for the murders. Since sleep would not come easily, Collier decided to review the research on the mind of a serial killer. Serial killers were found to be typically white males, between the ages of 20-30 years. Their main motive was usually sex, with power, manipulation, control, and domination. Victims of serial killers were usually found to be prostitutes. Between the murders, a cooling off period was usually in evidence. To avoid detection, disposal sites were commonly selected on the basis of the killer's convenience and awareness of the layout of the streets. Collier's idea was to apply research on the mind of a serial killer to Steve's tape recordings for comparison with the unsolved White Chapel murders associated with the Jack-the-Ripper case file.

# Chapter 13

Steve met with Dr. Collier shortly after noon on the following day. They quickly settled in the routine to induce hypnosis. Collier was all business it seemed to Steve and preoccupied with his thoughts. While he was friendly enough and said the right things, there seemed to be something different in his actions. Maybe it was his feelings of insecurity, he did not know. The session went as before and again Dr. Collier did not discuss the content of his dreams.

"Will you play back the tapes for me at some point in time?" Steve felt compelled to ask for he was interested in the content of his dreams.

The question caught Collier by surprise. It was an appropriate question given the circumstances and Collier was challenged for a response. He did not want to lie to a client. He was aware of his therapeutic responsibility his to client. Collier now realized that Steve was picking up on the non-verbal communication between them and was aware of a change in his demeanor or attitude.

"Steve, I have resisted making any interpretations regarding the content or subject matter in your dreams because I questioned the relevance," Collier said. "Frankly, I don't under the dynamics to develop a treatment plan." Collier replied honestly for the case was most puzzling. "My best impression is that you are having an out-of-body experience as far as your dream state is concerned under hypnosis."

"I do feel like I am floating outside my body sometimes in my dreams, but I never have any sense of time or place," Steve replied. "I would just wake up feeling a sense of dread and anxiety."

"I see," Collier said. "Have you experienced these feelings lately?"

"No, as a matter of fact," Steve said. "Outside the usual headache, I don't have any physical complaints after sleeping at night."

"How do you feel about me taping your future sessions, without interpretation, until I can formulate a treatment plan?" Collier asked.

"I have no problem with that; I have full confidence in your judgment."

Later Steve reflected on his counseling session and decided that he would not tell Barbara of his discussions with Dr. Collier relative to the content of his dreams. He felt it best not to worry her, since Dr. Collier did not represent any serious medical or psychological problem that would require treatment.

True to their word, the boys did not say anything to Barbara about the incident at practice the day before. Beginning to feel a little upbeat about the prospects of coaching a little league football team, Steve decided to draw up offensive and defensive schemes for practice the next day. Because he would be spending more time with the boys, he knew Barbara was happy for he had been so distant in the past and busy with his work when they were younger.

As he pulled the Bronco into the parking lot next to the stadium, Steve was concerned regarding parents' reaction to his coaching the team and his incident with Jim Champion.

"Hi, Coach," several parents greeted him as he walked by the stands, so he knew the word was getting around, at least among the players' parents. The players waited for him with wide-eyed expectations.

"O.K., I want everybody to get in a circle," he said.

The players started breaking up into small circles and Steve laughed.

"Not that kind of circle, circle around me," Steve instructed the boys. All the players laughed nervously and saw the joke.

Practice went well and he was feeling good about himself until he saw Edith Jones waiting for him at the gate.

"Coach, can I talk to you?" she said.

"Sure, you boys go head and get in the truck."

Edith Jones was the widow of a well-liked policeman in Hattiesburg who was killed in the line of duty.

"Coach, Johnny told me what happened at practice. He told me you would be the new coach. I just want you to know how much it means to me to see that Johnny has a good role model, now that his dad is gone. He was really scared of Coach Champion and only went out for football because he wanted to wear a football uniform with the other boys," she said teary eyed.

Steve was almost moved to tears as Mrs. Jones hugged him, while the boys in the truck watched. Steve reflected on what Mrs. Jones told him about her son on the way home. What she said now made his coaching the team all worthwhile, and that was what the Pop Warner League was all about in his mind. Steve did not discuss with the boys what Mrs. Jones said to him, he felt they probably already knew. Of course, Barbara had to inquire later how the first day at practice went with him being the new coach. Bruce took the opportunity to tell her he saw his dad hugging Mrs. Jones.

"What," she said, "hugging Edith Jones?"

"Wait a minute, Barbara," Steve replied defensively.

Barbara was beside herself laughing at his embarrassment.

"Did you really think you could keep something like that quiet?" she laughed. "Steve, it is all over town how you knocked Jim Champion on his ass," Barbara replied at his naivete. "I had at least four women approach me at the grocery store to tell me about it this morning. Not only that, but Julie Champion called me after you left for practice and asked me if you would take Rocky back on the team, that he was crying his little eyes out."

"Well, I'll be," Steve replied.

"Now tell me about Edith Jones," she said, while hugging him close. Barbara was as proud of Steve now as she had ever been in her life.

# Chapter 14

Collier could not believe the fanciful tale Steve represented on the tape. He replayed the tape recorder several times and each time he was astonished by the content. The fact that Steve had no recollection of the content or the subject matter on the tape was intriguing. Was the answer to the most gruesome, bizarre series of murders in English history revealed in the narrative of the fourth session? Collier could only speculate. He reasoned that the killer's traits, motivation and disposal of the bodies were consistent with research on serial killers. He was committed to playing the tape one more time, before he called Osmond to proceed with their plan.

The fourth recording session was spellbinding for Collier as he listened intently to the obsessive, imperative recurring theme of Steve's dream fancies.

"I have been a lover of keyholes and spying almost from birth. I guess it is related to my small stature and insignificant personage as far as the Royal family is concerned. I see myself as an elusive and mysterious figure, obsessed with moving from keyhole to keyhole to liberate my repressed emotion. I derive a keen satisfaction from viewing for it satiates my curiosity and adds to the thrill for erotic exploration. My fear is of being caught and punished for my surreptitious, voyeuristic nature has been a lifelong concern. I feared that solitude would be imposed by my father as punishment for my malign curiosity and peeping.

"My father has a room with the walls filled with pictures of nude women in erotic poses. He is preoccupied with leisure pursuits. He has an enormous appetite for pleasure and amorous adventures and is given to hedonistic nihilism. Leisure and pleasure are a rule of life among the upper classes you know.

"I have been the problem child for my parents, since birth and cannot live up to their royal expectations. Others perceived me as temperamental and sullen with no capacity to interact with other boys on their terms. My father's friends refer to me as the prodigal son and the princeling heir.

"My tutor, James K. Stephen, turned out to be a political opportunist, who was quite willing to exploit our relationship to advance his position in the community. He was at the same time quite willing to promote my developing sexual orientation by introducing me to the coarser, physical side of life, since he was given to luxurious habits. Higher sodomy was an art form and gilded vice at Cambridge according to James. He implied that one was required to sally forth among the common folk, as a form of hazing, to develop one's sexual proclivities, even thought homosexuality was against the law for the nonce. James himself was taught by a faculty member and noted writer at Eton, who, it was said, invited sailors and members of the lower class to his rooms. He was later dismissed from the faculty when the gossip became commonplace.

"James himself passed from one lover to another, and changed his lovers as often as his cravat. 'Dearest cakes,' he called them. He admitted to me later, in our relationship, that his bent had led him to men he otherwise would loathe and despise.

He once described a sexual misadventure in Felixstowe along the seacoast, when he attempted to satisfy his appetite for big, crude hairy men for sport. He suffered a lifelong injury after he was hit over the head by a mariner with a rum bottle in a low dive along the coastline. But he loved the slangy Queen's English spoken by the sailors in the pubs along the docks in Felixstowe. He loved to watch the rolling gait of the mariners and told of his misadventure one night while under heavy drink. He spoke of overhearing one mariner say to another, 'Your arse or mine?' while they were skylarking with one another in a pub.

"Noted for his public speaking and writing, James, to his credit, continued to write and work as a journalist long after his suffered injury in Felixstowe. He returned to Cambridge in the spring of 1891 and lectured on constitutional history and later published the *Living Languages.*

"James' father accepted his fancies, as long as he did not involve the family in a scandal. The Royal family soon learned of our misadventures and took efforts to dissolve the relationship for a time. But as any two delinquents, we were soon back together again, after I served my time in the service of my country. We reunited again at Cambridge, but James had developed a darker side to his nature since last seen by me. He had developed a pathological hatred of women and represented them as being the downfall of man. He hated whores and Jews with equal vigor and had developed an uncommon streak of malice. Still the Jews come to settle the East End, he opined like fleas to a dog with their Yiddish dialect and dark, gloomy Semitic looks. I wondered at times how a man like Sir James Kitzjames Stephen, lawyer and jurist, who wrote, *Liberty, Equality, Fraternity,* could have borne such a son as James K. Stephen with his views towards foreigners.

"James once described whores as trading ladies who only wanted an opportunity to establish their fortune, captivate your heart, and then your purse. Many a whore walked the streets of

East End in the hope that they might find themselves under Royal patronage, James opined. All the while James assured me that he was on to all the whores' tricks to make use of cock oysters and lascivious pictures to gratify a man's carnal lust and libidinous appetite. None can deny he opined their sly attempts to tactfully tighten up those little physiological flaccid problems with alum water to heighten a man's pleasure.

"They truly lay a cunning trap for an innocent like you, he told me once, after I professed my agony of shame and remorse over a hideous mistake of sexual weakness. He cautioned that every prudent man would do well to learn the mysteries of a whore's trade to avoid the cheat and those who can destroy you with a simple embrace.

"My life, of course, has been one of conflicting interest and perils; loyalty to my family and the ease of sensual pleasures that flourished in the East End caused me to have passing moods of despondency and truculence for my habitual life of luxurious indolence. Since our last association, James began to voice strange, obsessive, bizarre ideas and became twisted of mind, so I thought. He had cruel wit about him that made him distasteful at times. Dr. Gull, the Queen's physician, had a practice at Finsbury Square that bordered on central London and the East End. He was seeing James for his malady and me as well to determine my need for regular arsenic treatments for annoying rashes and pimples on my body. Gull was seen by some as a political opportunist, but I only saw him as a friend of the Royal family.

"James continued to use Netley for his forays into the netherworld of London and the East End. While an obsequious, servile character on the one hand, Netley was not one to eschew physical violence if the need arose. It was said that he could put such a fear in a man or woman that they could not spit dry rice. The idea being that fear dries up the saliva, and one cannot spit out dry rice. He was always involved in some perfidy or imbroglio and I never truly understood the relationship between the two.

"He was however familiar with the stews as it was called in the East End. He knew all the dimly lit streets and open coal-holes; and how to avoid being trapped in a cul-de-sac to carry out his evil intent. We never had problems with the lower class or meaner sort while visiting the East End. Slums of the East End was a challenge to aristocrats to seek out the sexual subjectivities in their nature without recrimination and for some it was called slumming. While prowlers and idlers were all about, the Jews and the Irish made up the main of the populace in the East End with immigration being what it was in London at the time.

"Prostitution was more prevalent than ever with whores on nearly all the streets in the East End given the hard times. Blackmail was becoming a marketable source of income in London to extract money from the wealthy for their misadventures or even the specter of gossip in some case. Bastards and unwanted infants that could establish a legitimate claim before the courts were the main source of blackmail in the East End for the times. Heirs of a morganatic relationship could not establish a claim against the crown of England and any threat could become fatal. Many a man would recognize a bastard son in his will if the person distinguished himself on the field of battle or had become famous for some literary or business endeavor. One could be a man of poor birth but not of breeding, it was said of some men at the time.

"On my frequent visits to the artist colony in the Cleveland Street area, I met a young, attractive Catholic girl who lived with an artist that was known to the Royal family. Since we shared common interests based on our youth and artistic interests, I enjoyed the company of the family and felt more accepted in their humble surroundings than I did the royal estate. The young girl later had a daughter out of wedlock, and over the years, it was rumored that I was the father. As times passed, the rumor grew wings in large part because of the artist's friendship with my mother. The gossip soon reached the ears of Netley that a member of the Royal family was being blackmailed by whores in the East End. When Netley learned that I was the target of the blackmail conspiracy, he reported the rumor to James. Out of some misguided sense of loyalty to me, the Royal family, or his obsessive hatred for whores, James decided to avenge the Royal family's honor after Netley conveyed the blackmail scheme. Netley was commissioned by James to find out who the whores were behind the blackmail scheme. Vowing to avenge me, James charged Netley that he would stop their malicious tongues with the bite of sharp steel. I, of course, was unaware of the dimension of the scandal and did not have knowledge of the plan until the deed was done. James knew of my weak constitution and inferred that he felt I might give the plan for retribution away. Later he professed the planning in detail to accomplish his ghoulish aim to kill the five whores who dared to blackmail royalty.

"The five whores were identified by Netley. He recorded their current lodging to James in time. Because most of the lower class would be in from hard slavish work or revelry the night before, the plan was to kill all five whores on a Friday, Saturday, or Sunday in the early morning. The hearse would provide the means and give them protection from scrutiny, since no one would question a hearse in the early morning hours or even care for that matter, according to James.

"Meat wagons were known to regularly carry the dead off the streets at night in the East End and disposed of them. For most of the residents in the East End, a hearse would appear to be an ambulance with a surgeon who always accompanied the driver to pronounce a victim dead. It was far better than throwing the dead bodies in the Thames, which was already populated from dead animals and sewage from the city. The River Thames' stench was so bad at time that it interfered with Parliament being in session during the summer months.

"Netley knew of a store room for iron works that was abandoned since the tenant let the license lapse. The store room was near to the London Hospital and a slaughter house. Both locations would serve to avoid detection from prying eyes to carry out their foul deed. James was aware that medical students and surgeons at the London Hospital had a lucrative trade with grave robbers for cadavers in order to develop their anatomical knowledge.

"The 1832 Anatomy Act allowed unclaimed dead bodies on the street to be sent to hospitals for the study of anatomy. The worst that could happen was that they would be taken for grave robbers and, of course, we would feign that it was just a lark, a practical joke to entertain our Royal friends. Netley made arrangements to pick up the victims in a regular Hanson to take them to meet a gentleman at an appointed time. The practice was not an uncommon one, for a prudent man who knew of these things and was given to frequenting the East End. The evil plan was to chloroform and strangle the victims, while dissecting the bodies and transporting them back in canvas slings in the early morning hours to some designated locales in the hell of East End.

"Horse-drawn carts, drays, van and wagon were common place in the East End, and ladies of the night whose maidenhood long vanished often complained to their trade of almost being killed in the street by horse-drawn traffic. Netley himself complained of having to work around the all night tram way that was under construction on Aldgate and the seedy nail gropers who were about on the streets in search of nails and old iron.

"Polly Ann Nichols was their first victim with the body being disposed of close to the warehouse and London Hospital. A practice run, James would say later when he told of their misdeeds. 'We cut the whore from ear to ear,' he said, 'and gently laid her out in a canvas sling on the street as the blood pooled under her head and neck. The body cold except for the heat from the intestines. Black cloaks and black hats were reportedly worn to escape detection in the din around them, with the fighting, screaming, and children squalling at all hours of the night. The inhabitants could care less if someone was being killed or knocked about. James implied that he had to remind Netley of their mission not to rob the wretches and made him return the whore's rings. We carefully place them near the feet of one of the whores we had disemboweled with my surgical knowledge and skill,' James offered pridefully, as he saw himself as a most skilled and learned surgeon.

"I begged not to hear more, when informed of the villainy of the world. The details in the newspaper were far too graphic for my taste. My youthful inexperience hindered me in these matters. I felt a sea of foreboding and feelings of despair. My sense of victimization was powerful, much like a desperate housewife in the East End with five kids and an abusive, out of work, alcoholic husband with no prospects in sight. James mentioned in passing that he saved the best for last, and that the whorish and hideous conspiracy was over. By now I was suffering from the vicissitudes of my own condition, diagnosed as extreme dementia and syphilitic cachexia to express any moral indignation of the conflict-ridden humanity and suffering in the East End.

"Later while I was in a lock hospital and in my own private hell, James came to see me. He seemed remarkably calm for one who professed to having committed a bizarre series of crimes and was still going unpunished. When I questioned him regarding his conscience, he said he was loyal to England's monarchs, and that England's ruling class must be preserved at all cost.

"Dr. Gull, the Queen's physician, was apparently aware of the conspiracy to kill the whores in the East End, from what I could discern. I suspected he was treating James to eliminate his vicarious impulses. Gull was an authoritarian figure that James respected in large part because he was close to Queen Victoria.

He was, to his credit, successful in controlling James' immature explosive reactions and impulses when temptations threaten him to act out. The key was environmental manipulation and medication, from what I understand. To remove stress, Gull instructed James not to frequent the East End and to develop his literary interest and talent. James admitted that he threw himself at his work as if he was the devil himself. Truer words may never have been spoken, I thought at the time as an acting sycophant. I freely admit that James was a libertine good at wicked work, just like his poetry, but I was not aware that he was capable of murder. The idea is nauseating and would make any man's blood curl in his veins. He talked of returning to work as Clerkship of Assize, and later to Cambridge where he was sought after as a public speaker. He seemed to me to have resolved some inner conflicts and saw himself as less contemptible and despicable for his actions. James and I had a special friendship that only he and I could appreciate.

"History will judge us badly, I am sure, but James will leave his mark with his prose and poems for the entire world to see. He was my keyhole through which I viewed the world at its worst and on this score I cannot protest innocence for any court in England would find me guilty. I was molded clay in James' hand, and he was the frame to the world for me at times. He was essentially a gateway to excitement and sexual excess, a keyhole that allowed me to wander through the unconscious mind. I could never assuage the horrors conjured up of the tormented memories that would haunt me to my dying days.

"Later I heard gossip that James had become depressed and was wildly acting out to the point that he was not permitted access to his own club. His mania and violent scenes resulted in his being hospitalized at Bethlem Royal Hospital or Bedlam to my royal staff. Sir George Savage, the Stephen family physician, treated James for his malady. Dr. Savage himself had a questionable reputation for excessive use of physical and chemical restraint of his patients at Bethlem.

"The last word I heard of James was that he was doing badly and refusing to eat. What a shame, I thought at the time, unmindful of my own history. Sadness overwhelmed me I must admit. In this melancholy state, I felt constrained to reflect on my poor judgment and ruminate over my cruel fate. To dream a dream, to peep once more I thought ruefully, as I heard my own death rattle and the horror of my soul."

# Chapter 15

"Oh, my God," Barbara called out to him.

"Dr. Collier was brutally murdered last night," she cried out from the kitchen.

"What!" Steve yelled as he emerged from the bathroom with a towel around his waist.

The small television set in the kitchen reported that Dr. Raymond Collier, a psychiatrist from New York and a resident of Lake Serene in Lamar County, Mississippi, was brutally murdered in his sleep around 5 this morning according to investigators.

The telephone rang as Steve and Barbara stood transfixed in the kitchen listening to the latest report.

"Brad, please answer the phone," Steve called out to his son who was getting ready for school. Brad had rushed out in the hallway when he heard his mother cry out.

"It's for you, Dad, it's the sheriff."

"The sheriff?" Steve replied brusquely. *What does he want this time of day?* Steve said to himself as he headed to the phone.

"What can I do for you, Lewis?" he said, not connecting his visits with Dr. Collier and the killing.

"Steve, we need you to come down town to the office as soon as possible, we need to ask you a few questions," the sheriff demanded.

"Questions?" Steve inquired. "What kind of questions?"

"We will talk about it once you get here, Steve," the sheriff said authoritatively.

"Why is Lewis calling you?" Barbara asked, now standing by Steve's side.

"He wants me to come down to the office as early as possible; he wants to ask me some questions," Steve replied his voice strained.

"What kind of questions?" Barbara asked wide-eyed and with concern.

"I may be one of the few people locally that have been on the property when you think about it," he replied grudgingly not wanting to think about the consequences.

"How did the sheriff know that you were seeing Dr. Collier professionally? That information is privileged," Barbara said uneasily.

"Osmond could have told him, I guess." Steve with a sigh.

"Do you trust Osmond?"

"Yes," he said without any hesitation, but not really thinking why.

"I want to go with you," Barbara said with concern still in her voice.

"I don't think that is necessary," he said brusquely.

"Good, then we will go together," she replied cheerfully.

"Barbara, you know that they are going to want to interview me alone," Steve stammered sharply.

"That's O.K., I will talk to Sally," she replied, trying to be cheerful.

Steve knew he was not going to win this discussion, so he headed to the bedroom to get dressed feeling the strain now.

The first person they saw in the sheriff's office was Sally. She was a fixture in the community now since her husband died in the line of duty as a policeman. Widowed with two children, the sheriff took her on as his secretary more than ten year ago. One of her sons was still in college, while the daughter was now a practicing lawyer in Memphis.

"Hello, Barbara," Sally said, like she was expecting her at a church social.

"Let's have some coffee while the boys talk," she said politely on seeing the Haralsons enter the office.

"Thanks, Sally," Barbara replied for she and Sally had been friends for a number of years. She hit the telecom and Barbara and Steve heard her say, "Sheriff, Steve is here."

"Send him in, Sally," the sheriff replied.

Steve headed for the sheriff's private office that was behind the front desk and set off to the right for privacy.

"Come in, Steve, want some coffee?" Lewis Carroll, a garrulous retired Marine Corps veteran, greeted him politely. His office was adorned with Corps memorabilia and war trophies.

"Fine," Steve replied as he eyed the Congressional Medal of Honor that was prominently displayed behind the sheriff's desk.

Steve recalled him admitting one night at the American Legion Club that he actually considered refusing the medal because he did not feel survivors of the war were the real heroes. He reconsidered because he felt an obligation to live an exemplary life for the men who died in service and that was the motivation for him running to be elected sheriff.

"Two coffees for Steve and me, Sally," the sheriff bellowed on the telecom. Steve smiled; he didn't know why he felt the need to use the intercom, as one could hear him all over the office.

Lewis Carroll knew that Steve took his coffee black and that he was in the Intelligence Service while in Viet Nam. Both men had served in Viet Nam, but different tours of duty. The two men had been friends for years and Steve helped the sheriff get elected when bootleggers killed the former sheriff in Kelly's Settlement.

"Steve, I wanted you to come down, right away, because the Negro man on the property said you were the only local that had visited Dr. Collier since he came back from New York."

Steve made no acknowledgment of that fact, he just waited until the sheriff went on with his questioning.

"Steve, we found your name in Dr. Collier's appointment book, and you obviously met with him four occasions. The problem we have is the fact that there are no tapes of your conversation with Dr. Collier and further there are no tapes on the property as far as we can tell or psychiatric notes," he went on to say.

Steve felt the need to be open with Lewis, they had been friends for a long time and they were both in the Rotary Club together.

"I was seeing Dr. Collier on a referral by Dr. Knox because I have been having night terrors and waking up anxious in the morning. I had four sessions. Dr Collier made a tape of each session, along with psychiatric notes that I saw him write. Dr. Collier hypnotized me in all four sessions."

"Why did the killers take your tapes and psychiatric notes?" Lewis asked.

"I don't have a clue," Steve said. "Maybe they were looking for something in particular, and felt Dr. Collier's tapes or notes would help them in their search."

"That is what we surmise also," Lewis said, as if they were confidantes.

"The Negro man on the property said he saw two men in the early morning hours as he was out walking the dogs on the lake. He described a black rental car with out-of-state license parked about two miles from the property lines on Lake Serene. We have an all-points bulletin out for the car now since it is registered in Tennessee," Lewis confided.

"You know, Dr. Collier is pretty much a mystery man here in Forrest County. We don't really know that much about him, except that he is native of Mississippi and a psychiatrist."

"I don't think I can add much to that myself, Lewis. He was a very cordial, helpful individual, as far as the times I met with him on the lake," Steve replied honestly. "Osmond, the caretaker on the property probably has more knowledge of Dr. Collier than anyone else in town," Steve went on to say. "How was he killed?" Steve asked.

"Shot in the face and the body with 12-gauge shotguns, we suspect. They used slugs and were not concerned about the noise the 12-gauges would make apparently. The body was unrecognizable, a bloody gory mess. It was a gruesome sight and Hank, my deputy, got queasy and emptied his watery stomach on the lawn outside." Lewis offered as a matter of fact.

Lewis had experienced some of the most repulsive and nauseous sights a man can envision in Viet Nam so he was not aghast at what he saw.

"The Negro man you call Osmond identified him from the rings he wore and the general body type," Lewis offered pausing for effect, for he was reading Steve's expression.

Noting no response by Steve from his body language, Lewis probed further, setting his coffee cup down on hid desk. "You know we always suspect family and friends first, Steve. What do you know about Osmond?" Lewis muttered dropping his voice.

Steve's facial expression changed quickly and his eyes narrowed as he looked at Lewis. Never in his life did he think he might be a murder suspect and now the sheriff was making a veiled reference that Osmond might be involved somehow.

"From my meetings with the doctor, I learned that he was a loyal caretaker and a long-time personal friend of the Collier family in Kentucky. Surely you don't suspect him. You said two 12-gauge shotguns were involved in the homicide," Steve questioned, his voice rising.

"Don't get worked up. I have to ask, we have a gruesome

murder here and the media will jump all over this for sure. Questions and rumors will run rampant here at the courthouse if I can't offer some rational for the killing. I trust your judgment and I want to be in a position to know the facts when called upon if this thing goes unsolved for any length of time," Lewis replied almost apologetically to his friend.

"I understand and I appreciate the situation you are in on this one," Steve acknowledged.

Paranoia would soon take the town over in Lewis' mind. People feared the unknown, and a homicide in their midst would surely make them uncomfortable if something was not done in short order to clear up the murder case. Lawyers would make the most of it, and every reformed bootlegger in the county would relish the opportunity to run him down or run for sheriff themselves. Klan remnants would charge racism from some backwater community to stir up trouble if a black man was within fifty miles of the crime scene.

You only had to scratch a man or woman's arm in Mississippi to see racism because of the propaganda and political bigotry still being fostered to make Mississippi the scapegoat for racism and slavery. Special interest groups were actively working to absolve themselves of past sins to maintain power in the Democratic party. "Johnnie jump ups" could be found everywhere now politically ready to criticize the state's past.

"Frankly, it looks like professional hit men, but we do not understand why they did not use silencers to avoid detection. My theory is they wanted to make an example and send a message for some reason or other," Lewis said, taking Steve into his confidence. "The New York office gave us the name of his solicitor in London who handles his affairs and he will make all the arrangements regarding burial. I am glad you came down, it is good to see you again. I wish the circumstances would have been better," Lewis said as he took Steve's hand firmly. "By the way, everyone in the office heard about your encounter with Jim Champion, and we all had a good laugh. You know, we think a lot of Edith Jones and miss her husband. He was a good law enforcement officer," Lewis said, escorting Steve to the waiting room.

While Barbara was waiting patiently, she did not seem worried from the smile on her face. He assumed Sally had assured her that there was not anything to worry about as far as his being questioned by the sheriff.

# Chapter 16

The Alamo Plaza Motel in Jackson was once a high-end motel and restaurant complex in its day, but now the motel was seedy, cheaply furnished and run-down with small cabins that had individual window air conditioning units. The rooms were damp and smelly and the beds lumpy from too much abuse on the weekends. A single wall lamp provided light between the two double beds, seemly as an after thought by maintenance.

"Damn, Mario, why do we have to live like this?" the man said, as he tested a soiled lumpy bed in the dimly lit room.

"We don't, Earl, we could just advertise to these rednecks here in Mississippi that we are in town to do a job," the big, hairy Italian snorted.

"No one will be looking for us in this damn fleabag, that is for sure," Earl replied, as he unpacked his suitcase on the bed.

"Did you notice the swimming pool in front; I saw several dead animals that must have been overcome by the stench from the pool," Earl complained.

"Quit bitching, we will be out of here early in the morning on the way back to Memphis to catch a plane to Chicago," Mario growled in disgust.

He hated to work with these small-timers today, they all see themselves as bigger than life, and want to make a show in public rather than take a low profile. They would not last six months in the old days. Mario missed the old days, the Teamsters union and the control they had over business and the politicians in Chicago. He was a twenty-year-old kid, just back from WWII, when he joined the Teamsters union to become a truck driver. With a chest full of medals and a good-natured disposition, he was well received by all the local members. Mario moved up quickly through the ranks and an over the road truck driver and then union representative. The money was good and he traveled extensively for a while seeing all 48 States. While he was not a loner, the road helped him cope with some of the emotional and physical scars he suffered in the war.

A mob boss on the south side of Chicago soon recognized Mario's loyalty. He convinced him that his talents were going to waste as a truck driver and union steward. Later Mario received an invitation to meet with Jules Scarbone at his country home on the outskirts of the city of Chicago.

"We will keep you on a retainer at $100,000 a year, plus expenses, to work for the family exclusively, just like we do our trial attorneys." Mr. Scarbone offered.

"But I am not an attorney," Mario replied, to test the offer.

"You have special skill that we need in our business," he said dryly with no apparent emotion.

Mario was not a stupid man; he could see where this was going. While he was never actively involved in any criminal enterprise, nor had he any direct contact with know Mafia members until now, he had heard stories on the docks. Mr. Scarbone had invited him to have dinner in his home to discuss a business arrangement regarding the union. Mario never imagined in his wildest dreams that it would come to this. Mario was careful not to offend Mr. Scarbone or show any disrespect. He had been invited him to his private residence to meet his family, and Mario was smart enough to know that was not the order of the day for the Mafia. Mr. Scarbone was well respected by the union membership and the community at large in Chicago. He was actively involved in community affairs and gave generously to charitable organizations in the city.

"I graciously accept your offer, Mr. Scarbone, and hope I prove worthy of your confidence," Mario replied with sincerity knowing full well he had no other option.

To Mario, it was like being drafted into the Army during wartime; there were not too many options at hand. Mario never saw or spoke to Mr. Scarbone again in person, his contact with the family would be with his son, Geno Scarbone.

* * *

Mario was now 64 years of age and given another contract, one of many with his years as a Mafia hit man. He had won medals for killing the enemy for his country in WWII, and now he was killing the enemy for the Mafia. The war had scarred Mario emotionally; he had lost the ability to feel love or have compassion for others, wondering at times why he even existed after seeing brave men die in battle. Some men wept and that seemed to help them. He could not find it in himself to cry, possibly because he was devoid of emotion or fearful that he might lose all control if he expressed himself freely. He masked his feelings to present an easygoing personality, taking no offense with other Teamsters in the union. Mario was recognized for his ability to accommodate a situation for the better, and men respected and looked up to him.

When Geno called to say he had to meet him, Mario knew it was another contract. Geno asked to him to meet in his office downtown. It was an unusual request given the fact that contracts are usually negotiated in secret. Geno's office was located on the 17th floor, the penthouse suite of Scarbone Towers in downtown Chicago. The receptionist was truly an attractive, young blond named Silvia, who ushered him right in to see Geno on his arrival.

"Have a seat. We have to seriously discuss a matter that is extremely important to the family," Geno explained without any need for pleasantries between them.

He was a dark-haired, good-looking, gray-eyed Italian who wore expensive suits and shoes and looked like a Madison Avenue stockbroker or bank official rather than a mobster.

"We have a job in Mississippi that needs to be attended to right away. Some preliminary work has already been completed by our friends in Memphis and Jackson to facilitate the plan for security. Instructions are for you to make an example of the mark for others who have a mind to cross the family. News reports will be viewed to determine how successful a message we are able to send to those who may be tempted to work against our best interest," he explained in military like fashion. Geno allowed for a long pause to let the message sink in.

"Earl Hart will be your backup," Geno ordered.

"Earl Hart," Mario muttered under his breath.

"You have a problem with that?" Geno said, looking at Mario over his expensive dark Italian glasses that he wore all the time, even inside.

"No," Mario replied, knowing that it would not do any good at this point in time. He was too good a soldier at this stage of the game to resist any orders, especially from Geno Scarbone.

"You will fly to Memphis and pick up a rental car that has been negotiated by one of our contacts. He will report the car stolen to one of our insurance carriers two days after you pick up the car to cover our tracks. Weapons will be in the car at the time of pick up. The Dixie group has hunting licenses for you and Earl in your names. It would be too dangerous to do otherwise if you are fingerprinted for some minor violation or picked up for some reason by local authorities carrying shotguns," Geno explained patiently.

"What about hunting clothes and gear as a cover?" Mario offered uneasily.

"That has been arranged and will be in the rental car when you pick it up. Make sure you check your clothes not to leave anything that might be traceable," Geno cautioned.

Mario was a professional and did not need Geno to give him instruction on cover or deception, but he elected to take orders and do the job as required.

"The mark's name is Dr. Raymond Collier; he lives on a lake called Lake Serene in Lamar County near Hattiesburg, Mississippi. Here is a map of the state, spend one night in Jackson and return to Memphis the next day. Do not take anything in the doctor's home, get in and get out. The site has been scouted out and you should have no trouble getting on the property. There are two German shepherds, but they are put up at night on Saturdays by the caretaker. Do you have any questions?" Geno growled, taking off his shades to read Mario's expression.

"No, I have been South before, so we should have no problems," Mario responded with authority.

"If you are picked up for any reason, call this number, the chicken man's attorney down South will make arrangements to get you out on bail right away," Geno offered to satisfy any concern Mario had.

Mario smile and wondered who the chicken man was, but he learned a long time ago not to ask too many questions. The less you know the better off you will be if there is a foul up, the family does not like to have loose ends on any job.

"Mario, I know you probably would like to retire from this line of work. Do a good job and I will recommend retirement perks for you and a dead-head salaried position with the Teamsters union so you can retire for life," Geno offered as he placed his hand on Mario's shoulder.

"I will take you up on that," Mario said, smiling as he got up to leave to leave the office, trying not to show the concerns he had over the job.

*  *  *

Before he left Chicago, Mario noted that Jackson was not too far from Monroe, Louisiana, as he studied a map of Mississippi. Monroe was a "safe town" for the Teamsters in the old days when the heat was on and they had to lay low for a while. Mario missed the dark-haired, pretty, Cajun women. They knew how to treat a man, not like these whores in Chicago who had their hands in your pockets before you had time to get your pants off.

Mario studied his partner as he lay on the bed snoring loudly. He was a slender man with dark auburn hair and ruddy complexion. His face was pockmarked and that made him savage around women because of his insecurity. Nevertheless, he thought of himself as a ladies' man. His lithe, quick body suited him well for his line of work, but he was lacking in the intelligence department as far as Mario was concerned.

The only reason he worked for the family was the fact his brother Red Hart was high up in the Teamsters union and made a place for him. Earl was feared, disliked and mistrusted by most of the Teamsters in Chicago for his quick temper and mean disposition. The Italians called him "Dago Red" behind his back. While Earl was a destructive, sarcastic bastard, he was good with weapons and that appealed to the dons who passed on the contracts.

Sleep did not come easy for Mario, so he turned on the cheap radio for relief from his splitting headache. He had been in the business too long to have any sense of guilt or feelings of remorse over the job that he and Earl and just done on Dr. Collier in the wee hours of the morning. It was a brutal way to go, but their instructions were to send a message for others who might be tempted to play fast and loose with the mob's money.

Of course he did not know any details and did not want to know. The family was forgiving when it came to indiscriminate behavior, but you did not mess with their money. They were like the charismatic evangelist in that regard, Mario mused, from his visits to Monroe in the old days, where preachers expressed contempt of money, but always closed the service with an overpowering need for the Lord that usually involved cash or a donation to a worthy cause.

Earl's snoring was pealing off the cheap wallpaper in the small cabin. The constant snoring caused Mario to become agitated. There was no way he could go back to sleep. He found the half pint bottle of whiskey in his coat pocket and poured himself a shot in a plastic cup. As he sat in a hard straight back chair, he wondered what life would have been like if he had gotten married and settled down on a regular job on the docks or had driven a semi across country. The mob discouraged marriage for younger members, he recalled.

A senior member of the mob professed one night while they were playing cards that there were two things that a hit man did not need to be successful, a watch and a wife, because every town had a town clock and a town whore. That attitude alone should have deterred him from joining the mob, he now thought in retrospect. Experience is a hard taskmaster, he knew. It was better to take advice from those who had been there and bridged over than to swim against the tide in his mind.

Mario began to reflect back on his conversation with Geno and his admonition not to take anything. Earl had acknowledged on the way back to Jackson after the hit that he found tape recordings in the doctor's desk drawer. Mario was too strung out at the time to think straight or he probably would have killed Earl on the way back to Jackson and just left his body and the tapes in some wooded area, he mused as he poured himself another shot.

He knew it would be the electric chair for both of them if they were caught with incriminating evidence to tie them to the murder. Not only that, but the dons would snuff out your life it they felt there was any danger of the contract killing being traced back to them.

He wasn't about to get caught with tapes in his possession. Slipping on his pants, Mario stuck a half pint of whiskey in his back pocket. Fumbling through the idiot's suitcase, Mario found the tapes. "Jeeze," he muttered to himself. While he did not know what was on the tapes, he did not wish to know because it was incriminating evidence. Curiosity killed the cat, he thought to himself, and this cat wasn't going to get caught with the victim's tapes in his possession. Slipping his bare feet in shoes, he quickly slipped out of the room to find a place to dispose of the tapes.

*What a dump,* he thought to himself as he stood momentarily outside the room. A yellow mangy-looking cur dog was sniffing at a garbage bin that had not been picked up in weeks. A thunderstorm had passed over earlier that night and a gentle breeze blew paper and trash in front of him as he shuffled down the concrete walkway to the back of the property. One tall light pole glimmered with a single flickering light bulb in the central parking area surrounded by cabins.

Locating a large metal drum in the darkness that was used as a trash bin behind the maintenance shop, Mario dropped the tapes in the metal drum and used his lighter to light a greasy newspaper to torch the tapes. A fourth of whiskey was poured from his half pint to stoke the crucible. The plastic tapes caught on fire quickly and blazed away in the metal drum to his satisfaction. He stood and watched the tapes until they turned to a molten black mass.

On his way back to the room, Mario noted the Mexican night attendant was sleeping with his head on the counter in the office. There were only a few cars still parked at the motel; most of the occupants had shacked up and left from signing in earlier. Retracing his steps back to the room, Mario entered without waking Earl, who was still snoring loudly his mouth gaped open wide enough to draw flies.

The tile floor was wet now from water that was slowly seeping out of the window air conditioner. The tile underneath the air conditioner was already peeled back from the water and the humidity in the room. Earl may have been right—why should they have to live like this? he mused.

Exasperated with Earl's snoring, Mario slipped off his pants and shoes and took Earl by the arm and turned him over on his side. If they were fortunate enough to make it back to Chicago, Mario promised himself that this would be his last contract regardless of the offer by Geno. He had saved some money and if nothing else he could relocate South and live in Monroe. The climate was sure better than Chicago and he could stroll down to the riverfront and enjoy his retirement. Maybe he could find a sweet Cajun girl who would appreciate a war hero.

# Chapter 17

Feeling apprehensive, Mario awoke early. He had a splitting headache and his mouth was dry. The air conditioner was sucking out all the fresh air in the cabin. The cabin only had one window and half of it was enclosed by the window unit; it was impossible to get any fresh air. His watch read five o'clock and Earl was still sleeping like a petrified log with one leg hanging over the bed, a socked foot almost touching the floor.

"Get up Earl; it's time to get on the road." Mario said kicking Earl's bed with his foot. Mario cracked the door for some air and announced to Earl that he was going to shower first. "You check with the Mexican up front to see if they have a daily paper," Mario called out from the bathroom.

"Gees, Mario, what time is it?" Earl asked sleepily and sitting up on the side of the bed.

"It's time for us to hit the road," Mario growled from the tiny bathroom.

"Damn! it's hot in here." Mario muttered to no one in particular because Earl was already out the door on his way to the front office.

Mario was dressed and packed when Earl made it back to the cabin.

"The locals don't distribute the newspaper here according to the Mex at the front desk," Earl offered almost apologetically.

"What the hell have you been doing all this time?" Mario snapped suspiciously because it was not that far to the front office.

"I was invited to have coffee; the Mex is not a bad guy," Earl explained.

"We are not here to socialize, we need to get out of town as soon as possible. Someone may have recognized the rental car's license plate at the lake."

"Is there any hot water?" Earl asked as he headed for the bathroom.

"The bathroom is hot enough to heat the water. Let's get your thin ass cracking. I want to eat breakfast and get on our way to Memphis. I will be outside in the car listening to the radio for news."

Mario started the car ignition and turned the air condition on high. He was still sweating from the humidity even thought he had just taken a bath. His bark tree camouflage hunting shirt was sticky and stuck to his chest from perspiration. He turned on the car radio and searched for news but all he could find was gospel and early morning church services. Maybe that was a good sign for the time being, he thought to himself. The mob would get the word out one way or another that the contract had been consummated.

As the rental eased on Highway 80, Mario was feeling a little better. He saw the Alamo Plaza Motel sign in the rear view mirror and the white Mexican archway that must have been something in the early thirties.

"Buckle your seat belt," Mario said. "We are not leaving anything to chance on our way back to Memphis."

Earl was busy fumbling under the car seat for something as Mario turned left off Highway 80 on to Interstate 55 North to Memphis.

"I thought I had some tapes in my suitcase but I could find them in the cabin when I packed," Earl said, turning to look in the back seat.

Mario did not feel a need to respond to Earl's question because he did not want to acknowledge the existence of any tapes.

"Look there's a Toddle House, let's stop for breakfast," Earl exclaimed almost childlike. He had already forgotten about the tapes.

The two of them stepped out of the car wearing their hunting shirts and pants in the parking lot of the Toddle House. The hunting gear should give the locals the impression that they were hunters and would account for the two 12-gauge shotguns on the back seat if they were stopped for any reason by law enforcement officers. The arrangement to get them Mississippi hunting licenses was a good cover.

As the two men entered the Toddle House, they seemly fit right in with the crowd. There were several other men in bark tree camouflage hunting shirts and pants who had been on a dove hunt late Saturday afternoon and were up early for breakfast.

Mario ordered a pecan waffle and coffee and Earl ordered the house special, waffles, eggs, bacon, hash browns, toast and coffee. The stringy haired blond waitress noticed Earl's gold chains and New Jersey accent right off as she placed their plates in front of them later.

"You boys are not from around here, are you," she said. She made it a statement and not a question as she leaned forward to allow her full breasts to strain against the fabric of her Toddle House uniform. Earl smiled and wondered what she would be like in bed as he looked up from his waffle.

"No, we are just down to do some hunting," Mario responded quickly before Earl could make a play.

"Shit," Mario muttered to himself, if the dumb, horny waitress could make them, what would they do if they were stopped by trained law enforcement officers?

"You have another order, Josie," the short order cook called out, relieving Mario from having to offer any further explanation or make any comments. The waitress looked back at him disdainfully like she had lost a john and tippy-toed her way back down the aisle to get the order.

Mario's thoughts turned to the Cajun girls in Monroe who came up from Baton Rouge and talked about banana pies at the Toddle House and servicing the governor.

Life was better back then, less complicated in his mind. While people may have been less tolerant in the old days, there was also less in-your-face immorality than you have now. Normative behavior by today's standard was shocking even to Mario.

All the movie stars' social relationships were below the waist now and their children were seen as computer giga-bytes on a string to be plugged in when needed. San Francisco was so plagued now by homosexuals, drug abuse and social disease that a drunken sailor was fearful of waking up in bed with a banker's wife.

"By the way, one of the guys at the club mentioned that the CEO of Federal Express is subject to an indictment for fraud to obtain a bank loan and that he was also the one who founded the Toddle House restaurant chain in the South," Earl muttered as he was pouring a half gallon of syrup on his waffle.

"Geez! Earl, cut that, we don't need to be talking about that in here," Mario cautioned.

"O.K., I just remembered what the guy said," Earl replied wading into his waffle that was now free standing on his plate.

"It might be best for you if you kept your mouth shut until we get back to Chicago; the blond had already made you wearing that gold chain around your neck and your shirt wide open to show your skinny chest," Mario snapped angrily.

Mob informants were everywhere Mario knew, looking to make a buck and blackmail business executives if the opportunity presented itself.

"Let's go," Mario said after Earl finished wolfing down his breakfast. Mario paid the cashier and noticed the blond waitress was still eyeing them as he pushed Earl out the door.

"Let me make a call," Mario said as the two stepped outside of the Toddle House. He used the pay phone to call a private cell phone number in Chicago.

"Geno here," the voice answered on the other end of the line.

"We have completed the order and are now on the way home," Mario said.

"Good," Geno replied and hung up.

* * *

Earl was snoring away in the front seat. The big breakfast had made him sleepy. The rental car sped north towards Memphis. Mario was cautious and drove within the speed limits. The fact that his anxieties were now belied somewhat allowed him to think about retirement. It also helped that the interstate highway was becoming monotonous. What would Geno do for him if he was successful in carrying out his assignment? Could Geno be trusted? He began to feel apprehensive about the future when he noticed blinking tail lights on the cars ahead of him as they neared the outskirts of a town called Southhaven. Cars were being routed off the highway up the side road to cross over the overpass or continue on down the frontage road to Memphis.

As the line of cars moved slowly ahead of him, Mario realized it was a road block. He could see the Mississippi State Highway patrol cars blocking the road ahead underneath the overpass. A patrol car was parked off to the right of the interstate to track cars as they approached the overpass. Mario turned his rear view mirror to view the patrol car. He saw the officer read the license tag on the rental car and turn on his blinking light and siren.

"Shit," Mario cried out.

He realized that he was trapped like a wolf in a snare. Turning the steering wheel hard to the left, he drove on the grassy median with the intent of reaching the southbound traffic lane going the other way. The sedan spun sideways and slid on the wet grass as he pushed the accelerator to the floor.

"What the hell?" Earl snapped as he awoke when the car left the pavement and fish-tailed out of control on the wet grass.

A shot rang out. All hell broke loose then. A sniper stationed on the overpass shot the left front tire and the heavy sedan skidded to a stop on top of a concrete drainage culvert in the median. The front windshield exploded and sprayed flying glass over Mario's head as he instinctively ducked below the dash on hearing the first shot.

Struggling with his seat belt, Earl slumped forward, his chest and head turning crimson red from the gun fire that was now peppering the sedan. His bladder emptied all over the front seat. The smell of urine was strong in Mario's nostrils. His mind flashed back to D-Day and Omaha Beach and the suffocation and fear of being on a Higgins boat taking fire with nowhere to go or hide for cover The floating corpses, body parts, smell of urine, vomit, diesel fuel, and death was everywhere. Men cried out, some for their mother, others profanely.

As the high-powered bullets continued to spray the car, Mario felt tired and weary. He knew he had been a dead man walking for a long time. Mario still harbored guilt over the loss of his comrades in battle and wondered why he was spared for the wretch that he had become. He wondered if history would record whether he was a hero or a villain as he raised his head proudly for the last time for the soldier that he was.

# Chapter 18

The evening news reported that two men attempted to run a road block at Southaven, Mississippi, and were gunned downed by the Mississippi State Highway Patrol and local police. They were driving a black rental car with Tennessee license plates and spent the night at the Alamo Plaza Motel in Jackson from a receipt found in car. Two sawed-off 12-gauge shotguns were also found in the car after they attempted to run a road block. They were suspected of having killed Dr. Raymond Collier at his lakeside home near Hattiesburg. News report indicated that there was no motive as far as the murder was concerned and local law enforcement authorities still had the case under investigation.

Months later, Steve and Barbara later received a written invitation to attend a private memorial service for Dr. Collier on the estate at Lake Serene. The invitation bore the name of Philip Collin, Solicitor, of London, England. Collier had left instruction to have his remains cremated when they were no longer useful as a cadaver for the University Medical Center. He desired that his ashes be spread over the clear blue waters off the pier at Lake

Serene. Only a small number of people were invited to the service and Steve felt honored to be one of them. Osmond gave a heartfelt eulogy on the deck of the home and one could tell the love he must have had for Dr. Collier.

Steve and Barbara met Philip Collin and his wife Lisa before the service. Barbara and Lisa hit it off right away because of their common roots in Mississippi. Steve enjoyed talking to Philip Collin, the solicitor. He seemed to be the English gentleman who was so well-educated and conversant on any subject. Naomi Selber probably drew the most attention from all those gathered at the service. For one thing, all the women were jealous of her dark, good looks and refinement, while the men were drawn to her sensuality not completely hidden by the expensive black dress and veil that hid her tear-stained eyes.

She was a mystery woman, but she seemed to have an unusual relationship with Osmond and looked to him for support. She was seen by Steve and Barbara later in the evening hugging the two German shepherds without regard to her expensive dress. They in turn seemed to be showing her an uncommon affection for two highly bred and spirited German shepherds.

Steve felt he knew Osmond well enough to ask him what would happen to the property and he said that Dr. Collier had left the property to Naomi Selber in his will.

"Who is Naomi Selber?" Steve asked.

"She is a corporate executive from New York who was a close friend of Dr. Collier when he lived in New York." Osmond replied.

Steve felt he had to ask because Barbara would never be satisfied until she knew something of the dark, beautiful, Jewish woman who attended the memorial service. Osmond informed the group that he would personally spread Dr. Collier's ashes with Naomi Selber later that evening as the sun set on Lake Serene.

Osmond and Naomi enjoyed their reflective time together on

the lake. She would have to leave soon. Before she left to return to New York, Osmond made her promise that she would return in several months to spend Thanksgiving Day with him. He promised to do all the cooking and told her she would be impressed with his culinary skills. It went without saying that Osmond had a place at Lake Serene for the rest of his life.

# Chapter 19

Naomi Selber flew in the night before Thanksgiving Day to be with Osmond at Lake Serene. She awoke early the next morning to smell the aroma from the kitchen that was invading the house. She found Osmond and a black lady in the kitchen cooking.

"I thought you were going to do all the cooking, Osmond?" She laughed.

"We all have to have help every now and then," he said grinning. "This is my sister's first daughter; she is the best cook in Hattiesburg. Mamie, this is Naomi Selber."

"Howdy, Miss Selber, we hope you will have a good Thanksgiving with us."

"Why, thank you," Naomi responded almost tearfully.

"Let me fix you a cup of coffee while you sit on the deck and watch the sun rise over the lake," Osmond offered, reading her mood.

"That would be nice," Naomi replied while opening the French doors.

"What would you like for breakfast?" Osmond asked as he set her coffee down on the table. She was looking at the lake deep in her own thoughts and said, "Anything would be fine, Osmond."

"We will fix you some ham and eggs, but we plan to have a big Thanksgiving meal," he said smiling to himself.

Naomi had her breakfast outside on the deck and enjoyed the cool breeze from the lake. The pines swung back and forth, and the huge oaks billowed every now and then from the wind. The deck offered a wonderful view of the clear, blue lake. In the late afternoon the sun would create a fireball on the lake as it set in the west. She pulled her housecoat around her and thought of Raymond and how much he loved this place. For the past four months she did nothing but work to take her mind off Raymond and his untimely death.

*How cruel life can be sometimes,* she thought to herself. She now had wealth, power, and constructive work, but it was not enough without someone you love. She was deaf to the many suitors in New York that tried to call on her. She even revisited some of the spas in Europe and visited old friends there, but life did not seem to hold much promise for her without Raymond. Who would believe that two people from such different backgrounds could find common ground for love?

She asked to help out in the kitchen, but Osmond and Mamie would have none of that, so she retired to her room to read before dinner. At first she thought she would sleep in Raymond's bedroom that they shared together, but she could not bring herself to do it. The room was left just as it was; all of his things were left in place, except the bed. The bed now had a deep maroon bedspread and pillow cases. His house slippers were peeking from under the bed. A book, with a page marker, was still in place on the bed stand to show the last page read.

A soft knock at her door caused her to sit up and put down her book. "Yes," she called out.

"It's me, Miss Selber," Mamie said. "Osmond, wanted to know if you would like to walk Heidi and Karras before dinner."

"Oh my, yes," Naomi replied, jumping up from the bed. "Let me, put my slacks and boots on, and I will be right down."

Heidi and Karras were all over her as she reached the first landing of the deck.

"I think they missed you," Osmond said as he made them sit.

"Dinner will be ready in about an hour, it's nice on the lake this time of day, and they love to walk the shore line," Osmond told her.

He watched her leave with the dogs in tow. He knew they would look after her. She was a beautiful, Jewish girl from New York, who really knew little about the South, he thought to himself as he watched her and the dogs make their way to the shoreline of the lake. As Naomi walked the shoreline, she began to feel an inner peace with the dogs now nipping at her hands as she walked.

Karras would range far and wide and cut a path back and forth across their trail, while Heidi stayed closer, looking back every now and then. Lake Serene was a lake within a lake, with a water fall across the road dividing one side of the lake from the other. The evenings were beautiful at Lake Serene. The lake had been formerly known as Lake Shady, before it was sold to a combine owned by Lady Bird Johnson, the wife of Lyndon B. Johnson, President.

According to Osmond, Collier had bought the first piece of property on the lake with a colleague from the University of Southern Mississippi. He purchased a lot sight unseen on the other side of the lake because of the large number of dogwood trees on the property. It looked like snow to Collier from his vantage point looking across the lake. Since his property was not accessible by car, the property was under development, he opted to help his friend build the first private pier and boat dock on the lake.

A man casually walked towards Naomi on the shoreline. Not knowing the property line, Naomi was concerned that she might be invading a neighbor's private property. Karras and

Heidi gave a protective bark to let her know that someone was approaching her on the property. As the man came closer, Karras broke and ran for the man. Heidi soon followed. Naomi was terrified, and she did not know what the dogs would do. The man was not close enough to harm her. She felt they were acting out of instinct to protect her and she knew she could not control them.

She saw Karras leap up to the man's face as he stood his ground. The man held Karras from him, as if they were in a dancer's embrace. Karras was now standing on his hind legs and they were face to face. Heidi soon joined the fray and was jumping up in the same manner as Karras. The man patted the two dogs for a moment and said, "Down." They obediently responded to his command.

"Oh, I am so sorry, "Naomi said to the man.

"I don't think they meant any harm," he said.

The dogs now moved between them still very excited and demanding attention.

Naomi's attention was drawn to the dogs and she really did not look at the man other than to note his disposition. Maybe it was her New York training not to make eye contact with a stranger. She looked at him for the first time and noted that he was an uncommonly handsome man with a small moustache and full head of dark, auburn hair.

A strange feeling came over her as the man's attention was directed towards patting Karras and Heidi. He was a strong-looking man, with good features and a square chin. He was shorter than she was in low-heel boots. As he leaned to pet Karras, she noted his legs in tight blue jeans and he seemed slightly bow legged like an athlete. A sense of panic almost overcame her. She felt flushed, like she was going to faint. Her face turned red and her knees buckled. The man caught her in his arms and held her close to him.

"Are you alright?" he asked.

She let her arm slip around his neck to keep her balance, and the physical contact caused the hair on her skin to stand up.

"God, Naomi, are you alright?" she heard him say with alarm in his voice, as he clutched her waist tighter.

"Raymond, is it really you?" she asked instinctively pulling him closer to her.

"Yes, my love," he said and turned her face to kiss her.

"Oh, God, Raymond, we all thought you were dead," she cried, as she broke off the kiss.

"Let's get in the house and I will tell you everything," he said, still feeling somewhat guarded even now.

# Chapter 20

Osmond and Mamie did not seem surprised when Collier and Naomi returned to the house arm in arm.

"We will be in my room. Call us when dinner is ready," Collier said to Osmond.

"What is going on and why do you look so much younger?" Naomi asked as they entered the master bedroom.

"It is a long story," Collier replied.

"I have the time," she said giving him a disapproving look as she lay down on the large king size bed.

"As far as the looks," Collier said, "I have had plastic surgery and had a hair transplant to make me look different. I have also lost some weight to help alter my appearance."

"You are a handsome man, why did you fabricate your death and lead us all on? You know how much I loved you," she said, crying now, recalling his untimely death and the grief she suffered.

"Let me explain," Collier said tenderly as he sat down next to her on the bed.

"Years ago," he went on to say as he sat next to her on the bed, "I had a patient that was suffering from a sense of guilt and depression, and voicing suicide. Peter Meyer was his name and he was referred by a Jewish doctor for psychoanalysis. Peter was a fifty-three-year-old Jewish man, who was highly intelligent, small in stature, who was born in Havana, Cuba. He immigrated to the United States with his mother when Castro took over Cuba in 1957. He and his mother lived very well at the Hotel de Nationale until they relocated to New York. Peter reportedly never knew his father, but they lived well and his mother had money to send him to college. After college he developed an expertise in finance and banking and worked for some of the best corporations in New York as an accountant. Later he became comptroller of a financial institution that catered to overseas clients. He never married and lived with his mother until she died. His case appeared to be a fairly typical with the dynamics being suitable for psychotherapy and hypnosis. After a number of sessions and under hypnosis, it was revealed that he was the illegitimate son of Aaron Meyer.

"Aaron Meyer was a notorious gangster during Prohibition, who opened up gambling in Cuba. Peter found out that Aaron Meyer was his father when his mother died and he went through some of her old packing trunks. He found pictures of her and Meyer in the penthouse suite with celebrities and a number of high level government officials from the United States and the United Fruit Company. Peter refused to accept the fact that Aaron Meyer was his father and suffered considerable guilt for a long period of time. He had always been suspicious of his accelerated rise in the corporate world and some of the accounts that seemed to follow him. Since he had developed a software program to use code words and encrypt financial records and files for security, his skills were sought after by corporate America. Little did he know that he was working for a corporation controlled by the Mafia and was transferring huge profits from the opium trade overseas to banks in Switzerland. The Mafia trusted him with the numbered accounts. Since this information was gleaned while he was under hypnosis and as a source of his conflicts, I could not divulge the information to anyone.

"On the other hand, when he accepted the fact that his illegitimacy and moral conflict were the source of his depression and suicide ideation, he decided to transfer the funds to other financial institutions without the Mafia's knowledge. Peter was able to get around the banks in Switzerland's Chinese wall to withdraw and transfer funds, because he knew the numbered accounts and the account holders' names. Since he was well-known to most of the account managers, they saw no violation of security. Later Peter made the decision to set up individual trust funds with different financial institutions to manage drug rehabilitation centers.

"Since Aaron Meyer was still living in Miami and was being prosecuted by the Justice Department, Peter was aware that he was putting his life in danger to follow through on his plan. Lansky made an attempt to avoid prosecution and fled to Israel, but he had his visa revoked and was forced to return to the United States to stand trial. The Justice Department had problems tying him to the Mafia directly because he was not an Italian and could not be formally initiated as such. Aaron was able to avoid prosecution because he had friends in high places in the government.

"Many former CIA officials and officials of the United Fruit Company were in bed together in Cuba in the 1950s. The unholy alliance profited from American tourists who went there on fantasy holidays for gambling, night life, and the cheap sexual pleasures, while exploiting the poor for cheap labor. The cocaine trade was allowed to flourish openly under a European fascist type regime. Castro's rebels took over the island in January of 1959.

"Meyer had earned his dues with the mob years earlier by forming Murder, Inc., that specialized in contract killers for hire. His business skills were later recognized and he earned money for the mob through gambling, prostitution and drugs in Cuba,

South America and Hong Kong. As a result of the empire he built, he was able to form legal businesses like hotels and golf courses. While he was in Cuba, he built the Hotel de Nacional and the air-conditioned Havana Rivera that is still in operation today.

"Peter and I agreed that my life would be in danger if he disappeared because the Mafia would suspect that I was seeing him for psychiatric treatment. I would be seen by them as the intervening variable, so to speak, for the change in his behavior and their loss of funds. Therefore, I was confronted with the need to change my lifestyle and my identity. Philip was calling regularly from London indicating that Interpol was on the case, so I knew it would not be too long before they found me. That is why I sent you back to New York, for your safety," Collier explained in detail.

"Dinner, is ready, you all," Mamie called out.

\* \* \*

Osmond had prepared Collier's favorite Thanksgiving meal, turkey, stuffing with giblet gravy, cranberry sauce, candied sweet potatoes, green bean casserole, sweet white corn, and home baked soft rolls.

"Did you cook the turkey in peanut oil in a brown paper bag?" Collier asked. Osmond and Mamie smiled, as Osmond nodded his head.

"The table setting is beautiful, Mamie. This will be the best Thanksgiving I will ever have in my life," Naomi said tearfully.

Collier kissed her on her tear-stained cheeks and said, "Now is the time to be joyous and happy that we can share Thanksgiving with family and friends."

"Thank you," Naomi said and kissed Osmond and Mamie.

"Osmond, why don't you say the blessing?" Collier asked.

"I cannot eat another bite," Collier later declared.

"You have to try my chocolate cream pie," Mamie said.

Osmond smiled and brought them coffee to have with their pie.

"I am now addicted to Southern cooking because of you two," Naomi said, hugging Mamie and Osmond.

Collier announced that he and Naomi would do the dishes later, and told Osmond and Mamie to take the rest of the day off to visit their family and friends.

Collier later drew the drapes in the master bedroom as Naomi was changing to put on a maroon velvet robe. He changed clothes in the bathroom and put on his green cotton robe. Naomi was reclining on the bed on a pillow with one arm raised above her head. Looking like a high borne Jewish priestess with her dark, ebony black hair and dark eyes, Collier thought how fortunate he was to have met someone like Naomi, and for her to love him. She had truly become a loving person and he had decided early on, that he wanted to share his life with her.

"Raymond, I won't be able to sleep until you tell me the rest of the story," Naomi pleaded. "Why did Peter decide to betray the Mafia at the risk of his own life, and for you to have gone along with his plan?"

"I think it was his Jewish conscience and his overpowering sense of guilt over the fact that he was managing the Mafia's finances," he said. "I am not sure why I decided to go along with his plan. We both knew, of course, that the Mafia would suspect that I had a hand in his decision to withdraw the funds. The fact that Peter disappeared and could not be located to explain what happened to the money meant that the mob would be looking for me."

"I was ready to change my lifestyle, so I agreed to become a co-conspirator," he went on to explain. "I began to have reservations after you were able to locate me so easy. Interpol was also aware that Mafia funds had been transferred out of the banks in Switzerland and that they were making inquiries. That is the reason I wanted you to go back to New York, because I knew the Mafia was making efforts along with Interpol to locate my whereabouts."

"But the newspapers said a body was found in your bedroom riddled with shotgun slugs," Naomi said. "I died a thousand deaths when I heard you were murdered," she said as she hugged him to her.

"I know, I had real concerns over the fact that I might lose you in the long run, if I was reported dead," he said as he took her face in his hands and kissed her. "I had to take the chance; the Mafia would never give up until I was dead. I also wanted to spare you from any future danger, so I took drastic measures to make sure the Mafia thought I was dead."

"But the police found a dead body."

"The Mafia keeps assassins on retainers, like corporations keep lawyers on retainer, so I knew it was a matter of time before they found me. So I called my secretary to inform her that I would be at Lake Serene in Lamar County, Mississippi, for a period of time before I returned to New York. I knew the Mafia would tap my phone lines. It was just a matter of time before they put out a contract on me."

Collier went on to explain how he and Osmond made arrangements with a personal friend at University of Mississippi Medical Center to have access to a cadaver. They had prepared a cadaver in cheesecloth at the university that day, which would pass inspection by any coroner as a real body based on the water content. "Given the mob's past experience, I knew that the assassins would use a gruesome method to kill the victim to make an example for others if nothing else. The coroner did not have a problem supporting the cause of death to warrant an autopsy.

"Of course, Osmond was here with the sheriff and coroner to give them a legal document which I had prepared to donate my body to the University Medical Center. The coroner, as predicted, said it would save the county money to just have the body transported directly to the medical center as soon as possible. I knew that cadavers were not useful if they had undergone an autopsy previously."

Naomi snaked her arm around Collier's neck as he continued to unfold the remarkable story.

"Later, I made arrangements to have plastic surgery to change my looks. An overseas client was contacted earlier to provide me a new identification and passport to travel overseas. I had Philip Collin, my solicitor in London, make you executor of my estate. So I am totally in your hands," Collier said.

"Raymond, that is a fantastic tale and Osmond went along with you?" she inquired.

"Yes, I could not have pulled it off without him."

"What about Philip and Lisa, they seemed like such a nice couple?"

"I imagine they will be surprised at your new boy next week, when we fly to London," Collier laughed.

"What do I call you?"

"You can call me Ray, you call me Ray Ray, just don't call me..."

Naomi interrupted him and said, "You are crazy, Raymond, but I love you."

"Do you love me enough to marry me and honeymoon in Taormina, Sicily?" Collier asked.

"I love you enough to marry you any place," she said, "but where is Taormina?"

"Taormina is on the slope of Mount Tauro in Sicily and offers a panoramic view of Mt. Etna's snow-covered volcanic cone as a backdrop to the Ionian coast. There is a wonderful Greek theatre that sits atop the highest point on the island to give one a spectacular view of the Ionian coast and Mt. Etna. I think it is one of the most beautiful spots in the world," he offered.

"Oh, that sounds wonderful, darling," Naomi replied, as they hugged each other before sleep took them over.

# Chapter 21

"Steve, telephone call," Barbara called out to him.

"Who is it?" he asked on his way to the phone.

"You know, Steve, I don't ask, unless it is a woman. It is a man and he speaks very precisely," she said, as she handed him the phone.

"Hello," Steve said.

"Steve, this is Osmond, I just wanted to call and thank you and Barbara for attending Dr. Collier's memorial service."

"Thank you, I appreciate you calling. You know how much I thought of Dr. Collier, and we considered it an honor to be invited," Steve replied.

"Naomi Selber wanted me to express her appreciation also. She regretted not being able to spend more time with Dr. Collier's friends, but she was heartbroken over his untimely death."

"I can understand that. We were shocked as well," Steve said.

"How is your health?" Osmond inquired.

"I feel much better now than I have in a long time. I don't know what Dr. Collier did, but I sleep better, and I don't have those awful dreams."

"I am glad to hear that," Osmond replied.

"Will you be staying on at the house?" Steve asked.

"Oh, yes, Ms. Selber plans to visit from time to time, and we will look after the place for her," Osmond said pridefully.

"Osmond, if there are any business affairs or anything I can do to help Ms. Selber or yourself, please call me," Steve said.

"Thank you, I appreciate that," Osmond said.

"By the way, Osmond, is Karras neutered?" Steve asked.

"No!" Osmond laughed. "Why? Do you want a puppy for the boys?"

"I sure do."

"You will have the pick of the litter. I will let you know," Osmond replied smiling to himself.

Appreciative of Steve's interest in the German shepherds, Osmond knew that it would create a bond between the two families, one that Dr. Collier would appreciate.

Later that afternoon, Steve, Barbara, and the boys loaded up in the Bronco and headed out for the stadium for football practice. Barbara sat with Steve in the front of the Bronco, while the four boys teased each other in the back. Steve wondered on the way what he was letting himself in for on his decision to coach in the Pop Warner League.

Sam Price agreed to be the team manager and help the boys with their gear, and keep up with the substitution during the game. Steve had already decided that everyone on the team deserved to play. He planned to let individual players play earlier in the game, but he wanted the best players on the field in the fourth quarter, because that was when most football games were won or lost. Steve wanted to make sure that there was no finger pointing at individual players for losing the game because that could demoralize a team.

Barbara looked eye-catching in her cheerleader outfit, Steve noted on the way to the stadium. Her charges demanded to see her dressed in her old cheerleader outfit. It was a way of establishing her credentials in their minds for they could not fathom their parents as teenagers or college students, for that matter, so great the divide and cynicism of youth in today's world.

"Are you going to tell the boys about the German shepherd puppy?" Barbara whispered in Steve's ear.

"No, I want to surprise them; I know they have wanted a dog for a long time. I think they are responsible enough now to take care of a dog," Steve replied.

"Our yard is really small and any dog is going to dig, especially a German shepherd in this heat in the summer," Barbara whispered.

"I know there are several houses on the market now which have acreage that I would like for you to look at next week. You have wanted a bigger place for a long time. I feel better now and am ready to make a commitment," Steve acknowledged.

"There's Mr. Champion and Rocky standing at the gate," Brad shouted in their ear.

Steve notice that Jim Champion was in his Mississippi Highway Patrol uniform and that Rocky was not wearing his football uniform.

"When this truck comes to a stop, I want you all to get out and not say a word to anyone but go quietly in the stadium, do you understand?" Steve said turning to the boys in the back of the Bronco.

"Yes, sir," the boys said in unison; they had seen that look and that tone of voice before.

"That goes for you, too, Barbara," Steve said as he turned to her.

"Yes, sir," she said, returning his look.

Steve waited until Barbara and the boys were inside the gate before he approached Jim Champion and Rocky. Jim Champion spoke first as Steve approached.

"Steve, Rocky wants to play if you will have him."

"Get your gear and join the team," Steve replied without hesitation.

Rocky ran to the patrol car for his gear as fast as his short, stocky legs would carry him.

"Your mother will pick you up after practice, Rocky," Champion said as Rocky ran past them at the gate.

"Steve, I want to—" Champion started to say.

"There is no need for that," Steve interrupted him in mid-sentence.

"I think Rocky is in good hands, Steve," Champion said, extending his hand.

"Thanks, I appreciate that more than you think," Steve said, shaking his hand.

Later that afternoon on the way home, Steve found himself in high spirits; the practice had gone well and the players were focused to be as young as they were. Even Johnny Jones was improving at the guard position and learning good techniques to offset his limited physical ability. It was apparent to Steve that his weight was attributable to a lack of self-confidence and his emotional state over losing his father so tragically. The team seemed to appreciate the idea of strategy and teamwork that was involved in football. Sam Price had his company copied all of the plays. Each player was given a notebook with offensive and defensive schemes and plays they needed to learn for their respective positions.

"Look, it is just like college ball, with the plays and all," Brad said as he thumbed through the playbook.

"I like the Green Bay Packer Sweep," Bruce said with enthusiasm.

"My dad put it together," Tommy Price chirped in with a newfound respect for his father.

Steve was encouraged by the positive way Jim Champion handled their confrontation. In retrospect, he wondered if he could be as big a man as Champion proved himself to be today. Of course, Rocky rejoined the team as if nothing had happened, and the team accepted him in the same manner. Edith

Champion hugged Barbara at the gate as they were leaving and exchanged comments. She did not say what the conversation was about, but seem satisfied with herself and him, he assumed, because Barbara was not one to suffer in silence.

As they pulled into the driveway at home and the boys said their good-byes, Barbara told Brad and Bruce to go into the house and put up their gear because they were spending the weekend with their grandparents on the lake.

"Let's go change, Bruce. We're going to have a great time on the lake," Brad said, as he jumped out of the Bronco and raced his brother to see which one would get to their room first and change.

"Can't a girl have a date with her football hero every now and then?" Barbara said, after seeing the quizzical look on Steve's face.

"Well, I'll be," Steve said, smiling at her.

# Chapter 22

Collier encouraged Naomi to retire early, because he knew she was emotionally spent on learning that he was still alive and had not suffered a brutal death. It was a cruel hoax, but one that was necessary to protect all the parties concerned, he thought to himself. Both Naomi and Osmond would have been at risk given the cruel nature of assassins, since murder, terror and intimidation were their stock in trade. While Peter Meyer may be a noble man in retrospect, Collier knew the criminal world was unforgiving when it came to money.

It was his hope that the U.S. Justice Department would be able to protect Peter in the witness protection program, but he did not want to trust his life to government bureaucrats. There were too many sycophants in government service that would give you up for a dime or an IOU if it would advance their career or provide some monetary gain. He preferred to trust his instincts and his friends to ensure his safety and the safety of others.

Osmond was waiting for him in the den and had set out his favorite drink and cigars. They sat for a while, not saying anything, just savoring their drinks and cigars.

Osmond respected the fact that Collier seemed to be in a mood and deep within his own thoughts. Because he knew Collier would be leaving soon, he had questions of his own regarding the future.

"Osmond, you know how I convinced my friend, the dean at the University Medical Center, to grant me access to a cadaver?" Collier offered breaking the somber silence that seemed to hang over the room.

"No, but I wondered about that," he laughed, stretching out his legs that were now growing stiff from sitting.

"I convinced him that he would be getting two for one, that I would donate my personal remains to the medical center. I assured him that the cadaver would be returned to the center, but worse for wear."

"I am surprised that your offer did not arouse his curiosity, especially if you mentioned worse for wear," Osmond countered sipping his brandy.

"Well, he was smart enough not to ask too many questions. He did offer, given the violent and traumatic injuries that the medical staff was encountering in the center's emergency unit, that the physicians needed training on gunshot and knife wounds."

"So, he had some idea that violence might be done on the cadaver," Osmond muttered.

"Yes, but I think the reason he was willing to go along was the fact that the man in question was homeless and had no identity. The Hinds County coroner immediately offered the man's body up as a cadaver when no relatives could be located within a reasonable time. The timing was just providence for me under the circumstance, otherwise my friend would not have offered just any cadaver for ethical reasons, I am sure," he acknowledged.

"What about your plans for the future?" Osmond inquired, twisting in chair from discomfort. He usually did not stay up this late at night and his rheumatism was paining him somewhat. The brandy was helping ease the pain he had to admit.

Osmond knew Collier only required four hours of sleep. He pressed the issue of the future so he could retire for the evening because he was fearful that Collier was in a talkative mood.

Collier stood and poured himself another brandy and offered Osmond the same.

"You know, Naomi has come to identify with Mississippi and has instructed her board to survey a location to build a department store in Hattiesburg. That move will give me cover as Naomi's husband here in the Hattiesburg area and satisfy the community's curiosity regarding the new inhabitants on the lake. The airport in Hattiesburg is large enough to accommodate Naomi's private jet, so we can travel and see the world."

"So you do plan to return to Lake Serene after your honeymoon?" Osmond asked with interest.

"Very much so, I guess we could live in New York City, but I think Naomi is about ready to turn over the corporate reins to someone else. She like me, seems to have fallen in love with the lake, you and Mamie."

Osmond was somewhat embarrassed over that admission by Collier. He knew Collier was not one to throw the word "love" around so easily.

"Do you think the tapes of your sessions with Steve will ever be recovered?" Osmond asked to change the subject.

"I honestly don't know; that is a good question, and one I have not thought about recently. If I were still in practice, I would desperately want to find the tapes for research purposes. Talking about the subject matter without the tapes would be like trying to explain that you had contact with an alien being from another world," Collier laughed. "By the way, how is Steve coming along? I regret our sessions had to be terminated, but under the circumstances it was the only way."

"He seems to be doing very well now, he indicated that he no longer has the headaches and is sleeping more soundly now than before," Osmond replied.

"I guess the cathartic release of the emotional material freed him from discomfort and belied his fears," Collier opined clinically.

"He asked for one of Heidi's pups, by the way."

"He did, now that is a good sign in more ways than one, since I will be able to maintain some contact with the family. Feel free to invite Steve and his family to visit here on the property in my absence. Steve is very perceptive, but I don't think he would ever betray my trust if he learned of my identity. I will take a low profile on the lake, and just be Naomi's husband for all intents and purposes."

"I appreciate that. Steve and I have become pretty good friends since he started visiting," Osmond replied truthfully.

"Naomi and I will spend some time in Europe visiting with Phil and Lisa and then return here to the homestead. I want you and me to do some real fishing off the Gulf of Mexico when I get back. I would like to see what Naomi would do with a big, blue marlin on the other end of the line."

"That would be fun to see," Osmond grinned.

"You did a good job mounting the bass in the den for her, I know Naomi appreciated that. I like the inscriptions also. I hope it won't be the last for her because I still treasure the sight of her catching her fist bass."

"I think she feels that way, too, she has really grown to love the lake and the surroundings," Osmond admitted.

"You don't think she will become a damn Yankee, do you?" Collier laughed. A Yankee was a person who visited the South and went back home, a Damn Yankee was one who visited and wanted to stay. Osmond laughed at the old Southern joke about Yankees and realized that sentiments had not changed much in the Deep South except that the populace could now make jokes and not war.

Later after Osmond retired, Collier sat in the den alone, swirling the brandy in the bottom of the cut glass snifter. Burnt wine, the Dutch called it. He drained the last of the cognac and walked to the liquor bar and washed the small snifter in the sink. As he was washing the cut glass snifter, he noted a Vat 19 rum bottle on the bar along with other vintage liquors. Whether it was a reminder of Peter Meyer and Cuba or his life in the Navy, he was not sure, but his thoughts turned to Cuba and Demon Rum.

He had seen Demon Rum drive many a swabbie crazy while on liberty in Cuba. It was considered a fighting man's drink in the West Indies by the old Tars. It was strong enough to make a rabbit bite a bulldog. The best rum was distilled from sugar cane juice and was especially strong and pungent to the taste. Drunken sailors sang "Rum and Coca Cola," a tune made popular by the Andrew Sisters. Sailors on liberty joked about the native Creole girls in Trinidad who had too much rum to drink and were too fat to polka. We were all sailing the world in search of mo' love in the late 1950s the old sea dogs among us decried.

Collier was assigned as a yeoman to the USS *Ranger*, a super carrier, when it was commissioned in 1957. The carrier was manned by over 3,000 sailors and airmen when fully deployed for a shake-down cruise. Some of the best sailors the Navy had offered to manned the Ranger, when it left Norfolk, Virginia, along with the dregs of the fleet that had to be conscripted to fill out the ship's complement of sailors. No naval commander with any salt would volunteer to lose good sailors to a newly commissioned ship in the Navy.

The *Ranger's* first port of call was the United States Naval Base in Guantanamo, Cuba. The crew was not aware that liberty was cancelled for all Navy personnel in Guantanamo or "Gitmo City" as it was called by the locals. The small town was invaded three months earlier by Fidel Castro's rebel insurgents posing as U.S. Navy sailors. Naval authorities at the base later realized the public relations coupe of granting liberty for the *Ranger* crew since the small town had suffered considerable economic loss as a result of rebel insurgency. The crew of the *Ranger* had long waited for liberty and had money in their pockets to spend freely. Rumor had already spread over the ship that Gitmo City was a sailor's paradise with the Cuban's liberal attitudes, pretty native girls, plentiful rum, and cheap sex.

Sailors were all over the town like sand fleas on a dog. Some old salts never reached further inland than the first bar, while others could be found atop the highest mountain peak for a view of the island. Money was spent freely. The exchange in currency was so great for the dollar that sailors were advised to take small ditty bags ashore to just carry the Cuban currency and small change while on liberty. The Cubans welcomed the sailors with open arms and the sailors returned the hospitality by being civil and generous with their money.

Sailors could see the physical destruction on the town and the emotional scars that still lingered in the minds of the Cuban people. The Arizona Bar was a popular hangout for sailors with its Western motif, long ornate bar, brass fitting and swinging batwing doors. The interior was riddled with bullets holes behind the bar, along the walls and ceiling. The wagon wheel style chandelier overhead was broken and the small stage lights were damaged beyond repair. Sailors left the port city better than they found it and no major incidents were reported for Captain's mast on the *Ranger*'s departure.

# Chapter 23

Life can be cruel, Collier learned as the *Ranger* steamed out of port in Cuba for the Dominican Republic. He was informed by the commander that his best friend and classmate in high school had crashed his jet plane just off the coast of Cuba while the *Ranger* was in port. His friend's father, a tugboat captain on the Mississippi River, had actually come aboard the *Ranger* looking for him, but was informed that he was onshore on liberty.

The next day Collier wrote his friend's mother a heartfelt letter of condolence and his regret for not being able to meet with his friend's dad. The two classmates came from the same background and had shared many common interests. Collier himself had enlisted in the Navy to become an officer and a pilot. He suffered a penicillin reaction at the U.S. Naval Officer's Candidate School in Newport News, Rhode Island, and elected to join the fleet to see the world rather than layout and re-enroll in the next class.

Liberty in the Dominican Republic was dangerous to you health, since Pappa Doc was the dictator. Because of the social and political climate, sailors were briefed to go ashore in pairs and be careful of what they said in public. People in the

Dominican Republic were found to be far more poor and oppressed than the average Cuban in Guantanamo. It was not a fun island for liberty; if it had not been for the lone gambling casino with its huge colorful water display, it would have been a total bust. When the word got out aboard ship, a good number of the ship's crew elected to stay on board and wait until the next port of call for liberty.

The crew was in high spirit when they arrived in Trinidad on August 8, 1958. Trinidad, or Port of Spain, was an island that Columbus was given credit for discovering. Trinidad captured the America's imagination in 1957 with calypso music, steel bands, and lively dances like the limbo and others that were more emblematic of a drunken sailor's strut.

Harry Belafonte was popular on the island with his Banana Boat Song, "Day O, Day O, and I'm Gonna Go Home." American tourists were flocking to the island for the pulsating rhythms and the sensuality of that nightlife that was being depicted by the film and travel industry. The beautiful Creole girls on the island distinguished themselves by making color and class a priority issue.

While the island itself was beautiful, it was all an advertiser's facade as far as Collier was concerned. It was second only to Cypress Gardens in his mind, when he saw the lake one summer while working in Florida. The image that was promoted of Cypress Gardens was far different from the reality. The lone spot depicted in movie newsreels and photos of the lake's shoreline was actually only about thirty feet wide. The rest of the lake was typical of any number of lakes in Florida and Mississippi for that matter.

Collier and his shipmate Joe Duncan decided to go ashore on Sunday and conserve their dollars for a big night out on the town in Rio de Janeiro, the next port of call. Sunday was an interesting day in Trinidad. It was closed up tighter than a widow's pantry with five kids. Mississippi blue laws seemed to be in effect inasmuch as there was little commerce that could be transacted on Sunday.

Not to be outdone, the two made arrangements with a taxi driver to find a place that sold cold beer in order to escape the oppressive heat, since nothing was open. The cab driver drove through the small whitewashed buildings and narrow alleys in town at an amazing speed, all the while setting on his horn. He explained that Trinidad law gave the right of way to the driver who blew his horn first.

He later pulled up in the back of a large two-story white building and asked them to wait while he went inside to conducted business. Returning quickly, he advised that the establishment would serve cold beer, but that they could not carry on any commerce inside. Collier and Joe were hustled in the back door, beneath a stairwell that led to the second floor. The first floor was a large rectangular room that had tables and straight back chairs throughout. The room was stark by all accounts and had no pictures, flowers or ornaments of any kind. A large well-stocked bar was at one end of the room.

A man was sitting near the bar on a large, well-worn, maroon sofa. He had one leg propped up on an old packing trunk lined with empty beer bottles. A captain's hat was casually thrown over a bottle or two. He had a shock of white hair, thinning slightly on top and a full white beard and moustache. He was dressed in a white crumpled shirt and pants to match. His shirt was open at the neck to reveal a mat of white hair and he wore soiled white tennis shoes without socks

"Hello, mates, join me in a beer," he said when he noticed the white sailor uniforms.

"Raymond Collier and this is Joe Duncan."

"Mike Fitzwilliam's here," he replied, extending his hand for a handshake, but made no effort to move off the couch.

"White slavers are ye?" the captain offered apparently picking up on their Southern accents.

"No, we were both too young to make an option," Collier offered, with no emotional quality to his voice.

The captain roared with laughter and slapped Collier's leg as he sat by him on the couch. Joe pulled up a chair in front of the sofa and next to the brass bound packing trunk.

"Margarita," he screamed at the top of his voice.

A large, heavy-set, attractive black woman emerged from behind a door near the bar. She took one look and brought three cold beers and offered no glasses as she set the beers on the trunk.

"You fool with me, you catch one's royal," she snapped at the captain.

"Ah yuh swallow dat," the captain replied, smiling at her.

"Ah vex mad, I clout yuh one," she offered with a grin.

"What are you captain of?" Joe asked, noting the captain's white hat.

"I'm skipper of an old rust bucket cargo ship that hauls mobile offshore drilling equipment from one place to another on the island," he replied, offering no apology or offense.

"What's the name of your ship?" Joe pressed him with mild interest in his history.

"The *Carriacou*," the jack tar said, swigging down a quarter of his beer. "My ship was in the movie *Fire Down Below* that was filmed here in Trinidad several months ago. You boys should have been here to see Rita Hayworth, she was a real beauty," he went on to say with a grin.

"Who else was in the movie?" Joe asked rising to the bait.

"Robert Mitchum and Jack Lemmon played the male roles. Margarita's daughter was in the film, too, with some other locals for color. The movie company even wanted her to relocate to Hollywood, but Trinidad law will not allow its citizens to emigrate off this damn island." He snorted in disgust for there was little opportunity for most natives of Trinidad to rise above their birth station in life.

"That's too bad," Joe replied sympathetically.

"What's your steaming route when you leave Trinidad?" the captain inquired with interest.

"We are bound for the West Coast, with ports of call in Brazil, Chili, and Mexico," Collier replied.

"Leaving the Caribbean to the Irish are you?" the captain grinned.

"We noted Irishmen in Guantanamo, Cuba, Haiti and Santo Domingo, Dominican Republic. How is it that Irishmen are all over the West Indies?" Collier asked.

"You mean you never heard of the Irish slaves in the Caribbean?" the captain replied, as if he was amazed.

"No, I guess not," Collier replied, looking at Joe for confirmation. Joe nodded his head in agreement.

"Then let me tell you the story." Mike snorted for emphasis as he finished off his beer, before telling us his tale.

"Queen Elizabeth, Charles I, Charles II and Oliver Cromwell nearly exterminated the Irish on during there regime It all started in the 17th century when the English created a policy of banishment for the Irish. 'Wild Geese' they were called for the capturing to be sent to New World colonies. When banishment did not serve their purpose, the British crown resorted to selling the Irish as slaves to plantations in South America and the West Indies. While African Negroes were better suited to work in the tropical climate of the Caribbean, the Irish made better mistresses, cooks, clerks, and house servants,.The Irish were transported in the same manner and style as Africans. In many cases the Negro slaves were treated better than the Irish, especially the men. A black slave had value, while an Irishman had no real value for the planter. He was given dangerous and hazardous work to perform to protect the African slaves to work the sugar cane and tobacco fields. Irish women were used as breeding stock with selected African men to produce better looking slaves to be sold at auctions in the West Indies. Descendants of the union were known as Black Irish. Most had lighter skin and were sold at a higher price at slave auctions. A bill was finally passed in England in 1839 forbidding slavery as a form of commerce. The story of Irish slavery has yet to be told in large part because the British were careful not to keep records and the public does not have the stomach to hear about England's sordid history in this regard," the captain explained pedantically in the manner of a college professor.

"I don't think I ever heard that story, of course, I am aware of African slavery, being from the South," Collier replied. Joe, who was from Georgia, nodded his head in agreement.

"Margarita, my dear, another round of beers for my mates," the captain called out.

Margarita had been busy scurrying up and down on the stairs on some mission. She reappeared from upstairs and quickly brought three beers to the table without a word to anyone. Margarita seemed distracted as she took a dozen or so empty beer bottles back to the bar in her soiled calico apron. The captain seemed to note her behavior but said nothing, which was not in character. He watched her as she left with the bottles with a quisling look on his face.

"Don't go outside, make him come in," a woman's voice was heard to say from upstairs.

A few minutes later the front door opened and a young black man in a neat robin's blue suit came in with garden flowers in his hand. He wore a white shirt open at the neck and had on white buckskin shoes. He stood nervously at the foot of the stairs when he noticed three white men observing him. Undaunted, he stood smiling with pearly white teeth showing when a figure appeared at the top of the stairs.

A pretty black girl stood momentarily at the top of stairs dressed in a red and white form-fitting dress with shoes to match. She smiled and spun her red and white parasol a time or two before descending the stairs to meet her black swain. He handed her the garland of flowers with eyes only for her. She took his left arm and they proceeded to march out the door unmindful that anyone was in their presence. Not a word was said by the three men who watched this uncommon scene play out in a Trinidad whorehouse.

"Where were we?" the strangled voice of the captain was heard to say as it broke the silence in the room for the three men.

We all felt to a man, like intruders, and laughed at our embarrassment, Collier recollected.

# Chapter 24

While the remaining ports of call provided sailors on the *Ranger* considerable pleasurable experiences, the experience that was etched in their minds was the "Crossing of the Line." When a Navy or any other vessel crosses the equator, it is cause for a celebration. The ceremony is a pagan initiation with its origin in Viking rites to test a man's mettle to meet the hardships at sea. The Royal Court of Neptune initiates those members aboard ship who have never crossed the equator.

No one is special when it comes to the imitation, whether one is an admiral or a common seaman. If one has not crossed the line, he is a Pollywog in the eyes of the Royal Court of Neptune. Shellbacks serve the court to ensure that Pollywogs are severely beaten and humiliated to meet standard to become a Shellback. There was the Royal Dentist who sprayed evil smelling juices in your mouth, The Royal Barber, who cut your hair in several directions so that your own mother would not recognize you. The Royal Baby, who was usually the fattest Shellback aboard the ship who was naked on his throne except for his diapers.

Each Pollywog had to kiss the Royal Baby's huge belly that was covered with the most distasteful smell one can imagine.

The Royal Baby would hold your head close to his belly, and when you gasped for air when he released you, he slapped some foul greasy pellet like stuff in your mouth. One then was bathed in the Royal Coffin, which was a huge canvas bin filled with water, raw foodstuffs and evil smelling juices and odors. The last rite was the most punishing. A run through the Royal Gantlet as Shellbacks took a position on either side armed with canvas fire hoses filled with cotton batten soaked in brine water. It was like being hit with a baseball bat or sling, Collier recalled, and left bruises and welts the next day. You can to this day find sailors in and out of active service who still carry the certification in their wallet that they crossed the line and are Shellbacks.

* * *

What a glorious moment it was later when the USS *Ranger* steamed up the narrow straits of San Francisco Bay. The crew saw the orange vermilion Golden Gate Bridge with its art decor form and sweeping cables in the early morning sunlight. It was a photographer's dream and could not have been better choreographed by a Hollywood producer as the sailors in their whites lined the deck of the carrier.

The flawless blue sky and the early morning sun shown brightly on the Coit Tower on Telegraph Hill as the ship steamed into harbor. Coit Tower was a memorial to San Francisco firefighters and built by Lillie Hitchock. The top of the tower was built like the nozzle of a fireman's hose.

Every crewman aboard the *Ranger* felt that San Francisco was welcoming them with open arms. It was like a siren call in Greek mythology beckoning sailors with beautiful music, except in this case it was the city of San Francisco and not the Daughters of Achetous who desired that ships sail on to cliffs and the sailors, drown.

San Francisco and Alameda, California, was the last port of call for Collier. He would have a few months before Christmas in California and then he would be eligible for an honorable discharge from the Navy.

He was determined to shed his military look as soon as he had liberty in town. His head was now bald since the penicillin reaction took a heavy toll on his hair, so he decided to have his head shaved. He had the look of a hard-nosed Marine recruit and not a sailor. His skin was drawn tightly on his face, and he had wide shoulders and narrow hips. The sebaceous cyst scar was still evident on his left cheek. The Navy doctor pulled out a slow growing benign cystic tumor with a curette and hemostat pliers. The corpsman who was assisting hit the floor when the doctor evacuated the contents and removed the cyst wall to prevent any chance of recurrence. The cheesy and offensive smelling contents were too much for the corpsman.

"What's that?" Collier recalled saying, as he lay on his side under a local anesthesia at the Naval Hospital in Norfolk, Virginia.

"We just lost the corpsman," the doctor replied, tugging at the lining of the cyst wall with pliers.

As soon as Collier hit the beach, he looked for a place that had lockers in town for Navy personnel who wanted to shed their Navy blues and start wearing civvies. He made a quick tour around town and located an upscale men's store called the Cable Car Clothiers on Bush Street. He went inside the well-appointed haberdashery and informed the store manager, a handsome, older man with a pencil moustache, that he was in need of civilian clothes.

"I have been at sea for over eight months and need for you to advise me on the latest men's fashions. I am not interested in tailor-made suits, but prefer something casual that will still allow me access to San Francisco's finer dining establishments and night clubs," Collier offered.

"I think we can outfit you nicely," the store manager said, admiring his physique taking note of his handsome face and a visible scar on his left cheek.

"Fine," Collier said. "I am looking to get out of these blues for a while now that we have made port."

"I understand," the store manager said as if there was a confidence between them that was unsaid.

The store manager outfitted Collier in a beige shirt which had a rolled type collar and was open at the neck. He selected a darker, tan colored jacket and gabardine slacks of the same color as the shirt. He selected a pair of light tan suede shoes that matched the trousers and a light tan woven grass belt with a brass buckle. As he stood in front of the shop mirror, he wondered how he would be received in Mississippi wearing this get up, but in California he knew he was in high style.

"I want to wear the clothes now and return my Navy blues to my locker, do you have a garment bag I could use for that purpose?" Collier inquired of the manager.

The manager was admiring the change in his client's appearance. Clothes do make the man, the shop manager assured himself taking a measure of pride in his ability to serve the customer. "Certainly, that will not be any problem," he said, as he strode purposefully to a small curtained-off room in the rear of the store. When the store manager returned with the garment bag and his Navy blues and black shoes neatly bagged, Collier thanked him for his assistance.

"I will be leaving San Francisco in a couple of months and before I go I would like to commission you to make me a suit out of this material," he said, handing the store manager a bolt of olive green and black flecked silk that caught his eye.

"Of course, sir, that will be no problem and you have made an excellent choice," he replied. "Come in any time and we will be happy to tailor the suit for you. I will set the material aside in your name." He took paper and pencil to write down Collier's name.

"What is you name?" Collier asked.

"Shelton Polk, at your service, sir," he said with a toothy grin, which reminded Collier of an old movie star.

"Until then, Shelton," Collier said, addressing the older man with a familiarity uncommon in San Francisco.

Shelton Polk walked to the front of the store and watched Collier make his way down Powell Street with the garment bag casually thrown over his shoulder. He was impressed, to say the least, with the young man and his manner. He thought he detected a Southern accent, but felt it was inappropriate to question a customer. Nevertheless, he felt some attraction for the young man, not like the snotty nosed Hollywood types who were incessantly trying to impersonate someone with their importance.

Like a bird dog on the loose for the first time in the City of Lights, Collier took to dining at fine restaurants and staying in expensive hotels. He had saved up his money for this splurge of extravagance before he would be discharged from the Navy in December. October and November were wonderful months for spending time in San Francisco. The air was clean and fresh in the city. Lombard Street with its winding, twisting serpentine curves offered one the fragrant smell of flora grown in large container pots at every doorway.

Fisherman's Wharf was a great place to visit and have seafood while watching the seagulls snipe as they played over the blue waters of the bay competing for food. Simply walking the streets in San Francisco was an adventure for Collier. One night while strolling he noticed a barman setting up an outside bar next to a large building. On impulse he simple sat down on one of the stools and ordered a beer.

While he was seated at the bar, a door flew open and people started exiting the building as if there was a fire. Well-dressed men in tuxes and expensive tailored suits paced to the street and lit up smokes underneath the overhead street lamps. Beautiful well-gowned women exited with the men as well. One exceptionally beautiful woman sat next to him at the bar, with an older distinguished looking gentleman. As she took her seat, she turned and looked at Collier with interest in the glow of the lamp light, then she gave her full attention to her escort. It was only later that Collier recognized the woman; it was Martha Hyer, the movie star. It was apparent to Collier now that a play was going on inside and this was just an intermission. He recognized Red Skelton and several other character actors from the movies.

Later that night at the Black Hawk, a famous jazz club owned by Helen Noga, a young singer by the name of Johnny Mathis sang. Collier overheard a man at the bar say on his way to a table that Mathis was a local college student who held the high jump track record in California and was being considered to represent the United State in the Olympics.

"I will just have a draft beer," Collier told the waitress who hovered over his small table in the darkness of the club.

"Where are you from?" the waitress whispered as she set his cold frosty beer down.

"I'm from Mississippi," he whispered in kind.

"I'm from Alabama. I will talk to you later," she smiled and returned to the bar to wait on other customer because the club was filling up quickly with patrons.

He was seated in a small elevated area that offered a great vantage of the bandstand and the crowd down below. Johnny Mathis was outstanding and received applause after applause from the crowd for his performance. To Collier he sounded like a young Nat King Cole. With a room just up the street, he was in no hurry to leave the sanctuary of the club. He was thankful now for the respite from the regimentation of military life and the shallow existence of some of his fellow shipmates who saw beer and pizza as being the essence of life. The time passed quickly and the beer eased his pain for a sailor on shore leave.

"We have an exciting stripper that will close the show if you stay until closing time," the waitress whispered as she set another cold beer down on the table. While Collier picked up on her invitation, he was not interested in getting into some type of entanglement that would interfere with his going home for

Christmas. His DD-214 was almost in hand to support his honorable discharge from the Navy. He was not about to screw that up now with a waitress in a night club who may have some issues of her own that she would like to avoid or pass on to some sucker.

"We are not allowed to talk or date the customers," the waitress offered later, "but here is my telephone number. Call me Sunday."

Collier awoke late the next morning and noticed the waitress' note as he was picking up his wallet to go downstairs for breakfast, or brunch, as they like to call it in California. While it was not like the steak and eggs the Navy served on Sunday mornings it was good fare for a man who had been up half the night. He wondered about the waitress from Alabama.

What was her story? Collier felt everybody had a story. He could not help be curious about how a young, attractive girl from Alabama wound up in San Francisco. So he decided to give her a call later before he checked out.

"Hello," he heard her say sleepily as he reclined on the bed in his room after a sumptuous champagne brunch buffet in the hotel's Nob Hill restaurant.

"This is Raymond Collier, you asked me to call, did I wake you?" he offered solicitously, not sure of the course he was charting for himself.

"Well, yes, but I am glad you called. I just wanted to talk with someone from back home; San Francisco can be such a lonely place if you are not from here," she replied with a sense of urgency like someone who needed a friend.

"I can understand that, I am looking forward to going home before Christmas. I am in the Navy and due to be discharged sometime in early December," he patiently explained to make sure she understood his situation.

"You're a Navy guy, huh?" she asked still sounding sleepy and not totally awake.

"Naval Reserve after college, I'm eligible to be discharged after a two-year enlistment," Collier replied not feeling the need to go into a lot of detail.

"My name is Jolene, by the way; I would like to meet you to talk to someone from back home." She sounded vulnerable to Collier over the phone.

Anyone from the Deep South was a person from home if you were living below the Mason-Dixon Line or had crossed the Mississippi River at Vicksburg heading east. Sensing the desperation now in her voice, Collier could understand her feeling of loneliness from his being at sea for long periods of time between ports of call.

"Well, I don't have to be back to the ship until 6 p.m. Do you have a car?" he offered, not wanting her to know that he could report later if he really wanted to. Better to limit the time, he thought to himself like a schoolgirl on her first date, since he did not know what he was letting himself in for. Jolene Smith, she said was her name, when she picked him up with his duffle bag in hand in front of Mark Hopkins at Number One Nob Hill on California Street. He was still wearing his civvies, and would change at the locker later that night.

Jolene was driving a light green 1950 Ford with the slickest tires he had seen on a car since he left Mississippi. She was still an unaffected Southern girl in his eyes as he sat next to her in the front seat.

"What's it like?" she said after they said their hellos and were driving down Powell Street later.

"What's what like?" Collier asked.

"The Mark Hopkins, of course?" she smiled.

"They have a sky bar lounge called Top of the Mark on the 19th floor that affords you a 360-degree panoramic view of San Francisco and they serve a great martini cocktail with vodka and dry vermouth," he replied, thinking he sounded somewhat like a travel agent.

Few sights could compare with Copacabana Beach and

Sugarloaf in Brazil for Collier. His decision to join the fleet was the best decision he would ever make in his life. The experiences were invaluable for he was exposed to a life that would ordinarily be unattainable and unaffordable for a person of his station in life. He saw wealth and luxuries as well as misery and poverty all woven together in one fabric in some countries.

Collier swore to never be a victim of the seductive trappings of power, wealth, political propaganda and greed after his experiences in the Navy. He would look to education in the future as the key to his salvation, for he saw the devastating influence of ignorance and illiteracy in the West Indies and the South American countries he visited while on shore leave.

"Let's go to Fisherman's Wharf," she said. "I know a spot where we can have lunch and just sit out in the sun and enjoy the bay," Jolene offered with a wide grin.

"That's fine with me," Collier replied cheerfully.

Later after lunch at a small café on the bay that served up a good shrimp po-boys, Jolene and Collier sat on a blanket near a private residence that had a great view of the bay. The house was vacant and there was only a private security guard who checked the front of the house and the main gate regularly.

Apparently a young security guard had told her about the place one night at the Black Hawk Club. The house was formerly owned by some old movie star who had fallen on hard times and the estate was tied up in the courts on some kind of settlement issue by the heirs.

Jolene's story was pretty much what Collier suspected on the telling of it. She was born poor in Prattville, Alabama. Her father, a landless tenant farmer, raised cotton and was a slave to the natural elements of Mother Nature and a large unforgiving plantation owner. The family lived a miserable existence trying to grub out a living on ten acres of hard-baked Alabama dirt that had long been farmed over. Jolene was the oldest of Ray Smith's issue who lived in a five-room clapboard house that was cold in the winter and hot in the summer. No longer able to stand the sight of her mother slaving wearily over a black wash pot stirring clothes with a stick in hot scalding water like a soul that had lost its heart, Jolene looked to move on.

Kissing her younger brother and two sisters sweetly on the cheek, she silently crept out of the house after dark and crossed the open cotton fields to Highway 31 South to somewhere. Emptying the small throw-away suitcase that she lived out of, Jolene packed a few things for the road. As she jumped the drainage ditch bordering the highway, the bailing wire cut her hand and arm. Clutching the suitcase tightly, for it was the only possessions she had in life, she made her way to Highway 31 South. People said the highway went all the way to Mobile and the Mississippi Gulf Coast.

Standing alone but determined, she faced the headlights of an oncoming car in her best short-tailed gingham dress. A big, heavy black sedan ground to a halt yards down the road and backed up. She stood on the gravel along the roadway that was now slowly washing away in the drainage ditch. As she instinctively backed off the graveled area alongside the highway, the tall Johnson grass with its sharp-tongued leaves bite at her legs.

The occupants of the car, a Canadian couple, were on their way to Mobile, and solicitously offered her help. So concerned was the couple that they both gave her money without the knowledge of the other when they heard her desperate story to make her way in life on the way to Mobile. Thanks to the generous couple, she was now in possession of more money than her father made in a month working the tenant farm in Prattville. With the money now tightly stashed in a bandana loosely knotted around her neck, she was "Nigger rich" as the Negroes would say in shanty town on a Saturday night.

Working her way southwest, Jolene saw the Gulf of Mexico in Mobile. The Canadian couple had advised her to go the traveler's aid section that was usually located in a bus or train station for assistance. They wisely cautioned her against hitchhiking and warned that it was too dangerous for a young girl. Jolene saw a travel poster of the Golden Gate Bridge in San Francisco in the bus station in Mobile, and knew that was where she wanted to go. Helen Nog, the owner of the Black Hawk Jazz Club, hired her as a waitress without experience because she felt the young, attractive girl from Alabama had pluck.

With four new tires that Collier later bought, he and Jolene took in the sights in and around San Francisco on Sundays and Mondays, which were her days off from the club. They visited Chinatown, Golden Gate Park, Union Square in the heart of San Francisco, Nob Hill, the hilltop estates, and North Beach. Jolene marveled at Collier's ability to hold the Ford on Lombard Street with just his foot on the gas pedal. He told her Vicksburg has some hills that would challenge any San Francisco cab driver.

Sausalito, a Mediterranean like village across the Bay, became Collier's favorite place to visit with its bougainvilleas that covered the hillsides as densely as kudzu around Vicksburg and Natchez.

As time passed, Collier intentionally introduced Jolene to his friends and spent time with her at the USO Club in San Francisco to help improve her self-esteem. She became a great dancer and was sought after at the club by the servicemen for her attractive looks and easygoing manner. Jolene made no demands on Collier, and he none on her as they developed a friendship that was more like brother and sister than lovers. She was smart enough to know that he did not want to make a commitment knowing that he would be leaving the Bay area soon to return home. They would become lifelong friends and write each other occasionally through the years. She later married a young artist from the South who relocated to San Francisco because the city was well known for its artist's colony in 1957. After Jolene's husband gained some prominence as an artist, they relocated to Sausalito and raised a family.

# Chapter 25

Collier was one for practical jokes. Before he was separated from service, he decided to take a  friend from Georgia and another shipmate to Finnochios, a famous tourist attraction on Broadway in North Beach. Well dressed in their Navy blues, they were escorted to a front row seat by design. Since he had visited the club earlier with Jolene, he knew the routine. That night, Laverne Cummings, a beautiful blond dressed in a pale green evening gown to the floor, opened the show by singing, "Everything Old Is New Again."

The audience clapped hysterically when the performer took a bow. Collier's two sailor buddies were impressed being so close to the stage and the performer, who was by all accounts a beautiful woman with long blond hair. After a long pregnant pause, the performer on stage rolled his shoulders forward and in a deep, masculine voice said, "We are all men, you know."

Collier laughed like a fool at his friends' reactions making the situation worse for them, for now the audience was in on the joke. All three threw their white hats in the air now that they had the audience's full attention. The variety show act that followed was unique, and Collier knew they would be spotlighted and made the butt of jokes all night long by the female impersonators. While his two friends did not go into a homophobia panic, they did decline an offer by the performers to visit backstage for a margarita party upstairs after the show.

Since there was an airline strike when Collier was discharged from the Navy, he had to seek alternative transportation home. The train ride home was eventful for Collier, because he met an interesting gentleman who got on the train late carrying a large expensive briefcase. He was a handsome older man of medium height, wearing an expensive, pin stripe suit, who proved to be an excellent conversationalist. Collier noted that the time passed pleasantly with his commentary and anecdotes after they introduced themselves on a first-name basis.

"Let me treat you to dinner?" Sam asked politely.

Retiring to the dining car, the stranger took the liberty of ordering for both of them. As the evening wore on, they had dessert and coffee, while the train made the click-clacking sound on the tracks beneath their feet. The dining car lights came on to signal that darkness was falling outside. A few travelers remained in the dining car, while others retired to their seats or moved to the club car.

"Why don't we retire to the club car and let me toast you on your service to your county?" he offered with a smiling.

While Collier felt stuffed from the large steak Sam demanded that they order and was sleepy, he did not feel he could decline the offer.

"That sounds good to me," Collier replied cheerfully, as they made their way to the club car in the rear of the train. The car was crowded with civilians and military personnel on their way home or to another duty station. The atmosphere was festive and Sam facilitated the conversation among the passengers, while Collier sat nursing his drink, observing the action. As passengers returned to their seats, the club car became less crowded leaving Sam the sole host over three couples besides he and Collier.

As the light dimmed to signal the club car was closing, Sam asked the porter if they could be allowed to continue the party. The porter grinned and replied that FCC regulations did not permit the serving of alcohol, but that he could dim the lights and the occupants could have all the ice and water they desired. Money passed hands to consummate the deal.

"Raymond, bring me my briefcase from the overhead if you don't mind?" Sam asked politely.

On returning to the club car, Collier learned that Sam had five fifths of bourbon whiskey in his briefcase. He smiled at Sam's resourcefulness for pleasantly passing time on a long train ride across the country. Sam was the ideal host. As the train railed on through the night, he drew out the couples on their relationships and interest in life. He was such an artful practitioner that he learned discreet details of their lives that they would not have divulged to their closest friends.

The chief executive officer of the Fortune 500 Company was living with his executive secretary in New York and had a wife and two children in the suburbs; the newly married couple were in for a surprise because he was a closet homosexual and she a school librarian; the former Marine drill sergeant was being transferred to another duty station for abusing a recruit. His companion for the evening was on her way to Biloxi to take over the club management that had fallen on hard times featuring down-and-out entertainers. While she was youthful in appearance, there were hard ridden miles in her history for which she was eager to forget as she looked forward to the opportunity on the Mississippi Gulf Coast.

Collier was not a party to Sam's skillful interrogation of the passengers. His time was spent in refreshing everyone's drinks at Sam's direction for most of the evening. He did not know how he made it back to the passenger section because Collier's first recollection in the early hours of the morning was Sam tugging at his sleeve urging him to get off on the train with him.

Struggling and half crawling, Collier made it to the Mission Union Station in Phoenix, Arizona.

The clear fresh air was intoxicating. Collier and Sam stretched and breathed in as much of the oxygen as their lungs would spare. The far snow-capped mountains were beautiful with the purple haze and clear blue sky in the background. Union Station with its mission revival architecture was a picture in itself with the red tile roof, stucco wall finish and curvilinear gables.

Sam was a master psychologist and foreteller of the future, and asserted on the way to the station in Jackson, Mississippi, that after Collier visited with old friends, enjoyed nights out on the town, and exhausted his unemployment compensation that he would have need of employment. Take my card, Sam told Collier, and look me up. We will have a place for you. Why would you hire me? Why not? Sam had replied laughing.

While Collier never took Sam up on his offer, he found the card later on his dresser at home. The card read: Sam Masterson, Vice President, United States Steel, and Birmingham, Alabama. Collier wondered years after what life would have been like working for Sam given his hypnotic charm and social brilliance. Their passing may have been the genesis for Collier's interest in psychology and psychiatry.

# Chapter 26

Practice was going well, Steve thought as he stood at the kitchen sink drinking a glass of water after practice. The team was coming together; they were more focused, and they were winning more games than losing. There seemed to be a comrade that was carrying over both on the field and off. Players were actually helping one another to develop their football skills and techniques and he even head a player or two offering to tutor other players in math or science in school.

It was a secondary gain that Steve never considered; he did not experience the phenomena while playing in high school or college. Maybe it was a value that one had to inculcate early in a child's life before they became self-centered and vain relative to their own individual needs or accomplishments. Bruce seemed more tolerant of Brad now he noticed, and there did not appear to be that infernal picking on one another that infuriated his wife. It was something he would discuss with Barbara later, when he heard the telephone ring.

"It's for you, Dad," Bruce called out.

"Hello," Steve answered.

"Steve, Osmond here, you still interested in that German shepherd puppy?"

"We sure are," Steve laughed.

"Would this Saturday be too soon for you?" Osmond inquired.

"Not at all, the boys will be real excited," Steve replied, smiling at the prospect.

Barbara was excited over the prospects of moving into a larger place with property and now was a good time to get a German shepherd for the boys. She had a German shepherd as a child and knew how protective they could be around children in the family. Since she and Steve had decided on a house and lot that had five acres, a barn and utility shed, the property would be ideal for raising two healthy, active boys. The acreage would allow plenty of privacy and give the boys an opportunity to learn how to operate a riding lawn mower and maintain the property. While town life had it conveniences, there was nothing like raising a family on property of your own, she thought. The boys would not have to change schools and they could still keep all their friends, while participating in the school and recreational events in town. Living in the county certainly had its advantages, Barbara reasoned.

"Boys, get in the truck, we are going to see a man about a dog," Steve called out to the boys who were playing in the backyard.

"Ah, Dad. You're always saying that," Brad said climbing over Bruce in the back seat.

"Yea, Dad. Why do people say that when they don't really mean it?" Bruce asked.

"It's just a Southern expression, boys, it means you are simply going to do business, the nature of which you might not want to offer for some reason or other," Barbara replied.

"I see we are going to do business, but Dad doesn't want us to know what the business is all about," Brad interjected with a wry smile.

"That's about right," Steve grinned.

Barbara looked at Steve, amused by his response and his unwillingness to tell the boys about the German shepherd puppy.

Later when the truck turned into South Lakeshore Drive, the boys noticed where they were.

"We are going to Grandma's house," Bruce offered as if he had discovered a secret.

"No, Grandma told me she and Grandpa would be out of town for the weekend," Bruce replied.

"There goes you're thinking, Brad, Dad didn't stop," Bruce snapped.

Stopping at the large iron gates to the Collier property, Steve pushed the electronic button to announce their arrival, but Osmond was already at the gate to meet them. He swung the gate wide to allow the truck access to the property and closed the gate behind the truck as Steve swung into one of the parking bays.

"Osmond, you know Barbara and this is Brad and Bruce, our boys," Steve said in the form of an introduction.

"They are mighty fine looking boys," Osmond replied, sizing the two boys up. "And how are you, Miss Barbara?" Osmond asked using an old Southern expression for greeting women.

"I am doing very well, thank you," Barbara replied smiling at his courtesy.

"I guess you want to see the puppies?" Osmond offered.

"We are going to look at puppies!" Brad cried out now making a connection.

"I have the dogs penned up; I think Heidi is ready to give them up; they have been so pesky since she weaned them," he said.

"How many puppies did she have?" Barbara asked.

"She had six, four males and two females," he replied. "I will let you pick out the one you want, but I will point out the alpha male," Osmond offered.

"What's an alpha male, Mr. Osmond?" Bruce asked, wide-eyed and with interest.

"An alpha male is the leader of the pack. I will show you the one I think is the alpha male." He smiled.

Karras gave a protective bark when he saw the party approaching. All the pups scrambled to the fence for attention and food since Osmond was feeding them puppy chow. Heidi followed the pups later and stuck her nose through the wire fence to smell Barbara's hand. Osmond noted Heidi's action.

"She likes women," Osmond smiled thinking back to Missy and their good times together.

The boys were wildly excited at the idea of picking out a German shepherd puppy of their own. "Which one is alpha male because they all look alike to me?" Brad inquired as the pups were nosing through the fence to touch or be touched.

"This one here, the big dude that is so aggressive," Osmond smiled.

"Boy, he is big. Look at his paws compared to the two smaller pups that must be females," Brad speculated, rubbing the big pup's ears.

"Yea, Dad, we want the alpha male," Bruce replied excitedly since they were picking out the most dominant male dog in the pack.

"That's alright with me," Steve replied, looking at Barbara. She nodded for she knew from her experience that it was easier to raise a male dog than a female.

Osmond opened the gate to the pen and picked up the alpha puppy for the boys. Bruce and Brad hugged the furry puppy and noted his peculiar smell.

"You need to train him to a box so he will feel secure. The box will replace his mother as his security blanket and help you to train him." He smiled at the youth.

The two boys sat down next to Osmond as he instructed them about house training a puppy, finding a toy for the puppy to cut his teeth, and leash training. Steve and Barbara watched as the boys were more attentive than they had ever seemed as of late.

"Remember now to get a book from the library and read up on German shepherds. It will be your responsibility to care for your puppy," Osmond admonished them as they were getting into the truck.

"Steve, I will get you the papers to register your puppy later," Osmond said.

"Thanks, Osmond, you have made these boys' day for sure," Steve smiled shaking hands with the black man.

Osmond waved to the boys and felt good about the puppy. He knew Missy would have liked for Heidi to have puppies and carry on the line because she made it a big deal to have both Karras and Heidi registered for she felt it was the responsibility of the breeder.

Later on the way home, the boys talked of Osmond and the instructions he gave them for raising the puppy.

"I like Mr. Osmond, Dad," Bruce offered.

"I like him, too, Bruce," Steve replied smiling at Barbara.

"What will we name him, Mom?" Brad asked.

"That's up to you boys, like Osmond said, he is your dog now," she replied, looking back at the boys' happy faces as they loved on their new puppy. It brought back memories of Kaiser, her first German shepherd, who followed her everywhere she went on their property.

# Chapter 27

The stewardess was envious of the well-dressed, dark-haired, beautiful woman in first class with the rose diamond. The diamond had at least twenty-four triangular facets that formed a convex face pointed at the top with a flat surface that splayed the cabin with northern light brilliance. Her companion aroused her curiosity. He was handsome enough, but wore rough clad jeans, cowboy boots and a blue denim shirt. Country comes to town, she guessed. She would love to ask the lady how she came by her diamond, but she did not want to appear as stupid as her roommate who asked the question once and was shocked by the curt response. The stewardess had some air miles herself and recognized the lady in first class was ostentatiously rich and respectable. She admired her tranquil appearance as that of a woman who was plainly happy and sexually content. A rare combination this day and time, she mused as she picked up the intercom to announce that they would be arriving at Heathrow Airport within minutes.

Restless and impatient, Collier could not wait to land for long flights were not his forte. He noted the stewardess giving them the eye and how attentive she was to Naomi's needs while in flight. To Collier, his prodigal affections and love for Naomi would last a lifetime. He was mindful of the story of Naomi in the Bible, a classic picture of a Jewish matriarch and a power behind her husband's throne. If that was to be his life, so be it, he had interests to keep him busy.

"I wish you could have convinced Lisa to let us stay in a hotel," Collier said in the baggage area.

"She would have none of it. When I called to inform Philip that I would be stopping off in London to sign papers regarding your estate on the way to Sicily, Lisa demanded that we stay with them and that Philip would meet us at the airport."

"I know Lisa, she just wanted to check out your new husband out of curiosity, not unlike the stewardess, I might add, that was hovering over us ever since we boarded the plane some seven hours ago," Collier offered wearily.

"You behave; the dear was just doing her job." She smiled contentedly but eager to stretch her legs as well in the baggage area.

Philip and the black cab driver were waiting faithfully for Naomi and Collier in the baggage area. Of course, Philip immediately recognized Naomi and welcomed her to London all the while looking like the urbane and refined gentlemen that he was.

"Phillip, this is my husband, R.C. 'Sonny' Randall," Naomi offered as she had agreed reluctantly to go along with Collier's deception.

"Sonny, this is Phillip Collin, Raymond Collier's solicitor I told you about."

"I see," Collier replied, extending his hand.

The two men briefly eyed each other like adversaries looking for a weakness as Collier played his role to the hilt. Sonny looked the stereotypical Southern male in his jeans and cowboy boots. Phillip was not impressed by Sonny on first impression. He wondered if Sonny had the stuff that a woman like Naomi needed in a mate. Immediately, Phillip turned his attention to

Naomi and opened the door to the black cab while Sonny assisted the driver in loading their luggage. It was an activity that no proper Englishman would engage for fear of invading a tradesman's space and interfering with his livelihood. Sonny finally settled in the back seat of the black cab. Black cabs in London had the reputation of being the best in the world. They could hold five passengers and reportedly could turn on a dime.

"We live in Hyde Park and Lisa would have it no other way than for you to stay with us while you are in London," Phillip offered in the way of an explanation while he completely ignored Sonny in the conversation.

Collier was amused that Phillip did not recognize him but it was not a fair test since he was so enamored of making a good impression on Naomi. True to Collier's opinion, Phillip would not recognize him if he was out of character and not of personage to impress.

"What's it to Hyde Park, Phillip?" Collier drawled in his best Southern accent.

"It is about forty-three pounds," Phillip replied without any hesitation.

Collier smiled to himself. It was interesting how the Brits measured distance in terms of cab fare.

"What about mileage?" Collier inquired innocently grinning all the while at Naomi.

"Oh it's about thirteen miles as the crow flies," Phillip replied a little piqued at himself for not appreciating the American tourist's need for the referential and inconsequential.

"Is this your first time to visit England, Mr. Randall?" Phillip smiled condescendingly.

"Yes, but call me Sonny," Collier offered to reinforce the stereotypical personalization of his role as a Southerner.

It might be helpful if Phillip learned of his identity because the Mob was sure to make inquiries about their former relationship in order to track funds missing from the Swiss banks. Phillip ignored Collier's presence on the way to London.

Instead he discussed matters related to Collier's will that would require Naomi's signature under British law since Collier's estate supported financial holdings in England.

Lisa and Phillip lived near Hyde Park in the prestigious Mayfair district. Their apartment was within walking distance of Hyde Park Serpentine Lake and Rotten Row. The four-bedroom apartment was well appointed with Italian marble floor and bathrooms. The bedrooms had crown molding covered headboards and pastel bed covers. The living room was painted light yellow with white striped walls, large heavily draped windows, and indirect lighting, while the kitchen was modern with light tan colored cabinets and appliances.

"Oh, I am so glad you agreed to stay with us," Lisa gushed on their arrival at the apartment. Naomi introduced Collier and Lisa took his hand in hers and looked him in the eye with no apparent recognition.

"The coffee pot is on and as soon as you have time to change, I will set our cups out here in the living room," she said smiling.

"Oh, would you help me Sonny with the coffee in the kitchen?" Lisa asked later as they were comfortably seated in the living room. Naomi and Philip were engaged in an exchange of views on the economy in the U.S. and the balance of trade.

"What the hell is going on, Raymond?" Lisa said as she turned to confront Collier as soon as they were out of earshot and the batwing doors were closed to the kitchen.

Collier realized that Lisa had made him as soon as she saw him in the living room but elected to keep his confidence for reason of her own. Without going into great detail, Collier explained the need to change his appearance and identity. Lisa was a quick study and appreciated the importance of maintaining his confidence. She was horrified to hear that the Mafia had made an attempt on his life.

"How did you make me so fast, Lisa?" Collier laughed.

"Well, for one thing, I was extremely curious about the man who married Naomi Selber, and when Phillip told me his name was R.C. 'Sonny' Randall, I knew it must be some kind of joke. I also wondered at the time what the odds were that Naomi would fall in love with another redneck in such a short period of time. When I saw your muscular build, strong chin, complexion and Southern accent, I realized you must have had plastic surgery to change your appearance." She laughed. "Of course, I didn't mention my reservations to Phillip at the time. He would have just put it down to my having grown up in the South."

"Philip apparently does not have a clue?" Collier laughed.

"How could he, he hasn't taken his eyes off Naomi since she's been here," she replied, feigning envy over the attention that Phillip was bestowing on Naomi.

Lisa was a beautiful, intelligent and competent woman in her own right and knew that she had no reason to be jealous. Phillip was a doting husband and they had two beautiful children. While their backgrounds were very different, they seemed to complement each other. Unlike some Southern small town women who had problems living away from home and their mommas, Lisa had the capacity to adjust and adapt to almost any culture or society, whether it be in Europe or elsewhere.

"What should we do about Phillip?" Collier smiled as if he did not know the answer.

"Let's play it out and see how long it takes for him to recognize you. Of course, I can support your Mississippi redneck role playing, since I am a redneck girl." Lisa's voice was soft and conspiratorial as she grinned with anticipation.

"The problem will be getting Naomi to go along." Collier grinned sheepishly, but his being able to maintain his identity was a serious matter in his mind. He knew that Phillip had a need to know, but if he could convince him of his new persona then it would be worth the effort for all concerned.

Lisa with all the aplomb of Loretta Young entered the living room through the swinging batwing doors and said that they needed to talk about plans for the evening.

# Chapter 28

As the black cab swung into the parking bay at 41 Dover Brook Street in Mayfair the occupants were already in high spirits from having a few toddies to fortify themselves for an evening on the town. London as usual this time of year was damp and overcast, making the streets slick and grimy for the unwary. The large, two-story brick building was not particularly imposing from the outside, but the large heavy black lacquered door suggested convenience and elegance.

Dressed to the nines, the two couples entered Le Blanc, an upscale restaurant famous for French cuisine. First established by Armand Blanc, it was now managed by his son Armand Jr. Phillip liked the traditional old school ambiance at Le Blanc. It reminded him of a gentlemen's club with the elegant, formal setting and attention to detail.

As the couples' table was being readied, they were ushered into the bar lounge with its rouged colored pastel walls and overstuffed chairs. Phillip ordered an aperitif for the four of them while they waited. Naomi noted the sumptuous padded seats, the drawings, cartoons, and expensive bric-a-brac that complemented the decor. Armand Jr. recognized Phillip, and their party was immediately ushered downstairs to the basement dining room that was darkly lit, heavily draped with rich green lacquered bamboo walls. Plush seats, skirted tables with napery and individual sculptures for ornamentation complemented the dining room.

Sartorially dressed, every eye in the house was on Naomi and Lisa as they gracefully entered the dining area. Naomi was beautiful and elegant in her form-fitting black silk chiffon dress and rouched top that complemented her full breasts. Matching high heel, black satin pumps and black velvet coat accentuated her appearance and dark good looks. Lisa was dressed in a rose silk dress, belted in the front, and matching stiletto heels. With her killing looks, graceful mien and her blond hair piled high on her head, she had all the ladies flushing with envy. Much speculation and titter could be heard as the patrons at Le Blanc's observed the two well-dressed women.

Both of the men who accompanied the ladies were dressed in tailored, expensive dark suits, white shirts, and ties. It was obvious to the locals that one of the gentlemen was British with his distinguishing good looks, salt and pepper hair and neatly trimmed white moustache, while the other gentleman, handsome enough, had the look of a stevedore that his Brooks Brothers tailor-made suit failed to hide.

Of course Collier was aware of the scene they were making. He was reminded of the old saw "clothes make the man" as far as distinguishing the wearer as a person of discrimination and taste. But Collier also recalled a friend back home commenting once, that "if you wanted to be impotent, you had to look impotent," when he was putting on airs, so to speak, in public. There is nothing like a redneck to remind you of your roots when you feel the need to make a statement in public.

Phillip was in his element and announced to the sommelier, "We will have Dom Perignon to petit four," and selected a 1992 vintage from the wine list.

"I wonder if they have wine-in-the-box," Collier inquired like a babe in the woods. The nattily dressed sommelier acted as if he didn't hear the comment and gave Phillip his full attention.

Lisa giggled knowing that Collier was putting Phillip on with his best redneck routine. Naomi gave Collier a look but smiled for, after all, it was not a night to be pretentious.

"Aren't you pushing the boat a little?" Lisa whispered, observing his extravagance.

"Not at all, we are here to celebrate Naomi and Sonny's marriage," he whispered in a resonant voice with good humor.

"You are right, Phillip, tonight is a night for celebration. It's good of you to think of same," she replied, as she affectionately kissed him on the cheek.

It was a practice not commonly found in British company and certainly not in public. But Lisa was not common by any standard and stood her ground with the Brits on any subject.

Phillip and Lisa's comments did not go unnoticed by Naomi and Collier. They were thankful that Phillip and Lisa thought enough of them to share their happiness. Since Phillip had command of the menu, he ordered for him and Sonny, recommending that they have the smoked onion soup, classic Caesar salad, and fresh lamb rack with Dijon mustard, garlic and herbs. Lisa recommended the chicken with rosemary, lemon, and garlic and thyme sauce for her and Naomi.

"We have to try the smoked salmon with our champagne," Phillip instructed the sommelier.

"A very good selection, sir," the sommelier offered as he openly admired the two women with the gentlemen.

Dom Perignon flowed freely and the couples enjoyed their dinner immensely. Armand Blanc Jr. made sure that the service was timely and the silver cloches covered the plates of food being served.

"Armand, our meal was worthy of Archestratus," Phillip commented. "I think we are ready for coffee and petit fours now."

"I will have it sent right out," Armand replied with a broad smile.

Another waiter was back in no time to deliver the petit fours on a burnished wooden trolley. Collier, into his chips now and devilish from the champagne that he had consumed, decided to act the role he was playing.

"Who is Archestratus?" Collier asked with a slack-jawed appearance of one lost at sea and out of his element.

"Archestratus was a Sicilian Greek who was considered the father of gastronomy and fine food. He believed in light, elegant style of cooking using seasoning in a sensitive manner not to spoil the roue," Phillip replied pedantically with an air of sophistication.

"I see, maybe Naomi and I can look him up while we are in Sicily on our honeymoon," Collier replied.

"I think not, he died in the fourth century," Phillip said almost scornful at the ignorance of Naomi's husband.

Naomi gave Collier a disapproving look. Lisa, on the other hand, was bent over with laughter, almost to the point of peeing on herself, over how Collier was putting Phillip on. She wished now that Collier could have attended her wedding; she would so loved to have introduced him around to the swells as her cousin. It would have been a hoot because Collier was so good at role playing. She knew he took a perverse pleasure at times in making the upper crust twist in the wind for their pompous views of the world inherited from abuse and misuse of wealth. Phillip was so into the wine and the spirit of the evening and intoxicated with Naomi that he still did not recognize Collier's black humor.

While Philip and Collier each selected the chocolate terrine and marquise au chocolate, Naomi and Lisa decided on the mini cake, triolette. Phillip noted the French waiter openly eying Naomi and Lisa as they made their selection of French pastry.

"The bloody bastard was lusting after our women, Sonny,"

Phillip growled in feigned indignation after the French waiter left with the trolley.

"'Tis a wise Frenchman that knows his own father," Collier offered without thinking and out of character.

Phillip howled with laughter and eyed Collier in a new light. Naomi may not have harnessed herself to a jackass after all, he mused, and at least her husband was literate. Lisa overheard the comment and recognized the source for the quote was from Samuel Clemens' impression of the French after visiting the country.

"A Frenchman's home is where another man's wife is," Lisa whispered to Collier and they both laughed heartily at Mark Twain's witticism of the French.

Giggling like school girls with their heads together, Lisa and Collier caused Phillip and Naomi to wonder about them. Maybe the Dom Perignon was getting to them, Philip postulated. So he suggested that they retire to the lounge to smoke a cigar and have a Marie Brizard to aid their digestion before departing the premises, for he knew they were fairly stuffed to the gills.

Later in the lounge, Phillip took the liberty of ordering a Pulco made of concentrated fruit juice and pulp, while the ladies retired to the powder room. Collier thanked Phillip for his generosity for a most satisfying meal and spirits as they smoked their cigars. By the time Naomi and Lisa returned to the lounge, Phillip and the imposter were arm-squeezing and back-slapping each other like two former classmates at a high school reunion. Finishing off their Pulco, Lisa announced that they had reservations for the late show at Ronnie Stout's.

# Chapter 29

Ronnie Stout's turned out to be a world-famous jazz club in Soho. The club level was small by American standards, but had a second balcony floor upstairs. The interior of the club was dark and smoky, with red tablecloths and pictures of jazz entertainer and notables lining the walls. Smoking was full blast in the dimly lit small room, as they were ushered to their reserved seats. Phillip ordered a light wine for the four of them. A light comedy act was preceding the jazz entertainment. The crowd was responsive and appreciated the comic's British humor, with a large number of tourists in attendance.

Lisa liked the club because it reminded her of the jazz and blues clubs that populated the delta and the river towns in Mississippi. A known black jazz singer was a featured singer at the club from time to time. But she became such a volatile and angry person she could never get over her resentment of racial discrimination in the 1960s in the South. Borne to a middle-class religious family, she ultimately lived out a tragic life and never realized her potential.

Ronnie himself was a poor, Jewish white boy from the East side of London. His family fled Southern Russia in the 1880s to escape persecution according to Phillip and changed his name for social acceptance in the entertainment field. Stout was later known for his willingness to give young entertainers a start. Some of the finest jazz musicians that Britain has ever produced had their beginnings at Stout's. Tragically, Stout was a heavy smoker and suffered dental problems that resulted in his having dental implants. The word in the legal profession suggested that he could not withstand the resulting pain from the complications of his dental work and that he suffered death by misadventure from mixing brandy with strong prescription pills.

Collier was not a jazz man, even though he loved the blues. Restless, he soon started to observe the patrons as his eyes adjusted to the dimly lit room and the white, smoky haze that was slowly enveloping the room. He suffered two idiosyncrasies in his youth—one, he never liked for his wife to enter an unfamiliar bar or juke joint without him going in first, and two, he always had a need to visit the rest room before he was seated for too long.

As he panned the crowded room, a strange sense of foreboding invaded his consciousness. The light hairs on the back of his neck felt stiff and he sensed that he was being watched. A common feeling he knew for those who suffer from paranoia. The front door opened and the splay of light flooded the far wall. A man was sitting with two older women against the far wall beneath the wall posters and framed pictures of celebrities. He turned as the light silhouetted his face and that of the two women. The two women appeared to be Jewish from the look of their Semitic nose and the man, looked...

"My God. It's Peter," he cried out silently as the words strangled in his throat. "How could it be?"

As he sought to gain control of his emotions, the fear was overwhelming him. Was this just a coincidence? "What are the odds of this happening?" he muttered to himself, as his mind raced for understanding. Fearful, he now began to scan the patrons in the room. Two men were sitting in the back with their backs against the far wall; they did not look like your typical jazz fans. One of the men was large, hairy with a full head of curly black hair and moustache, while the other man was bald, muscular, clean shaven with the skin taut and hard around his cheekbones an eyes. His face had a fiendish look under the soft light of the beer commercial overhead. Collier had seen men like this before in his travels all over the world — dangerous, strong, silent types, like vipers, with the capacity for violence and mayhem. But he had to be sure.

"Lisa, you see the two men with their backs to the wall near the door?" Collier whispered.

Without a need to question, Lisa turned and made out the two men with the sullen expressions on their faces.

"Yes."

"Do you think you could go the ladies room in the back and tell me what you think of them, the light is so dark, I can't make them out clearly," he uttered with a sense of urgency.

Without another word between them, Lisa informed Phillip that she needed to go the powder room. Naomi looked up and thought it strange that Lisa would go to the power room without inviting her. Because she saw him whisper something to Lisa, Naomi looked to Collier for reassurance. Taking Naomi's hand in his, Collier laughed openly at the comedian on stage and smiled at her.

By the time Lisa returned, the band was on stage belting out one of their favorite jazz songs that drew applause from the appreciative crowd. Seating herself, Lisa turned to face Collier away from Phillip and Naomi.

"They are from New Jersey from the looks of them and family. The fat one, with pinky ring and the gold chain around his neck is soft, but the other one looks mean and hard eyed. He could be dangerous?" she whispered.

"How do you know they are from New Jersey?" Collier asked with a hint of a smile on his handsome face.

"Because the fat one muttered under his breath, 'Jesus Christ,' as I shook my rose bush on the way by," Lisa whispered sweetly.

Collier knew Lisa was referring to her form-fitting rose colored dress with matching belt pinched tightly at her small waist. Naomi and Phillip were enjoying the music and were totally unaware of the undercurrent going on between Lisa and Collier.

"You should work for the CIA," Collier replied appreciatively.

"How do you know, I don't?" Lisa smiled wickedly.

His brain working overtime now, Collier was not aware of the retort. He couldn't approach Peter directly. The two men would be looking for Peter to contact someone. They probably knew the two older women were just family friends and that Peter was fulfilling some social obligation to entertain them. Collier gave a passing waiter the high sign to get his attention. As the waiter leaned over his shoulder for the order, he turned to him and whispered, "Give me your pen and your order pad." Quickly he scribbled a note, "Meet me in the men's room now R.C."

"Take this note with a bottle of brandy to the man with the two women seated against the wall beneath the cartoon pictures. When he asks you who sent the note, tell him the man standing with his back to him at this table. Don't point me out, just let him follow your eyes, do you understand?" Collier instructed the waiter firmly looking him in the eye. The waiter nodded his understanding from reading the look in Collier's eyes and feeling the sense of urgency. As Collier watched out of the corner of his eye, the waiter delivered the brandy and the scribbled note as instructed. Frightened, Peter looked into the eyes of the waiter and his body trembled after he read the note. Seeing the trepidation in Peter's eyes, the waiter realized this was no parlor game. Shocked by the note, Peter realized that it could be only one person, and that R.C. stood for Raymond Collier and that brandy was his drink of choice.

Peter instinctively clutched the waiter's arm and drew him closer. Nodding slightly, the waiter motioned towards Collier with his eyes as instructed. Trembling involuntarily, Peter followed the waiter's eyes and saw a man standing with his back to him across the crowded room. He was in the company of distinguished looking gentlemen and two well-dressed attractive women. There was nothing threatening about them. From the back and in the dim light, Peter could not make out the man except he was broad shouldered and had dark hair.

His mind raced to comprehend; was he a friend of Collier's or a federal agent? After the man was seen walking to the men's room, Peter offered his apologies to his lady friends. Smiling politely, they both turned back to the entertainment on stage. Fearful now, Peter made his way through the smoke-filled room, his eyes downcast so as not to draw any attention to himself or show panic. His hands were sweaty and his undershirt was now becoming wet under the arms.

Closing the men's room door behind him, Collier stepped inside and stood with his back against the wall next to the door. Two men washed their hands at twin wash basins along the wall. They eyed him speculatively in the mirror, but said nothing and left. The four stalls proved to be empty when he squatted down to look under the side panels. The white tile floor was damp. The mirrors over the wash basins were slightly glazed over from the humidity. Taking a step forward he saw his hazy reflection in one of the mirrors and his face looked strained with tension. Returning to the back wall of the men's room he took a position near the door.

Moments later the door opened slowly and Collier knew it was Peter. His hair grayer now and his shoulders a little more stooped, he seemed smaller and more vulnerable.

"Move to the back stall and stay there until I call you," Collier instructed him softly.

Peter flinched when he heard the man's voice behind him. As he walked to the last stall, he noted the man's reflection in one of the wash basin mirrors. Even with the scum and haze on the mirror, he knew the man was not Collier because he was younger looking and had a full head of hair. Not fully understanding and fearful, Peter did as instructed, almost instinctively, like a child obeying his parents without question.

Closing the toilet door, Peter took one last peek at the man and still had no recognition. The man appeared determined and purposeful as he stood against the wall. *He must have my best interest at heart*, Peter reasoned, trying to reassure himself like a child who turns to a stranger for help.

It seemed like an eternity to the two men waiting in the men's toilet, but it was only minutes before the door opened slowly. A bald-headed man with a thick neck and wide shoulders of an athlete cautiously entered. Stopping just inside the toilet, he peered under the side panel of the four stalls. Grunting like an animal, he stood up, pleased with his finding. He saw the feet of a man in the last stall wearing expensive, black leather shoes. The bald-headed man never saw the right arm that closed around his thick neck and hooked over the left arm of the man behind him. A triangulation was formed on his neck as the man behind him slowly squeezed and pulled him backwards and down with force. The gap narrowed until the pressure on the carotid arteries shut down the blood flow and oxygen to his brain. The bald-headed man lost consciousness in a matter of seconds, so effective was the shimewaza judo technique.

"Get out here quickly, we don't have much time," Collier called out.

Unconscious now, the man was flat on the tile floor, his head to one side and his powerful muscular legs flexed along the floor. Quickly, Collier snaked through the man's pockets and found no weapons. His wallet revealed a New Jersey address, credit cards and a wad of cash.

"Collier, is that you, is that really you?" Peter cried, still frightened.

"Yes, but we don't have much time, this man is an assassin, stand next to his neck and if he moves, step on his neck right here," Collier instructed, pointing to the carotid artery.

"We only have about thirty seconds before he regains consciousness," Collier explained as he stood back and looked at the man on the floor.

Stuffing the credit cards and money in his pocket, Collier noted that the assassin's heels on his shoes looked new compared to the soles that were worn and scuffed. Twisting one heel, he found piano wire that the assassin planned to use to strangle Peter. The other heel revealed twin metal rods that would attach to the loops on each end of the piano wire. In disbelief, Peter stared at the assassin's tools. He knew the man's evil intentions—he would have strangled him to death if it had not been for Collier.

"We don't have much time, go straight to the airport and book a flight to Toaormina, Sicily, and stay at the Mazzaro Bay Hotel. I will meet you there in two days. Ring my room. I will be registered as R.C. Randall. I will invite you up. We will work out details later," Collier instructed his friend breathing hard and almost out of breath.

"But, Raymond," Peter stammered, for he was still fearful over the prospect of almost being assassinated.

"No buts, you get out of here. I will take care of your lady friends. Don't speak or say anything to anyone unless you have to," Collier growled impatiently, for the assassin on the floor would be regaining consciousness shortly and his companion might come looking for him.

Turning to look at Collier before he closed behind him, Peter was still amazed by the change in his friend's appearance. Countless questions came to mind, but he realized that his friend was right as usual. But why Toaormina, Sicily of all places, Peter wondered as he hailed a black cab for the airport. All he knew now was that Raymond was a blessing.

Putting his heel to the assassin's neck for good measure, Collier took his money, credit card, and tore his wallet apart to give the appearance of a violent attack and robbery. Later he instructed the waiter to inform Peter's lady friends to take a cab home and not to worry, that he would contact them later. The assassin would not make an issue on regaining consciousness. The two would try to make it back to the States as quietly as they had come without drawing any attention to themselves.

Returning to the table, Collier complained how smoky the place was getting as he took his seat. Lisa quickly picked up on his comment and suggested that it was time to call it an evening for Sonny and Naomi were probably tired from their long overseas flight.

# Chapter 30

At the apartment later Lisa made mint tea. She assured everyone that it made them sleep better. As Lisa made the tea, she encouraged Naomi and Sonny to change clothes and get comfortable. After they were all comfortably seated, Lisa poured Phillip's tea in a dog house cup that simply read, STUPID.

"What have I done now?" Phillip asked plaintively when he noticed the cup.

It had been a long-standing joke between them for some time. It was their polite way of pointing out that one or the other had erred or made some miscalculation in judgment that day. Phillip was usually the recipient of the cup. As the boys got older, they questioned the role of the cup and how their parents could make light of faux pas situations and laugh about it later.

"What have I done now, Lisa?" Phillip exclaimed out loud when he noticed the cup sitting in front of him.

"Meet your old friend and client Raymond Collier," Lisa crooned while pointing her slender finger at Collier.

Phillip's mouth flew open like a barn gate and he blushed from embarrassment. His slack-jaw reaction reminded Collier of his pals in the Navy when they realized the performers at Finnochio's were female impersonators. Phillip apologized profusely to Collier for not recognizing him, while hugging him over his second coming. Collier laughed and put it down to the skill of plastic surgeons and the wonders they can perform these days. It was a wonderful way to end the evening for good friends. Phillip teased Sonny before they retired that he had a lot of explaining to do in the morning. Collier had no intention of besmirching or belittling Phillip for not realizing his identity, for after all was that not the scheme, for many a man has followed a simple suggestion without question, so strong is the mind to advance thought.

Up early the next morning, Phillip had coffee made by the time Collier arose. Pressing him for details, Collier laid out the entire story from the beginning and his need to change his appearance and identity. Philip was aghast to learn of the potential assassination of Peter Meyer that was foiled by Collier at the night club. After discussing the assassination attempt, Philip was amenable to having one of his firm's private investigators use the assassin's credit card to make large purchases in London. Collier explained that it would seal the assassin's fate for the Mafia, because they did not like to leave footprints. It was unlikely the two assassins would ever see the Statute of Liberty again for their failure to carry out the contract and the mob's need for security.

Since the girls were sleeping in, Phillip challenged Sonny to a cycle around Hyde Park to see the sights. While Phillip found it difficult to refer to Raymond as "Sonny," he recognized the need to maintain his identity a secret, even from the firm. They both agreed that Naomi would be the contact between them in the future. Using the boys' bikes, Phillip and Collier cycled around Hyde Park and the Serpentine Lake. They raced with the excitement and enthusiasm of a time past, the memory still imprinted on the brain from their youth.

The lake was home to waterfowl and a few sweating oarsmen

who were up early also on a Sunday morning to test their skill. Phillip pointed out the sights. Hyde Park was once a hunting ground for Henry VIII. As they cycled leisurely past Rotten Row, a famous horse-riding area, Phillip pointed out the soapbox orators at Speaker's Corner who were setting up their displays to banter back and forth with individuals in the crowd. Lisa was not averse to taking on a speaker if his fact were at odds with the truth.

While they were viewing the large statute of Prince Albert, Phillip recalled discussions with university professors at his club who were knowledgeable of the research on Jack the Ripper and the unsolved murders. Any numbers of dissertations have been written on the subject by serious researchers in law and criminology.

"By the way, Sonny," Phillip said, now trying to use Collier's new appellation in conversation as much as possible. "I have learned some interesting facts about the Jack the Ripper murder case. For example, James K. Stephen, Prince Albert Victor, and John Netley were about the same age. Peas in a pod, as they say."

"That is interesting," Collier replied.

"What is more interesting is that John Netley is hardly mentioned in any police investigations, yet he was known to Dr. Gull, the Queen's physician, James K. Stephen, and Prince Albert Victor, or Eddy, as he was called by his aristocratic friends."

"Friends of a feather stick together it seems," Collier replied.

"Very little is known of John Netley, except he died an untimely death when he was run over by his own coach."

"That is an unlikely occurrence in anyone's mind. It would be like having a cab driver run over by his own black cab," Collier snorted mockingly.

"No official report was ever found that Netley was interrogated by Scotland Yard for his role in the Ripper murders. Several researchers have speculated that James Stephen and Netley were co-conspirators, but no facts have ever been proffered to support that contention," Philip said bluntly.

"I find it strange that no historians have attempted to develop a time line for James Stephen and the murders. They seem to discount him as a suspect because of his accident at the town along the sea coast, yet he worked as a Clerk of Assize before he took a leave of absence from his duties in the summer of 1888. He conveniently returned to work after the last victim was murdered November 9, 1888," Collier acknowledged.

"You have researched the Victorian aristocrats?"

"Yes, and I find there was a strain of madness that governed the Stephen and the Woolf family genetics, from which, I might add, they all died. Of course, Virginia took her life, while James and his father died in an asylum," Collier asserted.

"So you know that James Stephen was a cousin of Virginia Woolf?"

"Yes, and given the current history of the Royal family, I think it is obvious to almost anyone why the Royal family wanted to keep the Jack the Ripper murder case sealed for these many years," Collier admitted bitingly.

"The thing that bothers me in retrospect is why the investigating authorities never considered the murders were committed out of the East End and later returned?"

"To do that would have suggested a conspiracy to murder. The idea that another man or men might be involved was too devious for consideration given the times. The East End was already a tinderbox and any suggestion that Royalty or nobility was involved in the murders would have created a riot in the streets of London," Collier replied.

"I had family that was in government at the time and they surely knew if there was wrongdoing in government and a cover-up," Phillip said uneasily.

"Don't react too harshly. Consider the handling of John Kennedy's assassination and the U.S. government's attempt to refute any allegations of a conspiracy for fear the American public would rise up and demand we go to war with Russia. The

U.S. was pretty much a tinderbox at the time, with the Cuban missile crisis and the Bay of Pigs incident where Bobby Kennedy convinced the President not to provide air cover for a CIA covert operation to take over Cuba. The Justice Department under Bobby Kennedy decided to take on the Mafia after the President was reported in league with the mob for the trade union vote to win the election. Hoffa was targeted by Bobby Kennedy to divert attention. Only a controlled media in the U.S. averted a panic among U.S. citizens for their willingness to sit on these stories at the time."

"The way you have chronicled the events, the media may have contributed to Kennedy's assassination by their silence," Phillip observed.

"You may be right. The conspiracy of silence may have given Kennedy's enemies freedom to operate for no one could imagine an American President being assassinated in modern times," Collier replied reflectively.

"I guess you wish you had the tapes now?" Phillip replied wistfully.

"I think it is enough that I have the Mafia on my tail. I don't need to be looking over my shoulder for the Royal Examiner," Collier snorted gruffly. "The matter is still sensitive to this day."

"You maybe right. I hadn't thought of that," Phillip observed.

"Let us get back to the girls, Phillip; I don't feel comfortable leaving them alone over what happened last night," Collier replied brusquely.

Lisa was curious about Naomi and Collier's marriage. So when Naomi entered the kitchen for coffee, she could not resist asking.

"Here, let me pour you a cup of coffee, Naomi," Lisa offered politely, wondering how anyone could look so beautiful this early in the morning. Lisa knew she was grumpy as a bear in the morning if she did not get a good night's sleep.

"We had a great time last night. I want to thank you and

Phillip for a wonderful evening," Naomi said as she sipped her coffee.

"Of course, we enjoyed having you, and Sonny was entertaining with his redneck routine putting Phillip on. I miss the South in a lot of ways living here in London with the constant mist and dampness."

"I understand. I have grown fond of Lake Serene. Raymond, I mean Sonny, and I plan to homestead there when we return from our honeymoon."

"I see; where did you and Sonny get married?" Lisa asked, trying not to be too obvious.

"We had a small wedding ceremony. Tom Haralson, a Methodist minister who lives on the lake, married us at the house with Osmond and Mamie as witnesses," Naomi replied, smiling.

"I guess with Raymond's need to go underground and create a new identity that was the best thing to do under the circumstance," Lisa nodded.

"Frankly, I would have married under any circumstance because I love the man so. He opened up a whole new world for me. Not material things, because I lived in a world where many people bought their fame or were apologists for inherited wealth or sought salvation in foundations," Naomi replied firmly and with conviction.

"The man has an inner drive that I have never understood. He dances to his own tune and seems to have an understanding of life that is a mystery to me relative to his background. He has been rudderless for a number of years now, since his first wife died. The Italians have a saying, he who has no wife, has no master." Lisa smiled thinking that Collier now had both an oar and rudder for his sails in Naomi.

"Lisa, he has shown me the satisfaction of simple things, a way of life. I now love to fish, eat hush puppies and catfish, read on a summer's eve or talk, just talk with Osmond or Mamie about things past or present," Naomi sighed, already missing the small family in Mississippi.

"Osmond, he is the caretaker at the lake, right?" Lisa asked, for she could see Naomi could be emotional when talking about her new husband. Lisa wondered about Naomi being Jewish and if that would present a problem for them in the future. For right now, it did not seem to be a matter that concerned Naomi. For she knew that her and Phillip's marriage was a mixed marriage to some people.

"Yes, we talked about his growing up in Ellisville, Mississippi, and his slave parentage."

"I know all about Ellisville, I wrote my master's thesis on the Free State of Jones and the life of Newt Knight, a Baptist preacher, former Confederate soldier, who later refused to fight in the Civil War for he considered it a rich man's war and a poor man's fight. Ellisville and Jones County was populated by yeomen farmers when the war broke out and only a few people owned slaves since the area was not tillable for cotton given the pine wood forests," Lisa replied.

Memories of her days in graduate school at the University of Southern Mississippi flooded her consciousness. She recalled meeting Ethel Knight, who wrote, *The Echo of the Black Horn* and descendants of the Knights, both black and white. Lisa recalled trudging through the deep thickets and tall pine trees with the Black Knights. They showed her New Knight's grave site that has been kept secret for all these many years for fear of vandalism.

"What a small world," Naomi replied.

Lisa only smiled and took out her big heavy bottomed saute pan for the Cajun omelet she was about to prepare. Her ingredients were laid out on the table top near her: eggs, chopped onions, green bell peppers, vegetable oil, butter, green onion tops, chopped parsley, Tabasco, pepper sauce, crawfish tails, smoked ham and milk.

"My goodness, what are you making?" Naomi asked after viewing the ingredients on the counter top.

"Cajun omelets. I had the ingredients special ordered when Phillip told me you were accepting our invitation to stay with us. Omelets are a favorite for cooks in the South on Saturday mornings when the family usually sleeps late."

"It certainly smells good. You know, I really never learned how to cook," Naomi offered apologetically.

"Well, most Southern girls don't when they get married, because their mothers do most of the cooking and don't want to be bothered with daughter's contention. Southern girls have a lot on their minds, and cooking is not at the top of the list."

"Is that really true?" Naomi smiled.

"Sure it's true. I would advise you to work on other things besides cooking. Leave that to Osmond and Mamie for the time being."

"Raymond and I have never really talked about having children."

"Phillip and I didn't talk about it, either; it just comes with marriage for most of us."

"You have two boys, is that right?"

"Yes, they are with their grandparents at their country estate. The boys love to visit because they can ride horses, fish and tromp the woods. Phillip's family was not quite ready to accept a country girl from Mississippi as his bride, but the boys helped bridge the gap and they have come to respect me I think. I remember hearing my father tell my mother when it came time for her son to get married, no girl would be worthy. Now that I am the mother of two sons, I see where my mother was coming from," Lisa replied laughing.

"Raymond and I are surely a mixed marriage by conventional standards but I haven't been into convention since I met him," Naomi giggled.

"You will love the South. The people, the climate, the hospitality. I miss it at times but the boys keep me busy and we travel often. My parents are deceased now and my brother was killed in Viet Nam so I have no real ties in Mississippi anymore."

"Well, this is an open invitation; I will invite you to visit with…my husband, Sonny, and I every summer at Lake Serene. Your boys will love Mississippi and give them and opportunity to identify with their roots. After all, listening to Osmond, I now see how important that is for people in their personal development," Naomi offered sincerely.

Lisa turned and hugged Naomi tearfully for the invitation, just as Phillip and Collier entered the kitchen.

"What's the matter?" Phillip snapped protectively when he saw Lisa sniffling.

"Oh! It's nothing, just girl talk" Lisa replied smiling.

"Lisa is teaching me how to make a Cajun omelet," Naomi offered to counter Phillip's concerns.

"That's wonderful. Lisa will have you barefoot, pregnant and in the kitchen in no time."

"You really are a redneck, Sonny," Naomi said as she hugged him in anticipation of their honeymoon in Sicily.

# Chapter 31

"Oh, Sonny, I love this hotel suite," Naomi offered as she looked out on Mazzero Bay situated high on the Mediterranean Sea. Mazzaro Bay is considered the most beautiful bay in the world with the colors of the Mediterranean on one side and Mount Etna, a snow-covered volcano, in the background. The suite had its own terrace and private splash pool that overlooked the sand beach with its sixty or more brightly colored parasols and sun beds for guests. Crater-like rocks formed a private inlet to the Mediterranean.

"I thought you would like it. I have always thought of it as a special place," Collier offered as he called out from the bedroom.

Appreciatively he noted the huge oversize bed with its covered headboard. Large oversize wall prints tastefully decorated the bedroom with big stuffed oversize chairs, fine furnishings, paintings, and antique statutes. The low ceiling and soft indirect lighting created a romantic cavelike effect within the heavily draped curtains in that separated the bedroom from the spacious entry room and sliding glass doors that led to the terrace.

Joining Naomi on the terrace with a cold beer from the well-stocked mini-bar, Collier hugged her around the waist, while pointing out the enchanting view of the Ionic Sea as it converged with the Mediterranean and Mount Etna, the highest volcano in Europe. Since the sun was twelve o'clock high overhead, Naomi whispered that she needed to work on her tan and show him her new swimsuit.

Enjoying the ambiance on the terrace while soaking up the sun, Collier clipped the end of a cigar with his sterling silver cigar cutter and rolled the cigar around in his fingers. As he lit the cigar he could not help but think of Peter and wonder whether or not he was registered at the hotel. He purposefully elected not to make any inquires at the front desk because he did not want to draw attention to himself or Peter as personal acquaintances. Since he had no contact with Peter from the time he went under the witness protection program, he was not sure what name Peter used to register. The Mafia would certainly learn that Peter made reservations for a flight to Taormina. The Corleone family was still active in Sicily and Toto Riina's gang was attempting a takeover from information Phillip leaned from informants on the streets of London. While there was a cloak of silence, there was no peace in the Mafia family in Sicily.

"What do you think?" Naomi said, posing in the doorway of the terrace, her knee bent in a feminine pose like a model, except her figure was more lush and mature.

"Oh, my," Collier exclaimed thinking the dolphins would rise out of the Mediterranean if she was on the beach.

"Don't you like it?" she said, arching her eyebrows in disappointment.

"What's there not to like, Naomi?" Collier grinned appreciatively.

She was breathtaking and divine looking in her dare to share swimsuit or lack thereof, he thought. Her bikini was made of strategically located pale cloth with bejeweled sequins and pearls supporting her breasts. She complemented her bikini with a silk scarf worn as a turban and silk champagne colored crocheted shawl that she wore off the shoulder and over her arms. Her high heeled molded sandals accentuated her height and made her legs seem longer. Here was a woman who at one time was shamed by her own nakedness. He thought back to their initial counseling sessions.

Smiling, Naomi put on her big dark, sunglasses that matched the champagne color of her shawl and stepped onto the terrace. She hugged Collier's neck before stretching out on one of the sun beds near the splash pool. As he sat puffing his cigar, he could not help but muse, this must be the la dolce vita lifestyle, or the sweet life as the Italians like to say. His musing was interrupted by the ringing of the telephone.

"Hello, Sonny Randall here," Collier answered for effect to assert his new identity.

"It's me, Peter. I am calling from the phone in the lobby," he whispered weakly.

"Come on up, Peter, the room number is 4223," Collier replied, relieved to hear his friend's voice.

"Naomi it's Peter, he's coming up. We will talk in the bedroom," he called out to Naomi sun bathing on the terrace overlooking the bay.

"Good!" she replied, for she was relieved herself after Collier briefed her about the assassin's attempt on Peter's life at the jazz club.

Naomi had a right to know of the danger involved for all of them. Being in a foreign country and not being able to control security was a concern for Collier, but under the circumstances he had no choice. A few minutes later there was a soft knock at the door. Opening the door, Collier let Peter enter. He still had a lugubrious expression and looked frightened, like a doe caught in the headlights of an oncoming car at night.

"Thank God you are here, Raymond. Every Sicilian has the look of a Mafia assassin for me now that I have become so paranoid," Peter admitted, openly hugging Collier. The show of affection and dependency worried Collier to some degree.

"Come on, let's talk in the bedroom, my wife is sunning on the terrace. We won't be bothered if someone comes in for any reason," Collier assured him.

"I can't believe it's you, Raymond, your looks—you look so much younger and handsome with hair," Peter gushed.

"Would you like a wine or a beer, Peter?" Collier asked, letting the compliment pass.

"A beer might help," Peter sighed as he sat himself comfortably in one of the over-sized chairs.

"Did you register under the alias that Justice established for you?" Collier inquired after returning with two beers.

"Yes, I had to, because of my passport," he replied, looking fearful.

"That's allright because I have made plans to create a new identity and passport for you to get of the country later. I have already called the front desk and reserve another room in my name. The room number is 4236 on this floor and here is the key card to the room. To make it appear that your room is still occupied, I want you to leave your suitcase and personals in your room. I will check your other room out, mush up the bed and so on, to make it appear the room is still occupied should anyone have a need to check," Collier detailed

"You have thought of everything, Raymond; I don't know what I would have done without you," Peter suggested, his voice laden with despair.

"From now on, Peter, call me Sonny, and remember my alias is R.C. Randall if you are questioned by anyone regarding our relationship."

"Do you have trust that my new identity and passport will be kept confidential from the FBI and Mafia?" he asked, still feeling pangs of uncertainty.

"Yes," Collier replied, "because my contact is Jewish and was active in the Italian underground during World War II." Collier explained his contact was a former member of the Sicilian underground in Palermo. The Sicilian Jew had worked with the Office of Strategic Services and was a master at counterfeiting postal stationary and German stamps. He was also active in black propaganda in Caserta, Italy, and was credited with disseminating information that Mussolini was acting under the evil eye of Hitler. A Jewish client put Collier on to the man when he learned of his interest in psychological warfare.

"We will work out a story line for you later. Right now we need to make arrangements for you to have plastic surgery."

"Plastic surgery?" Peter cried out from the emotional strain he was under.

"Don't worry, we are not talking about major reconstruction, just rhinoplasty to alter your nose, a chin tuck here or there, and maybe a dimple or two."

"Come on, Sonny, you are kidding now?" Peter laughed, feeling more relaxed now and remembering to call Collier by his new alias.

"Question, would you have recognized me if you saw me on the street?" Collier asked.

"No, you look great and much younger with the hair and all," Peter admitted with a smile.

"I have an Austrian friend named Marta Sacca who will see you in Catania; she has a clinic there as well as in Austria. You might be interested to know that the first nose job was done by a Jewish plastic surgeon by the name of Jacques Maliniac in New York around 1925."

"I really don't know how to thank you. I am nonplused as to how the mob was able to locate me," Peter admitted almost shamefully.

"The FBI kept pressing me concerning the source of money. Where was it now? Who had it and so on? Agents were dropping by my residence in St. Pete on a regular basis. My Jewish friends started to ask questions about those men. A number of unmarried Jewish couples who were living together to keep their social security benefits became uncomfortable having federal agents around all the time. It made me uncomfortable as well," Peter admitted almost sheepishly.

"We will be allright if we stick together," Collier offered trying to reassure his good friend who was still unsettled over the affair in London. Collier himself was fearful for he knew the Mafia creed: eliminate the body, and you eliminate the memory.

"From now on, stay in your room as much as possible and I will call you when they can see you in Catania. We do not need to be seen together while we are in Taormina. Call me on the phone if you need me for anything. Here is the number," Collier said, pointing to the phone for Peter to memorize. Since Peter was blessed with a photographic memory, Collier was not worried about him following instructions.

"Come on, I want you meet my wife," Collier said, patting his friend on the back to reassure him.

Naomi was entering from the terrace as Collier and Peter emerged from the bedroom.

"Naomi, I want you to meet Peter Meyer," Collier said.

Naomi had taken the silk scarf from her head and her raven black hair hung loose and uncombed to her shoulders. It gave her the appearance of a Jewish high priestess, regal and powerful with dark sensual powers.

"Peter this is my wife, Naomi."

Embarrassed, Peter Meyer gazed downward at Naomi's nakedness before him. Instinctively on seeing his embarrassment, Naomi pulled the silk crochet shawl with the scalloped beaded fringes around her shoulder and folded her arms over her breasts. The crochet shawl hung loose and did little to hide her lush figure as she extended her hand to Peter. The high heeled platform shoes made her appear more statuesque and taller in comparison with Peter's diminutive figure. With his eyes downcast, Peter took her hand and kissed it lightly. Peter's action embarrassed both Naomi and Collier. She looked to

Collier her eyes pleading, but he could offer no solace, because he was taken aback by the scene as well. Quickly, Collier stepped to Peter's side and put his arm on his shoulder.

"I am sure you two have a lot to talk about, so I will just change clothes in the bedroom. It was so good to meet you, Peter."

Peter turned away from Naomi as she exited for the bedroom. As he stood by Peter's side, Collier was aware of his maddening inner conflicts—feelings of repressed sexuality caused by his mother's sense of guilt over her past sins in the eyes of God and Biblical laws of sexual purity. Jewish psychotherapists were only now coming to grips with the conflicts between asceticism and sexual gratification, procreation, and pleasure with their clients in New York City.

Without another word between them, Collier led Peter to the door. Peter stood in the doorway and turned to Collier, a questioning look on his face.

"Naomi's Jewish?" Peter offered the question not so much as a question but as a fact.

"Yes," Collier replied simply.

"She's..." Peter stammered trying to find the words to express his sentiments.

"Yes, she is," Collier replied, smiling as he gently shoved Peter towards the door.

"A good wife is joy for her husband and she shall double the days of your life." Peter whispered an old Jewish saying in Collier's ear.

"I will call you later," Collier whispered closing the door.

Peter's comment caused Collier to reflect on his own attitude towards marriage. He espoused the sanctity of marriage and saw it as a covenant that allowed humans to rise above the animal kingdom. For Collier, marriage was unconditional love.

Naomi had settled in on the bed in her lounging outfit when Collier entered the bedroom later with two tall glasses of champagne from the mini-bar.

"Oh, Raymond, I am so embarrassed. I did not know that Peter was here with you. The look in his eyes when he saw me," she said apologetically as Collier handed her champagne that was bubbling and sparkling in a glass.

"I think he was more embarrassed over the fact that a Jewish woman of your status would marry a redneck from Mississippi," he offered, sipping his bubbly as he called it. He tried not to make any more out of the incident that was necessary. Like Naomi, he was embarrassed for Peter.

"You don't really mean that, you are not given to self-deprecation," she replied.

"Where did you learn that?" he asked with a puzzled expression on his face.

"From the books you asked me to read," she smiled.

"It's one thing to marry a Jewish woman; it's another thing to learn she is a psychotherapist," he laughed.

"Why are we having champagne so early in the day?" she questioned.

"Because it's Friday," he replied looking impish.

"What's so important about Friday for you?"

"The rabbis encourage love on Fridays," he smiled up at her.

Naomi could only smile and hold Collier's head closer to her breasts for she truly saw herself as Pandora for having received the touch of a divine hand.

"Raymond," she asked in a serious tone of voice, "do you like children?"

"Yes, my little chickadee," he replied, "boiled in oil."

The one-liner was from W.C. Fields and he recalled hearing it on television years ago. Why it came to mind, Collier was not sure.

"You are a redneck, Sonny," she murmured, hugging him tightly, giving him sweet kisses as her tongue gently glided within his lips.

Later as he stretched out his legs, Collier noticed the bed actually dwarfed the bedroom with its size. It was an obvious attempt at symbolism. In his mind, symbolism was but a thin, poor veil for sexual content for today's marketers. For some unexplained reason, he was reminded of a saying from the Sanhedrin: "If a man and a woman are truly lovers, they can make their bed on the edge of a sword; if their love goes bad, the best bed in the world is not enough."

# Chapter 32

The next morning after sleeping late from a sumptuous Sicilian dinner the night before on the terrace, Naomi was looking forward to a stroll in the Piazza IX Aprile in town. The hotel staff had adorned the terrace with flowers in a large ornate vase and with the palm, lemon and olive trees in bloom, the terrace was like a romantic tropical garden. Collier ordered up a typical Sicilian breakfast with espresso coffee, granites and brioches.

"Granites may seem like ice cream, but it's the way to go in this climate, especially after you have consumed a full course dinner the night before," Collier explained to Naomi as they sat on the terrace soaking up the morning sunlight and clean smell of fresh air driven by a friendly breeze from the bay.

"I like the granites, but the brioches are a little too hard for my taste as a cookie," she offered after sampling both.

"Well, the granite is crushed ice flavored with syrup, almonds, coffee or fruit mixed with water and some sugar. Sicilians stir and allow the mix to cool to make a dense granule. The brioches are simply cookies, cooked twice, thus the brittleness you find," he asserted while agreeing with her on the brioches.

"What is your pleasure today, love?" Collier asked, as if he didn't know. Like most women, she wanted to see what the latest retail shops had in store and have lunch.

"I thought we might visit the Piazza in town. I heard tourists on the plane commenting how beautiful the Piazza was in Taoromina this time of year as we were landing in Catania," she suggested cheerfully.

Collier himself was dressed casually in white pants, white cotton overshirt and light tan solar slip-ons. Naomi fetched her large raffia bag and hat to match. How she could get a hat that size in her luggage was a wonder to him. Locating his old, well-worn captain's white hat from his luggage, Collier announced he was ready. Slipping a multi-colored silk scarf around a strap on her bag, Naomi said she was ready as she surveyed the room and found her sunglasses.

On the way out Collier informed the concierge, an oily looking Sicilian at the front desk in the lobby that he was expecting a mail delivery and for him to make a special effort to see that it was delivered. The handsome concierge smiled his acknowledgment as he admired the American woman with Collier, thinking he would remember for sure.

The Piazza was, as Naomi predicted, the main social attraction in Taoromina this time of day. Plants were bursting into glorious color, the shaded walkways welcomed the tourist and visitors. A Dutch sailing ship was anchored in the harbor with its tall white sails billowing against the azure blue sky of the Ionian Sea. The Piazza offered elegant open-air bars and upscale shops to meet the needs of the most discriminate cosmopolitan shopper. The Church of San Giuseppe and the picturesque Corso Umberto complemented the scene with an arched entryway into the medieval town. Naomi was impressed with the Aragonese architectural style, the triumphal arch and lavishly decorated stuccos in the church.

As Collier sat at one of the outside tables covered with a bright blue tablecloth having a Sicilian cassata, Naomi shopped for a pair of sunglasses. Two attractive middle-aged women with Dutch accents approached him and called him captain. As he looked up to acknowledge the women, Naomi appeared from a shop nearby and glared at the two women. They quickly departed without another word.

"Those two women," he said, "mistook me for the captain of the Dutch sailing ship that we saw anchored in the harbor."

"I think not, I overheard them to say, 'Oh Captain, My Captain,'" Naomi snapped as she put her small package on the blue tablecloth.

It was the first time he had ever seen Naomi show any sign of jealousy in their relationship, and while he would like to have chided her, he thought better of it. He smartly opted to ignore her comment and asked if she was able to find a pair of sunglasses for him.

"Here," she offered pushing the small package towards him, acknowledging a twinge of jealousy to herself.

"Would you like a cassata?" he smiled at her to distract her from her thoughts. For he reminded himself of the advice one of the psychiatrists gave a young doctor at the hospital whose wife learned of his infidelity and was considering a divorce: "Go to the sporting goods store, buy a pair of knee pads, get down on your knees in front of your wife and pray that she takes you back." He was determined to never consciously make Naomi jealous as far as women were concerned. He knew his good fortune and felt like a blind hog that had found an acorn.

"What's that?" she replied more cheerfully.

"It's what the Sicilian's call melon jelly. I think you will like it."

"O.K.," she replied, "try on your sunglasses."

Waving to the waiter, Collier loudly ordered a cassata for his wife. Naomi noted his action and smiled to herself. Opening the small package Collier found a pair of black wire-framed sunglasses by Giorgio Armani. Slipping the sunglasses on over his eyes, they immediately block out the gamma rays and helped relieve his tension headache. As they walked arm in arm along the narrow walkways exploring the displays of ceramics, jewelry, clothing and art, the smell of bougainvilleas and jasmine petal wafted in the breeze and littered the sidewalks.

The Bay of Naxos and Mount Etna could be seen from Café Wunderbar where famous notables were said to have spent time. Collier and Naomi enjoyed a glass of wine and the concert in progress at the café. Later when Collier went to pay the check, the waiter, a Sicilian of many years, complimented Naomi and said she was the most beautiful woman to visit the Café Wunderbar since Elizabeth Taylor in her youth.

Collier steered Naomi to the Mocambo Bar where they had a better view of the bay and they enjoyed a ham and cheese sandwich on toast. For some strange reason, Naomi felt Collie was uncomfortable and she was sure the problems with his Jewish friend caused him concern. After lunch, Collier suggested they visit tour the Greek Theatre. The theatre was originally a place to stage plays and musical performances, but later gave way to gladiatorial contests, naval battles and hunting spectaculars involving blood sports. The panoramic view from the promontory was unlike any other in Collier's mind and the most beautiful place in the world based on his travels.

The concierge flagged Collier in the hotel lobby while they were waiting for the elevator to take them to their room and informed him that a delivery had just arrived for him. The concierge retrieved the package and Collier tipped him for his service.

Opening the package later in the room, Collier found identification papers for a David Kohl, a social security card, credit card, a Mississippi driver's license, birth certificate, library card, and a post office box in Hattiesburg, Mississippi.

"Naomi, I need to call Peter to tell him the package has arrived," he called out to her in the bathroom.

"Allright, I am going to take a hot bath, this Sicilian climate is something," she replied over the splashing of the water in the tub.

"Peter, this is Sonny, your package has arrived; I will be down in a minute to go over it with you," Collier commanded.

"That's good, I have been worried," he whispered.

As Collier stood next to the bathroom door, he could hear water splashing as Naomi was taking a hot bath. He wished he could join her now, but he had business. This thing with Peter was causing him some consternation. He wasn't worried about Peter as much as he was Naomi being caught up in this affair. Reservations had plagued him over his involvement in this whole affair. The mob was surely not likely to go easy on him because he now had personal concerns. They were strictly interested in recovering the money and nothing else. There was no turning back now, just play the string out and be as smart as he could. But innocent people like Osmond, Phillip and Lisa were involved in the affair and that was unfortunate.

"Naomi, I am going down the hall to see Peter. I will be back shortly," he called out to her through the bathroom door.

"O.K., don't you be gone too long," she crooned.

"I won't," he murmured wistfully.

While Peter did not look as anxious as before when he opened the door, he was still showing signs of fear in his eyes and that was good to Collier's thinking. We all need to be on our guard, he reasoned as he put the documents on the coffee table in front of the sofa for Peter to see. Amazed at the number and quality of the documents, Peter was inclined to want to go into the techniques of forgery and counterfeiting, but Collier headed him off with the admonition that the less you know, the better off you are. Privately, Collier was impressed with the forgeries. The signatures on the forged documents appeared as holographic with none of the characteristics commonly associated with forged signatures.

"Friends have been a great help in getting us feeder documents and that is all I say on the matter," Collier offered bluntly.

"I understand," Peter acknowledged, feeling chagrined because he knew that he was putting all their lives on the line.

"You need to review the documents, commit them to memory and use the hotel's computer to read up on the state politics in Mississippi, Hattiesburg, Lake Serene, and the Jewish community. Make yourself a representative member of the community," Collier ordered. "I am expecting a call from Marta tonight on you appointment for plastic surgery. Naomi and I will be leaving in the morning to return home. Use Marta's clinic phone to call me on my return if you need me. Marta will make arrangements for your new passport photo following your surgery. Otherwise it is best that we do not have any further communication. We need to limit our contact until you have undergone surgery and can meet me in Hattiesburg," Collier explained calmly.

"You know there is no way I can ever repay you, Sonny," Peter admitted, intentionally using Collier's new alias.

"Let's not worry about that, we can make this work if we hold together and follow through on our plans," he reiterated for effect.

"I know you are right, Sonny, and I will follow your instructions to the letter, for I have all the confidence in the world things will work out," Peter asserted firmly.

"That's the ticket," Collier smiled sounding like Phillip as he shook Peter's hand.

The locked clicked open to their room when Collier swiped the magnetic card to the suite. The door opened silently over the soft pile of the carpet. As Collier stepped inside the door, he instantly recognized a man, the concierge from the desk downstairs, standing with his back to him. The Sicilian sun from the terrace bathed him in brilliant light as he stood in front of the large table in the center of the room. *What's he doing here?* His pulse jumped when he saw the man and a chill ran down his spine as he feared for Naomi.

As he stole silently, moving forward, shortening the distance between himself and the man, he could smell his perfume. His hair reeked of oil. A ladies man in his off-white concierge coat, he was comfortable with young American women and their infidelities, especially the "porche-i-tutes," who married wealth and required his services while their husbands were deep sea fishing. Sicilians saw American women who liked to cuckold their husbands as "counterfeit whores" because they voiced dying ecstasies when beguiling and fanning their husband's feeble flame. European custom, on the other hand, favored marriage, family and children with mistresses for secret intrigues to satiate male lust.

Collier noted the concierge reaching inside his jacket, unaware of Collier's presence as he stood in front of the table.

"If your hand comes out with something other than five fingers, you are a dead man," Collier snapped, his voice ice cold.

The concierge turned with fear in his eyes, a handsome man by Sicilian standards, sculptured cheeks, wavy, jet-black hair that contrasted sharply with his neatly pressed white coat and dark slacks.

"I have a cable for you. I was informed you wanted your messages delivered as soon as they arrived," he said, his voice stammering.

He reached inside his top coat pocket and handed Collier the cable. Collier smiled provocatively as he took the cable.

"I was only kidding about killing you," he said pleasantly as he took the cable.

"One does not kid about a thing like that in Sicily," the concierge replied uneasily as he made a hasty departure, still shaken by the experience.

The cable was from Marta. Peter was scheduled for surgery at her clinic in Catania on Monday given the need for expediency. Collier phoned Peter the good news and wished him luck just as Naomi entered from the bedroom looking sweet and smelling fresher than the flowers that were changed daily at the hotel.

He decided not to describe for her the incident that just occurred. He was in need of a light repast of scrumptious large oysters on the half shell, shrimp, olive bread and a light beer. He would recommend the smoked tuna for Naomi, but for him Sicily was heaven on the half shell. Oysters were considered the best remedy to prevent a hangover and he planned to celebrate this night with his lovely bride on the terrace overlooking the crystalline turquoise Mediterranean Sea.

Long after Naomi had gone to sleep, Collier sat on the terrace, smoking a cigar while killing the last bottle of champagne in the mini-bar. With his planned surgery Monday, things seemed to be working out for Peter. Of course, he would need a recuperative period of rehabilitation before he could leave Sicily. While not subject to associating an elegiac intone for the past, he felt the need to simply sit and study his navel, a sure way to hell according to Buddha.

Since his first wife's death, he had devoted himself to his work and cut himself off from traditional social activities. Given his developing cynicism he saw groups, associations, conventions and people as well, as in terms of diagnostic psychiatric classifications—schizophrenics, manic-depressives, character disorders, addicts and neurotics.

His own trust in mankind was fractured by his observation of abuse and misuse of wealth and self-interest groups that had a hegemonic need to maintain control to foster their own personal aims and goals. While he realized that his outlook could be perceived as providential, he was like a rat departing a sinking ship. On the other hand, he had, through hard work, built an incredible life for himself, and no one could argue with his success.

What would the future hold for him and Naomi? A mixed marriage for sure, children, and a press for him to reconnect with the community at large. Likened to a comet, Naomi flashed through his life and brought two souls together. As he flicked a long gray ash into an ash tray on the table he was certain that Lake Serene would become their heart and soul in the future, where he and Naomi could live out the rest of their life in grace and peace.

# Chapter 33

"Telephone for you, Steve," his private secretary called out to him as he passed her desk on the way to his office. While Brenda Wilson was not unattractive, she was going on fifty-five years of age, a fact which was as closely guarded as the bank vault, because she appeared to be much younger and maintained a youthful appearance both in her dress and manner. Given to wearing scarves, she was called the "scarf lady" by some of the younger female tellers at the bank who were not above using their feminine wiles to succeed if the opportunity presented itself.

The turnover at the bank was high among the female tellers, since most of them wanted to take off early on Fridays and come in late on Mondays. It was a practice that the supervising loan officer permitted, especially if he had accompanied the female teller for a night out on the town over the weekend. Since his father was chairman of the board at the bank, his activities were overlooked by the bank president but not the hard-working loyal tellers who had to accommodate the situation.

"Steve Haralson here," he replied picking up the phone at his desk.

"Steve, it's Osmond, I have the papers on your puppy any time you want to come by the house."

Osmond's voice sounded soft and friendly to Steve. "Thank you, Osmond, I can come by after work, if that is convenient for you."

"We will expect you this afternoon and look forward to seeing you again," Osmond replied.

So accustomed to the sound of Steve's truck now, Heidi and Karras did not even offer a sentinel bark on his arrival. Osmond was there at the gate to meet him with a smile. The shepherds welcomed him with tails wagging as soon as he stepped out of the van, smelling his pants and his extended hand. Steve learned to extend his hand for them to sniff and they responded in kind with affection.

"I think they smell your puppy on you," Osmond smiled kindly as they shook hand and turned to walk to the house.

"I have the papers in the den," Osmond said as they reached the landing to the den. "Would you like something to drink?"

"Tea would be nice if you have it," Steve replied, feeling the need to accommodate Osmond, for he had grown to welcome his companionship.

"Tea it is then." He smiled. "The papers are on the coffee table for you to read while I serve us some tea."

"Have you heard anything from the newlyweds?" Steve called out to Osmond as he sat on the large oversize sofa reading the AKC forms. Osmond had already filled out the form for information required on the litter.

"Yes," Osmond replied from the kitchen, "they will fly in tomorrow on Naomi's private jet from New York."

Steve knew from his father that the newlyweds planned to spend a few days in London and then fly to Sicily before returning.

"Dad told me he married the couple here at the house," Steve offered as Osmond returned, setting down two tall large glasses of tea on the coffee table.

"Yes, since it was a mixed marriage, I think Naomi wanted a simple wedding here at the house. I understand it was a second marriage for both couples, so I think that played into the decision as well," Osmond confided. Steve observed that it was the first time that Osmond had ever addressed Ms. Selber as Naomi. Maybe it was easier for him than saying Naomi Randall, Steve speculated.

"What sort of man is he?" Steve asked directly because he did not feel Osmond would necessarily be offended by the question. No point beating around the bush, Steve thought, he might as well get the story now, for there would be considerable speculation and gossip on the lake regarding the newlyweds, especially since his father married them in a private wedding.

As he sipped his tea, Osmond smiled wryly at the question, for he was aware of the culture in the South and was not put-off by Steve's directness. It might be a blessing, since Steve was well-respected in the community.

"Well, I don't know everything," Osmond smiled to himself, "but what they tell me."

Osmond in his long life had learned to tell many tales about white folks. Having been born in the South, it was part of his cultural heritage. Negroes have always had a vested interest and curiosity about how white folks do things. Even thought the Negro may have no capacity by their station to change their circumstances, it was part of their education for good or bad in times past.

Sipping his sweet tea, Steve listened intently as Osmond spoke of his understanding of the relationship between Sonny Randall and Naomi Seller. "Naomi knew this Mr. Randall a long time, from what I gather, even before she knew Dr. Collier. He lived in New York City and worked for an import-export firm, traveling overseas a great deal in South America and the West Indies. Made good money from what I can tell. He and Naomi talked about retiring here on the lake with her giving up chairmanship of a large retail chain in New York. She would stay on the board in an advisory capacity for consultations and have corporate perks, like the corporate jet, at her disposal."

"I see," Steve replied on hearing the tale. "But what about the man, what's he like, Osmond?"

Steve was like a reporter to Osmond, he had to have the story. Of course, Osmond knew that in the South everyone had a story. It placed one in the community, not for good or evil necessarily, but knowledge and understanding that all could accept without fear or intimidation. "Bless his heart" or "the poor dear" could compensate for considerable misfortune, ill, or misadventures. But to lie or be caught in a lie was unpardonable for most of the people, even though the reformed sinner was always welcomed back into the community if one demonstrated reasonable penance and prayed for their sins to be forgiven by the Almighty.

"He is a Southerner by birth, likes to hunt and fish. Seems to have overcome his humble beginnings, appears to be conversant on most subjects and appears given to philosophizing at times. Nice looking, manly person, who seems capable of engaging himself in almost any situation. But most of all he appears totally devoted to making his wife happy," Osmond explained.

"Well, he sounds like the sort of man we can live with," Steve snapped, implying that he might have harbored some reservations until he knew more about the man.

Osmond was aware that Steve was loyal to the memory of Collier and that he personally liked Naomi from their brief contact. Given Steve's perceptiveness, Osmond was sure he would make a connection in time that R.C. Randall was in fact Raymond Collier. But only time would tell, he mused to himself.

"Mamie and I will be glad when they get back. We are getting tired of rattling around in this place by ourselves. Dr. Collier has a wonderful library and was an avid reader and book collector wherever he traveled. I still enjoy sitting up late reading and the shepherds keep me company," he laughed.

"My dad was really complimentary regarding Mr. Randall; he seemed to think he was a real gentleman," Steve offered, trying to lessen the loss of Dr. Collier. He was aware of how much Osmond cared for the man.

"Yes, as you say, he is a nice man and I think he will fit in well here. He seems happy with living on the lake. Mamie and I appreciate that, of course," he suggested.

"The boys are crazy about the pup," Steve said, wanting to change the subject.

"That's good. Boys need a pet to learn responsibility and accountability at an early age," Osmond observed.

Steve thought that was a pretty sage way to put it. He would have to remember that to Barbara later.

"Did you have a pet growing up, Osmond?" Steve asked.

"Yea, I had a pet pig. He was a pretty smart animal, too, went with me everywhere," he replied with a big grin from recalling his youth.

"What happened to him?" Steve could not help but ask.

"He grew up to be a big hog and my dad butchered him."

"Gee, that must have been terrible for you."

"It was, but it was the way of the world. Hard lessons learned early, like Future Farmers of America who raise livestock only to see the animals auctioned off to the highest bidder. Kids who grow up on a farm have experiences and knowledge far beyond their counterparts in the city from seeing nature at work," Osmond offered from his life experience with rural life in the Deep South.

"I guess I never thought about it that way," Steve replied.

"Farm kids know supply and demand, what it costs to raise wheat and what a loaf of bread sells for in the supermarket," Osmond snorted.

Steve liked Osmond. Osmond had a witticism about him that was uncommon for a Negro man in the South. He was painfully honest in some respects, maybe too much when it came to his own race. Not that he was disrespectful regarding his own race; it was just that he was so objective and not sensitive to criticism. He appeared to know who he was, what he was, and he did not have a need to be defensive or wear his feelings on his sleeve.

"How do your relatives feel about the race issue in the United States?" Steve felt compelled to ask.

"The question is probably too complex for me to answer for my relatives. I learned a long time ago that people in general have a view of race. In the North, to be specific, they accept the Negro race and not the individual, whereas in the South, they accept the individual and not the race," Osmond replied profoundly.

"I have never thought about that regard, but I can see the reasoning in your answer. Most Southerners truly have Negro friends because there is a common thread or understanding that goes beyond race. I hear my Northern friends talk of space when it comes to relationships and they seem hellbent to protect their space," Steve offered.

"That is mainly why I wanted to return to Mississippi. I wanted a simple life, a life where people understood me and I understood them. To go through life on the streets up North, for example, and never make human eye contact or let anyone enter your space seems to me to be a loss of humanity," Osmond replied grimly.

"I think you are right, Osmond. I see so many people enamored of wealth and power who are so unhappy in their relationships that they turn to drugs for solace of all things when they are the most successful," Steve acknowledged.

"Life is getting what you want and wanting what you get. The problem with today's youth is their need to resist exploitation, domination and neglect in our society. The basic single need for mankind is safety and it seems we are fearful of losing that," Osmond offered scornfully.

"I can tell you have spent some time in Dr. Collier's library. I don't know when I have had a more interesting discussion." Steve smiled. "But I need to get home; Barbara will be waiting for me."

Osmond smiled at the omission by Steve. He could see why Steve might be some type of receptor to the past for he was so basically honest.

"I am reminded that Naomi indicated that you and your family are welcomed to visit with us any time. As a matter of fact, it is my understanding that Naomi has invited Mr. Phillip Collin, Dr. Collier's solicitor in London and his family to visit here each summer. I understand they have two boys about the same age as your boys, so you may receive an invitation in the near future."

"The invitation would be welcome, Osmond," Steve smile appreciatively.

Because Barbara found Naomi to be such an intriguing woman, Steve knew she would be happy to continue their relationship with the Randalls.

# Chapter 34

As Naomi was packing, Collier told her he wanted one last word with Peter because he was concerned regarding his mental state.

"I will be right back, Naomi; I just want to reassure Peter," he said, stepping out into the hallway.

Peter's room was a dog leg down the hall. Collier noted the arrow 4230 pointing to the right. Just as he was turning the corner, he observed movement outside room 4236, the room he arranged for Peter for his safety. A young, pretty, dark-haired maid was talking to a man fronting her in the doorway. As the man leaned forward to whisper something to the maid, Collier recognized him as the same young concierge who delivered the cable to his room earlier in the day. The two stood for the briefest moment; the concierge stepped back into the room and closed the door behind him while the young maid took the elevator down to the lobby of the hotel.

Since Peter was not in his room, Collier was immediately suspicious. He must be downstairs in the restaurant having breakfast. Quickly Collier surmised the maid was to keep an eye on Peter while the young concierge went through his luggage for valuables. Apparently they suspected something with Peter occupying two rooms. What were they up to? Had the Mafia already picked up Peter's trail from the airport in London and tracked him to Taormina?

He was close to panic now, not for himself but for Naomi, for he could not bear the thought of her being hurt because of him. His face was reddening out of anger; he couldn't control his emotions as he stood outside the door. Using the magnetic card to unlock the door, he pushed the latch down quietly as he entered the room. The concierge was not in sight. Sounds of a suitcase being closed came from the bedroom. The bedroom door was partially open as Collier silently crept across the carpeted floor. The concierge could be seen with his back to Collier as he leaned over the suitcases on the bed. Apparently Peter had packed to leave by rental car for Catania for his surgery on Monday. As the concierge stood with his back to him, he was close enough for Collier to smell the aroma of his cologne.

"What's your game?" Collier growled angrily.

The young Italian concierge turned, his handsome face paled and grey-blue eyes widened in terror. His knees grew wobbly as he stepped back. The oversized bed pressed against the back of his legs. He felt trapped as panic began to take over. The color in his handsome faced drained as he read the grim expression on Collier's face. The man in front of him now looked mean and threatening

"I was only helping the gentleman pack," he replied, trying to use the patented smile he so often used for the wealthy ladies from America. From the look of the man's face, his eyes narrowing like slits, his nose reddening slightly, he knew he was not convincing.

"My ass, that's not what the maid said," Collier snapped scornfully.

Santo's life flashed before his eyes. What had he gotten

himself in for? He never thought it would come to this. What did Maria tell the man, and how much?

"I'm waiting," the man offered, looking menacingly.

Confused and scared, Santo instinctively tried to flee out of stark fear and panic. Lowering his head, he tried to use the bed as a springboard and race past the man before he could react. Anticipating his move, the man stepped aside and tripped him with his foot, sending him sprawling against the door frame of the bedroom. His head struck the door frame and his neck bent at an awkward angle and his body crumpled in a lifeless heap.

*My God, he's dead*, was Collier's first impression. He needed information. He didn't need a corpse on his hands, he thought ruefully as he looked at the young Italian on the floor in his white coat. Kneeling over the youth, Collier noted a pulse., Collier helped the young Italian to a hard back desk chair. With one hand, Collier held him in the chair and with the other, he untied the lace of one of the youth's shoes. Pulling his arms behind him, Collier tied the youth's thumbs together tightly with the shoe string.

Regaining consciousness, Santo felt the sting of his thumbs tied together as he sat in the chair and watched the man move about in the bathroom. He could hear the sound of running water and the rustle of plastic as the man moved about in the bathroom. *What was the man up to?* he wondered? Did he plan to kill him? The pain to his neck was excruciating now and his thumbs were swelling from being bound so tight.

The man returned with a glass of water in his hand and showered Santo's face with the water. The water felt good and caused Santo to regain a degree of consciousness. He sat across from him now looking mean and determined in one of the large stuffed oversized chairs.

"I will ask you one more time, what is your game?" the man demanded, his voice laden with anger.

"I don't know what you mean," Santo cried out, his voice

shaky and quivering from the emotional strain and the pain to his neck and head.

Casually and with no emotion, the man approached him and placed the plastic bag from the waste paper basket in the bathroom over his head. As the bag was being placed over his head, Santo now knew the man's intention. He was going to smother him to death. Blind now to things about him, Santo heard the sound of a curtain cord being ripped from the Venetian blinds. The cord was placed around his neck and over the bottom of the bag and drawn tightly. His body jerked horribly and twitched spasmodically as he was being slowly suffocated with the oxygen supply rapidly depleted. The pain in his thumbs was becoming unbearable as he struggled to fight off this horror.

Santo thought of his poor mother and father. They had been so proud of him because he had respectable work and was earning a good and honorable living. What would they think if he died like this? he thought as he began to lose consciousness. Again Santo felt a shower of water striking his face, causing him to regain consciousness slowly to things around him.

God, he was still alive, he thought after seeing the bright light of death old people talk about. The plastic bag and the curtain cord were neatly folded on one knee. The man sat across from him, his legs crossed one over the other casually, as he waited for him to regain consciousness. Santo was teary-eyed now; he had lost all resistance. What could be worse than this he thought? What if he man did know, what would he do with the information?

"What do you want to know?" Santo offered weakly, uncertain as to his future and willing to tell this man anything he wanted to know.

"What's your game?" the man asked scornfully. For he knew it would come to this, he could only wonder why the youth resisted for so long.

"What did Maria tell you?" Santo asked still negotiating.

"To hell with Maria," the man replied, showing his temper.

Santo realized that the man was becoming aggravated and would likely smother him to death if he did not give him the information he sought, and in a hurry. Santo never imagined that an American could be so cruel and brutal. Sicilians were capable of such brutality from years of occupation by foreign powers on the island of Sicily.

"Si, I will tell you," Santo offered weakly, for he had no more clay for the molding. Every man had his breaking point, and he had reached his. He would accept his fate as predetermined for his transgressions.

Santo poured out his and Maria's conspiracy to blackmail American and other tourists who visited Taormina. They systematically identified the home addresses of tourists and then mailed them incriminating pictures of their wives or husbands in compromising situations with either he or Maria. Most of the victims were willing to pay up as a price they had to pay for visiting a Mafia-controlled country. Since the victims would have a Mafia mindset, they could never be sure things might not get worse for them at home if they did not respond to the initial demand Santo suggested. If he had not been hurting so badly, Santo would have sworn he saw the slightest hint of a smile on the man's face as he told his story.

"What were you expecting to find in our rooms? We have no clandestine involvement with you or Maria since we have been here," Collier offered, trying not to appear too relieved at Santo's story.

"Maria questioned you asking for another room and she knew that another man was occupying the room. You made me suspicious that you had something to hide with the cable and your attitude. I knew you were not kidding at the time. So we decided to check out the rooms to see if there was an opportunity for blackmail. That's all, I swear," Santo said honestly, his dark eyes bulging with fear.

Thankful that their cover had not been exposed, Collier was

at a loss as to what to do next. He could not kill Maria and Santo to silence them, for they were innocent as far as his and Peter's situation was concerned. Collier knew that he would have to create such a fear in Santo's mind that he and Maria would never betray him or Peter.

"I am willing to let you and Maria live, conditionally," Collier offered as he untied Santo's thumbs. He wanted him free from pain for what he planned to explain to him. "That is, if you promise never to mention to anyone the names of the two people who rented rooms here at the hotel or the cable message. Do you understand?" he expressed emphatically.

"Si, Si," Santo replied with conviction.

"I have friends here in Sicily who will make you and your families pay if you do not. Are you aware of how they preserved the bodies of nuns in churches after they died in years past?"

"Si," Santo replied, wide-eyed.

"After the nuns passed away, the church let the blood drain out of their bodies within subterranean chambers or grottos within the church."

"Si," Santo replied, surprised that an American would have knowledge of such things.

"If you ever betray my trust, my friends will cut your hair, rouge your lips, dress you in a fine nun's habit and place your body in a subterranean chamber after they cut your throat. Your body will dry to the consistency of parchment in your religious habit as you slowly bleed out your last drop of blood. No Italian authority can intercede for it is the right of the church and we will offer the church a tribute for the privilege of giving you a holy burial to be interred within the chambers of the church." Collier slowly and patiently expressed his thoughts in an attempt to burn the image in Santo's mind, for Sicilians were prone to believe black propaganda and the curse of the evil eye.

Santo could not believe an American was capable of such horror. He sounded Sicilian with his monstrous tale. It was apparent to Santo that the man was well-connected and that he would be foolish to ever betray his trust. The fact that Maria and he were involved in a blackmailing scheme seemed to matter little to this man, which created some speculation in Santo's mind. It was a win-win situation in Santo's mind not to be exposed for criminal behavior in Sicily.

"I swear on my mother's grave that I will never betray you," Santo offered without being asked. Sweat beads broke out on his forehead and his face flushed.

"Good," Collier replied, "because I have friends here in Sicily and we will be returning from time to time. Any violation of our covenant will be reported to me and both you and Maria will pay the price. The choice is yours. It is my hope that you will have a long life."

"Si, you have my trust," Santo replied as he extended his hand. He was not a fool, he knew a bargain when he saw one.

While Collier had reservations concerning the covenant between him and the young concierge, he knew he had little choice but to trust him. Hopefully he had created sufficient fear and self-interest in the concierge's mind that he would maintain their secret.

Not wanting to cause Naomi any undo anxiety, Collier decided not to mention the confrontation with the young Italian on his return to their room. He found her still packing and informed her that he would need to meet with Peter before they departed Sicily. While he harbored concerns, Collier felt certain the concierge would keep his word given the possibility that he might lose his own life. He did not appear to be a career criminal, only a young man who saw a way to make easy money fleecing tourists who had questionable values and too much money.

"Peter is having breakfast now; I will call his room later and meet with him. We have plenty of time to catch our flight home," Collier assured Naomi. She had packed their suitcases like the good wife she had become.

"I will call room service and order breakfast for us on the terrace. It's such a beautiful day. We need to enjoy the view of Mazzero Bay and this Sicilian sun as long as we can," Collier crooned to her in the bedroom.

"That's wonderful darling. Can you order us an American-style breakfast?" Naomi muttered.

"Sure, how do you like your guinea eggs?" he said as he picked up the phone.

"You really do love your new role, Sonny," Naomi smiled mockingly.

"It comes naturally," he retorted kindly.

Naomi had finished her breakfast and was enjoying her fresh orange juice when Collier informed her that he needed to step down the hall to Peter's room. She acknowledged that she would soak up sun on the terrace and brush her teeth before they checked out of the hotel. Smiling to himself, Collier noted how domesticated they were becoming. For him it was a good feeling. He needed a sense of normalcy in his life and was looking forward to a simple life on Lake Serene. The incident with the young Italian was upsetting to him, but demonstrated how vulnerable Peter, Naomi and he were as far as their identity and personal safety were concerned.

"Pete, it's me, Sonny," he whispered as he knocked on the door to room 4236 later. As the door opened, Collier stepped inside quickly. Peter seemed more relaxed. His face, now burned by the Sicilian sun, made him look more youthful and in good health. Dressed casually, Peter wore a multi-colored shirt, white pants, and sandals.

"Are you homesteading?" Collier asked his friend to make him feel more comfortable and relaxed.

"When in Rome," Peter grinned broadly and did not finish the sentence.

Coming down the hall, Collier decided not to tell Peter of the incident in his room. It would only cause him anxiety. Better to keep the matter to himself, for the time being at least. Need-to-know situation, he thought. Scanning the room, Collier noted that the concierge had repaired the curtain cord and placed a new plastic bag over the waste paper basket in the bathroom. At least the young Italian was smart enough to cover his own tracks. That was a good sign in Collier's mind.

"Let's get down to business, Peter. Naomi is expecting me back soon, for we are packed and ready to leave," Collier said bluntly.

He noted Peter's brow wrinkle but there was no overt evidence of anxiousness. That was a good sign, he noted, as he sat across from him on the sofa. Collier wanted Peter to be relaxed and comfortable when he kept his appointment for surgery in Catania.

"You will meet an old friend of mine named Marta Sacco. She is competent and will perform the plastic surgery. Trust her and you will be alright," he commanded to reassure his friend. Peter sat quietly and heard Collier out. "Reservations have been made for you at the Katane Palace Hotel in the heart of the city. Here is the address of Dr. Sacco's clinic in Catania. She will be expecting you. Feel free to walk around the city like any other tourists after your surgery. Your rehabilitation should be of short duration, just guard against infection. You have your new identity papers and passports. You have my address in Mississippi. We will expect you in Mississippi in a couple of weeks," Collier ordered cheerfully.

"Thank you, Sonny, there is no way I can ever hope to repay you," Peter stammered softly, extending his hand to Collier.

"Just meet me in Mississippi," Collier replied, thankful that Peter remembered to call him Sonny. That was a good sign. It suggested to Collier that Peter was internalizing his identity and using it in personal conversation as a reinforcement cue. Peter was too fragile to learn that they had avoided another serious problem that might have jeopardized their security. He needed encouragement to just undergo plastic surgery. The idea of leaving the witness protection program was threatening enough, but fortunately Peter trusted Collier's judgment after the incident in London. He just wanted to bury the past now and the fact that he was the illegitimate son of a well-known mobster.

# Chapter 35

Peter boarded the bus in Toarmina for the 50 kilometer drive down Motorway A18 to Catania. While he considered a rental car, he realized that would leave audit tracks, but if he took a bus and paid cash, he would be just another anonymous tourist. His self-confidence buoyed now, he took a seat next to a middle-aged, refined-looking American woman. She had the look of a librarian with her small wire frame glasses and dark hair worn in a bun. As he took his seat, she smiled at him politely. It became apparent she was traveling with a Brown University charter group of noisy, ebullient students. They feverishly described their previous night's adventures to anyone who would listen as they boarded the charter bus.

"Good morning, Miss Claremont," a few of the coeds chimed in unison as they boarded the bus.

"Good morning, girls," she responded amicably with little vigor.

The students seemed to prefer the back of the bus, which was welcomed by Peter and Miss Claremont.

As the Sicilian bus driver pulled in a side mirror to make room for the bus to pass along a narrow winding passageway,

Peter's companion grew uncomfortable and felt the need to make conversation.

"Are you on your way back home, too?" She smiled at Peter. For some unexplained reason and without consciously thinking about the ramification, he pointed to his ears and signaled that he was deaf.

"Oh, my dear, I am so sorry." She blushed profusely and was genuinely apologetic. She turned away from him, so great was her embarrassment, and continued to stare out the window for the rest of the trip. While it might have been cruel and against his nature, he knew it was best given the circumstances. Until he had plastic surgery to change his looks and his passport altered, Peter felt it best that he not be identified or strike up conversations with strangers.

The bus was new and the driver aggressive as they made stops in Acireale and Giarre. Acireale was advertised by the station master as the most beautiful of carnival towns in Sicily. Sicilian workers could be seen preparing their wagons for the celebration. To Miss Claremont's chagrin, a few of the coeds at Brown experienced Mardi Gras in New Orleans and they took it upon themselves to describe their youthful misadventures in painful detail.

Giarre, a small town on the outskirts of Catania, was known for its antiques shops, clothing, ceramics and leather goods. The bus driver waved his arms and verbally threatened two coeds to leave if they did not get back on the charter bus. He vociferously charged that he had a schedule to keep and that he could not allow them to shop for goods no matter how reasonable they seemed for tourists.

When the party arrived in Catania, Peter tipped his straw hat out of courtesy to his companion. She smiled politely at the gesture. The bus station was located in the center of town, well within walking distance of the Katane Palace Hotel. Peter found the hotel was elegant and the architectural design pleasing. His room was large and well appointed with an oversize bed and padded headboard. The room was painted a deep yellow that glowed with the yellow lampshades and overhead lights. He noted the modern furnishing—mini-bar, satellite TV, modem jack and fax for the businessman.

Restless after unpacking his suitcase, Peter decided to take in the town. Nervous energy was working on him now, so he asked the concierge for directions to the markets. Catania was a populous town and well-known for its fish markets and handmade ceramic sunburst plates. He leisurely walked the baroque style Piazza del Doumoand and found that Catania was also noted for it production of jams and marmalades that were exported worldwide. The black elephant fountain caught his eye with its raised trunk as he strolled through the Piazza.

Peter marveled at the old churches and architectural designs from different periods. The Church of San Benedetto, an old Jesuit religious complex, was impressive. One could not but help marvel at the religious influence on Sicily and the wonderful architectural structures built by the masters. It's not an ill wind that doesn't blow some good, he reasoned, for if it had not been for the assassination attempt on his life, he would still be in London and would have never visited Sicily. Had he not taken a friend's advice to see a psychiatrist, he would still be imprisoned with his guilt and melancholy, notwithstanding the agonizing headaches he experienced from time to time. As for Collier, he owed his life to the man, a debt he could never repay in his mind. Strolling now without purpose, Peter realized he needed to get back to the hotel for lunch and a light nap later.

The next morning after a wonderful night's sleep on a full stomach from the excellent Sicilian cuisine served in the hotel's restaurant, Peter asked the concierge at the desk directions to a particular street without naming Marta Sacco's Clinic. He would check out of the hotel and walk to the clinic with luggage in hand, for when he left the clinic he would have a new identity and hopefully a new life.

He stopped at one of the sidewalk cafes and had a light

Sicilian breakfast and later strolled down the narrow passageways to the clinic. People were rising now for work. Small motor bikes were being towed out of doorways and alleys, large wooden shutters were being opened to let the early morning sunlight provide heat for floral pots that were set on the windowsills or attached to metal hangers on the wooden shutters.

The narrow passageway opened in to a large circular open space with a fountain in the center. Flower vases with brightly colored flowers lined the walkway and the office buildings were lined with balconies of ornamental iron work with large hanging baskets of flowers and vines. Peter noted a small brass plate that read "Sacco's Clinic" affixed to a large wooden door on one of the buildings. Depressing the heavy iron latch, he opened the large wooden frame door that entered into a small patio. A pergola was draped in ivy overhead and he could smell the aromatic lemon and fig trees. Peter followed the terra cotta walkway that led to another entryway with a smaller, brightly painted yellow door.

With some feelings of trepidation, he opened the door to the clinic and was met by a young Sicilian receptionist sitting at a desk in the foyer.

"My name is—" Peter muttered.

"Yes, we have been expecting you," the attractive receptionist interrupted him in a businesslike manner. "I see you have your luggage. Have a seat on the sofa and Dr. Sacco will see you shortly." She smiled.

Peter took a seat on the sofa, placing his suitcase next to his legs. He noted how modern and businesslike the clinic seemed by American standards. He smiled to himself at his ugly American bias, comparing everything to America, for his travel had already taught him that he had a lot to learn.

"Let me take your luggage to your room while you wait," the receptionist offered, taking the luggage in hand before he could respond. She closed the hallway door behind her, but Peter could see the clinic area and waiting rooms. Relaxed now, Peter took the time to observe the foyer and waiting area. He noticed an excellent painting of Mount Etna and pictures of the Sicilian sea coast and fishermen. Several works of Italian sculpture decorated the waiting room. Travel magazines of Sicily and Austria lined the table in front of the sofa. As Peter thumbed through a magazine featuring the Alps and famous ski resorts, the door opened, and an attractive dark-haired woman in a white coat greeted him.

"Peter, I am Marta Sacco," she said, extending her hand. Peter rose quickly and grasped her hand in a warm handshake. She lightly touched his arm with her other hand.

"I am glad to meet you, Dr. Sacco," Peter stammered.

"Call me Marta." She smiled broadly at his courtesy, while noting his Jewish features and gentle manner.

Marta Sacco was half Jewish and half German. Her mother was a Sephardic Jew who was married to an aristocratic German officer, Stephen Siears, who was on Field Marshal Erwin Pommel's staff in North Africa. Her mother was a great downhill skier. After WWII, she met her husband at a ski resort and continued to use her maiden name to compete in the Olympics in recognition of her Jewish heritage.

"Let us have a talk in my office, Peter, I am sure you have a lot of questions," Marta offered, taking him by the arm and escorting him to her private office down the hall.

Peter noted the white sterile wall and how clean the clinic appeared. The receptionist smiled as she passed Peter and Marta on her way to her desk in the foyer. He noted several medical technicians in white coats moving about down the hallway as they entered Dr. Sasso's office.

"Have a seat on the couch and let us talk," she said kindly, seating herself opposite him. She crossed her legs, revealing a black dress, black hose and high heel pumps. His eyes were drawn to her black stockings and slender legs and he felt uncomfortable in her presence. While not a beautiful woman,

Marta exuded a womanishness that attracted men, half mother and half mistress. Her dark black hair framed her face and her smile caused you to overlook the Semitic nose. Noting Peter's obvious discomfort, Marta tried to make him feel at ease by personalizing their relationship.

"Raymond has told me a great deal, Peter, and you can be assured of our confidence," Marta whispered.

"I owe my life to Raymond, I mean Sonny," he said in a strangled voice.

Marta smiled at the comment and replied, "I know, we will do everything we can to help you. Sonny gave me considerable instructions on how to assist you while you are in Catania," she offered, using Raymond's alias to make Peter feel more comfortable and to reinforce her own behavior, for she understood the serious consequences for all concerned. "Do you have any questions concerning plastic surgery?"

"How long will the operation last and how long will I have for recovery?" Peter asked, clearing his throat to compensate for his nervousness.

"Rhinoplasty is not involved surgery. It will take no longer than one to two hours, and we will perform the surgery here in the clinic. The surgery will be performed under general anesthetic. Following surgery you may feel tired for the first 48 hours. You will be asked not to blow your nose until we instruct you. You will have a nasal cast that we will remove after a week or two at most. There may be some swelling and discoloration that will clear in two to three weeks. Since we need a good photo of you for your passport, anticipate staying with us for three to six months depending on the swelling. I have an apartment for you here at the clinic. The main of my work is in Austria. I schedule special clients in Catania and use medical interns from the University of Catania to assist me," Marta patiently explained in detail.

"I see." Peter sighed to release the tension, for he had not anticipated staying so long in Sicily. But he could see that certain precautions had to be taken to assure his recovery while maintaining his identity and security. The idea of an apartment was a sound one. Marta seemed to not only be a dedicated professional, but a confidante he could trust to protect his identity.

"If you are ready, we will proceed with the surgery." Marta smiled, sensing his reservations, but feeling a need for expediency.

"I don't have any other questions; it seems I am in good hands," Peter replied weakly, for he had no other alternatives.

"Good, then let me change into my surgical gown, and we will get started," she replied touching his arm. Marta smiled at him confidently and used the intercom to inform the receptionist to escort the patient to the recovery room. Peter observed her movements and wondered about her relationship with Raymond, for she was a very attractive woman.

Peter noted, the surgical suite and the recovery room were state-of-the-art, immaculately clean and well-maintained. The technicians were young and bright and reviewed his post-operative care while they waited for the doctor. They assured him that they would attend his every need. Marta entered the surgical suite in her surgical gown and peered down at Peter stretched out on the surgical table under the overhead lights.

"Are we ready?" she asked, smiling down at him. Peter, mildly sedated, could only nod his head and force a smile.

Marta realized that she had not discussed with him any preference for reshaping his figure 6 nose which was commonly associated with the Jewish race. Of course she knew that was a myth. The Levantine nose, as it is called, is not universal among European Jews, but is commonly found among people in the Middle East.

"How do you want your nose to look?" she asked.

"Like Sonny's," Peter mumbled.

His answer caused Marta to smile. *Peter must have a great deal of confidence in Raymond Collier*, she mused as she nodded to the anesthesiologist and put her mask on. Marta recalled not going into a great deal in regards to Peter's situation with Raymond because she felt the need for confidentiality. While a medical record would be established for the patient, Marta planned to shred Peter's case file when he was discharged from the clinic. No medical or financial records would ever be recorded of the surgery. Marta assured Raymond that she would work the case off the books and that there would be no cost for the surgery. Marta would bear the expense based on their friendship with Raymond.

# Chapter 36

The routine nature of Peter's surgery caused Marta's thoughts to drift, like one driving the autobahn at 80 to 100 miles per hour, so straight and monotonous was the roadway. She was reminded of her first meeting with Raymond on the Swiss Alps. Marta was staying with her girlfriends at one of the traditional alpine ski lodges that attracted royalty and celebrities. The bars and restaurants were plentiful in the Alps. The stone and wood chalets offered luxurious apartments, exclusive shops, and recreational activities to suit the most adventuresome. Marta and her two girlfriends were skiing on one of the most challenging black slopes when Gretel Adler lost control and tumbled into a small alpine tree.

Gretel was a rich snob who coveted luxuries with the intensity of a jewel thief. Known for her rich and cultivated taste for expensive jewels, cars and dresses, Gretel lived off of symbols that created her personage in Austria, for she was regularly featured in Euro women's magazines for her face and figure. An entourage of sops promoted her parody all over Europe. Born of self-love and self-absorbed in her own vitality, she had no vocation or avocation. Euro magazines insinuated that she exuded sexuality in ever pore and that her figure could seduce a monk into obscene fantasies, so great was her ability to raise a luxuriant heat and sexual appetite.

When Gretel found herself lodged against an alpine tree in a snow drift, Collier was the first person to arrive on the scene to assist her. Marta and her girlfriend assisted Collier as he separated Gretel from her badly tangled skis.

"You have a broken foot," they heard the young man say on their arrival.

"Are you a doctor?" Gretel responded angrily. She was bitter because she felt she was too good a skier to have an accident.

"No, but I know a broken foot when I see one," he muttered gruffly.

The ski patrol arrived later and, after applying a box splint, whizzed Gretel to the lodge. Marta looked around to thank the young man but he had already joined his party to ski down the slope. Gretel's foot was x-rayed to reveal a fracture that would require titanium screws. Placed in a long-leg cast by medical staff, Gretel was advised to stay off her feet for two to four weeks. Determined not to ruin the ski vacation, Gretel decided to stay on at the ski lodge and "rough it" in the lounge. The three girls were partying with their friends days later, when Marta noticed Collier at a nearby table with two other young men.

"I am going to apologize to the young man," Marta told her friends.

"What do you have to apologize for? You just want to meet him because you think he is a young handsome American," Gretel snapped.

"Your hero," she stammered with disdain in her voice, scratching at her leg cast. For Gretel was not one accustomed to discomfort or being ignored.

Despite Gretel's protestation, Marta offered to buy the men a round of beer for their assistance. Smiling, the two men made excuses that they were just leaving, but that their friend was in need of another drink.

"What will you have?" Marta said, smiling, for she knew his friend departed in deference to him.

"A lager on tap, if you will join me," Collier replied, noting how friendly and attractive she was, dressed in her colorful alpine skiing sweater.

The two spent the next couple of hours talking about their interests and goals in life. Marta was studying to be a physician and Collier was working on a master's degree in psychology and working part-time at the ski lodge on the weekends to make money, while doing a practicum at the University of Vienna. He desired to study under Dr. Viktor Frankl to learn logotherapy, which postulated: A Will to Meaning.

"Es jock mich," Collier heard Gretel calling out from across the room. She was sitting with her leg propped straight out on an oversized foot stool.

"What's she saying?" Collier asked as Gretel vented her frustrations, for she was accustomed to being the center of attention everywhere she went in Austria.

"She wants me to scratch her leg," Marta replied, laughing at Gretel's predicament.

"Come on, let me introduce you," Marta said, taking Collier by the arm. The two joined Gretel with lagers in hand at her table.

"Gretel, this is Raymond Collier," Marta offered, smiling at her friend's predicament.

"I guess you see I got a second opinion?" Gretel quipped as she extended her hand to Collier. For Gretel, that was as close as she would ever come to an apology.

"So it seems," Collier replied warmly as he and Marta took a seat across from her.

"Where is Lena?" Marta asked.

"Oh, her boyfriend decided that he would come up and spend the rest of the week with us after all. He called her as soon as he checked in," she replied, smiling through pearly white teeth. Collier observed Gretel was an incredibly pretty girl who desired to hear out the story on people she first met who might become part of her entourage. She was taken with Collier for, unlike most men, he seemed indifferent to her, unlike the sycophants she was accustomed to meeting in Europe. Later Collier learned that it was part of her need for security and that Gretel's parents hired bodyguards to shadow her that would be a credit to the Secret Service in the States.

"I like you, Raymond Collier. I want to invite you to a party I am giving for some friends to celebrate my graduation from the university," Gretel offered as they sat chatting late into the evening.

Since Gretel and Marta were classmates from grade school, Marta was not one of her sops and for that, Gretel respected her. After they became friends, Collier had Marta agree to meet him at the university library so they could study together. Because some primary books on Freudian psychology were written in German, Collier had a need for an interpreter. Marta agreed to help Collier because he was so straightforward and direct relative to his intentions that he intrigued her. Their relationship allowed her the opportunity to learn about American culture from someone who was not considered an ugly American. Collier was accepted by Marta's youthful friends as well as older members of the family.

Gretel and Marta introduced Collier to elite Austrian culture. Since Vienna was the music capital of the world, he was invited to the famous opera ball attended by celebrities from all over the world. Both girls were great dancers and taught him the waltz and fox trots. They dressed him in traditional Austrian trachten suits and jackets. Hand-me-downs, they said, but Collier felt they were recently purchased.

While he was exposed to film festivals, concerts and pub crawling along the Danube Canal, Collier was also invited to parties in the 13th district, a fashionable garden suburb with splendid villas and summer residence of the wealthy. The atmosphere was all too heady for a youngster from rural Mississippi to comprehend, given the fact that America was such a young nation by comparison. Despite Europe's history and its wealth of culture, Collier knew it was the capitalistic system, technological advancements, and historical freedom's that made America great in the eyes of the world.

Years would past before Collier and Marta would see each other again because she became a successful plastic surgeon and he a psychotherapist in New York. Learning of Marta's clinic in Catania, years later Collier visited her there while on vacation in Italy and Sicily. They renewed their friendship and Collier learned of Marta's relationship with a shipping magnate in Catania. While he had proposed marriage, Marta had reservations since he was a widower with two teenage children, in addition to the fact that he was Catholic and she Jewish.

Marta recalled her conversation with Collier as they sat together in the Piazza del Doumo one evening enjoying the breeze from the Mediterranean.

"Tell me about him," Collier asked pointedly.

"Mario is a successful businessman here in Catania. He is well liked and involved in civic and community affairs. His two children adore him," she whispered.

"What about you, do the children like you?" Collier asked directly, observing her body language.

"Yes, they like me. Their mother has been deceased for some time now, and they seem well adjusted. Mario married his wife while they were young; they both came from wealthy parents who doted on the children."

"How old are the children?"

"Angelia is thirteen and Edmondo is twelve," she crooned.

"Do you and Carlos share things in common, or is he possessive?" Collier pressed her for details.

"We very much enjoy just being together and he is not the least bit possessive."

"Will he give you freedom to have a career?"

"Yes, he acknowledged that in his proposal," Marta muttered frankly.

"Would you consider him a friend if you were not married?"

"Yes, very much so," she replied smiling.

"Are you willing to raise the children in the Catholic religion?" Collier asked her.

He realized it was a practical question for consideration. Since the children were raised in the Catholic church, it would be unrealistic to ask them to change their faith in his mind.

"Yes, I knew that would be a consideration and I am willing to make the accommodation," Marta stammered, realizing that she was offering up reasons to get married.

"Do you love him?" Collier asked, putting his arm around her shoulder.

"Yes," she replied tearfully.

"Well?" Collier asked leaving the question open.

"What should I do?" she cried.

"I think you need to buy a lot of candles," Collier whispered kindly.

Marta laughed with tears steaming down her face. That was as close as Collier would ever come to giving her advice on marriage, for Marta realized how sensitive he was on the matter of marriage.

"Dr. Sacco, do you want us to close and bandage with the splint?" asked one of the medical students who was assisting. The question roused her from her intrusive thoughts.

"By all means," she replied, conscious now of her surroundings. She noted how well the surgery must have gone from the shape of Peter's nose.

# Chapter 37

The stewardess noted the handsome, sartorially dressed gentleman in a dark, handmade Italian suit. The silk tie alone would have made Countess Mara proud. She noted he was ticketed in first class as he boarded the overseas flight from Catania to the States. Carrying a book to read on the flight to pass the time away, he smiled politely to her and took his seat. Making himself comfortable, he folded his suit coat and stored it in the overhead compartment. Slipping off his Italian loafers, he sat in his stocking feet and rubbed his toes together.

A middle-aged female tourist later took the aisle seat next to him as the plane loaded for departure. She too had brought along a novel to read, by Jackie Collins. The two exchanged pleasantries before fastening their seat belts. As the lights dimmed to signal readiness for departure, the man turned to look out the window as the jumbo jet raced down the runway for take-off.

Smiling at the reflection, Peter took in his handsome features: silver grey hair and moustache, his face tanned from the Sicilian sun. Marta had even removed the wrinkles around his eyes and tightened the skin under his chin to give him a firm-looking jawline to go with his nose. While he was not a man given to vanity, Peter was appreciative of his looks and realized how differently people treated him after having his nose reshaped.

Marta spent considerable time with him talking in her apartment that was like Italianate grandeur to Peter. Mario, her husband, would join them occasionally and spoke highly of Collier. He acknowledged that he probably owed Collier for convincing Marta to marry him. While Mario gave Marta a simply band of gold on the day of their wedding, he later gave her an unmatched diamond that he called a flame of love. She seldom wore the diamond except on family occasions and parties in their home.

Marta was a wonderful woman and convinced him that his looks alone would not change his personality. He had to find a new personality within himself to improve his posture. He must carry his chin high to take the time to walk through life and not be self-conscious. During his rehabilitation, he observed the behavior of Italian men and their love for women of all shapes and sizes. Italians were passionate people who would kiss a stranger on the cheek as a form of introduction.

Most Italians lived a causal lifestyle and the young men seemed to sport a permanent tan, beaming smiles, and suave charm he noted as he sat in Piazza in the center of town following his surgery. Marta arranged for a new photo for his passport to establish his new identity while he was convalescing and made sure his identity papers were in order to travel internationally. Included in his portfolio of papers were business cards, and correspondence with some of Mario's business interests in Catania for him to carry with him on the plane.

"What a beautiful set of cufflinks," the lady next to him offered as she observed his white tailor-made shirt and rolled cuffs.

"Thank you, my dear, they are gifts from a dear friend in Catania." Peter smiled politely.

"I like to see a man who still dresses smartly." She grinned at his response.

Peter smiled to himself and thought it best to leave things a mystery. It would add some intrigue for his traveling companion to think about on the trip home and share with her lady friends in Saginaw, Michigan. She returned to reading her Jackie Collins book while he perused *The Golden Book of Taormina*. In his own mind, he would return to Taormina to experience the rich culture and its archeological and historical treasures.

The tedium of the flight wore on Peter. His thoughts turned to his own business interests as well as the trusts he established to operate drug rehabilitation centers. To his surprise, his rehabilitation program for drug addicts was becoming highly successful all around the country. His rehabilitation centers reported less recidivism than older, more established drug rehabilitation centers in the U.S.

The toughest nuts to crack, as far as heroin abuse, were the young Negro youths in the major cities where "speedballs" were the drug of choice. On Collier's advice, Peter instructed the rehabilitation centers to specifically target young, illegitimate, Negro males who were heroin addicts. Young illegitimate Negro males with their fear of inadequacy and weakness were driven to self-destructive an "acting out" behavior.

For one can only imagine what it must be like to not know from whence you come. To be perceived as an anonymous drop of smelly semen by some black walker in the neighborhood is a tragedy. Walkers in the South have indiscriminately serviced unmarried black women who have instinctual, maternal needs and vulnerable teenage girls in search of love and affection. The practice has served to raise poverty while creating a population of illegitimate Negro males who despise themselves and are made to feel worthless and shameful in the community.

Society's failure to deal with the pathological dynamics of the illegitimate Negro male has burdened and impacted the judicial and correctional system. An inordinate number of Negro males are being incarcerated every day as a consequence. Many a Negro youth has professed that he was in prison because of his mother, after acquiring knowledge of self and personality dynamics that drove his destructive behavior.

The key to success for juvenile addicts was to have them attend boot camps or ranches that specialize in residential treatment programs for troubled and rebellious adolescents, following discharge from drug rehabilitation centers. Counseling would determine a juvenile's need for placement in a camp or ranch. There was no better way to use the mob's money, in Peter's mind. But at the same time he was keenly aware of the need to maintain his identity secure, as well as Collier's.

After changing planes in Atlanta, Peter was finally on the last lap home. He was scheduled to arrive in Jackson, Mississippi, sometime around noon. The Delta flight was a "milk run" after having been on an overseas flight for some seven to eight hours. Just being stateside was a relief in some ways.

The squeal of the brakes awoke him later as the jet set down on the tarmac at Jackson International Airport.

Picking up a Jackson paper and a map of Mississippi in the small gift shop in the airport terminal, Peter noted an article in the paper on the Temple B'nai Israel in Hattiesburg. The synagogue, according to the paper, was having a reception for the new rabbi. The newspaper reported that the Hattiesburg Jewish community had roots that stretched back more than 100 years.

Collecting his luggage, Peter rented a car and looked for the shortest route to Hattiesburg from Jackson. As he neared Hattiesburg on Highway 49 South, he looked for a sign indicating the business district. The Temple B'nai Israel Synagogue was easy to locate for Peter after getting directions from a service station attendant across the street from the University of Southern Mississippi.

The synagogue was located in a shady subdivision off Main

Street near downtown Hattiesburg. While the rabbi was not available, a friendly secretary welcomed him to Mississippi and informed him that they had sixty members in the congregation. The small-town atmosphere appealed to Peter and he could see why Collier liked the people and the area.

Peter informed the secretary that he was in town on business as well as visiting friends but that he would be attending services while he was in town. The secretary was familiar with Lake Serene in Lamar County and gave him directions to South Lake Shore Drive, as it was on the highway to Columbia.

Peter located the property easily. He pressed the electronic button on the gate and heard two dogs barking off in the distance.

"Yes, what can I do for you?" he heard a voice say from inside the iron gates.

"I am a friend of Sonny Randall and would like to see him," Peter replied politely.

"Come in," the man offered cheerfully. The two men stood eyeing each other for a moment when the iron gate was swung opened. Two German shepherds sat on each side of the Negro man and made no move to interfere with Peter as he extended his hand in a friendly gesture.

"My name is Arthur Koln," Peter offered, using his new alias.

"Call me Osmond," the black man replied pleasantly as they shook hands warmly. The stranger was nattily dressed in a tailor-made Italian suit, with expensive shoes. His white shirt was loosened at the neck and he was not wearing a tie. While he was a handsome, distinguished looking man, he appeared tired and worn, like a man who had traveled far.

"May I pull my car in, Osmond?" he asked politely.

"Most certainly; this way," Osmond replied, motioning to one of the parking bays as he swung the iron gate wide to allow the rental car access.

Later, the two men walked together towards the lake house, the shepherds now sniffing at Peter's pants and handmade

Italian shoes. As they walked towards the house, Peter scratched the dogs' ears as they sought his attention.

"I am sure they are not accustomed to the smell," Peter muttered to Osmond as they walked.

"They have their own way of decoding smells," Osmond replied reflectively.

"It would be interesting if they could interpret for us. You know, the Russians at one time kept the smell of people for identification, like we keep fingerprints,"

"I did not know that," Osmond replied.

"Yes, they kept small tags of clothing with the owner's smell in glass jars in large underground storage bins for years until the Berlin Wall fell," Peter went on to say.

"I guess we never know what some governments are capable of," Osmond replied.

"That's for sure," Peter replied, smiling now, noting the beauty of the lake.

"What a beautiful view," Peter observed as he stood on the landing waiting for Osmond to announce his arrival.

"I don't know this man, Osmond," Collier mockingly cried out, standing in the doorway of the den in his stocking feet, dressed in a maroon pullover shirt and khaki pants. Grinning, Peter turned to confront his old friend. The two men hugged as Peter bussed Collier on the cheek in Italian fashion.

"My God, you have been in Sicily for too long," Collier jested as he held Peter at arm's length to review the transformation in his appearance.

"You look great, come on. I want Naomi to see you. We were just taking an afternoon nap," Collier muttered, taking Peter by the shoulder and escorting him into the den.

"Oh, I hope I didn't interrupt anything by not calling ahead," Peter blushed and apologized profusely.

"Heavens no, Naomi and I were just taking a little afternoon nap," Collier offered, smiling at the attitude of his friend.

"Look who's here, Naomi," he called out as they entered the den together.

Naomi entered from the bedroom, sleepy eyed, her dark black hair tousled now from napping. Barefooted, dressed in a long white pullover shirt and billowy white pants to match, she was as beautiful as ever to Peter.

"I'm so sorry to wake you from you sleep," Peter offered as Naomi approached him, smiling.

"Don't be silly, Collier has me sleeping my life away," she smiled, noting Peter's dark Sicilian tan, a handsome appearance.

Hugging Peter, Naomi whispered how wonderful he looked and so Sicilian. Collier saw that Osmond was taking in the scene before him and called out to him.

"Osmond, do you think we can plan an old-time hog killing and invite all our friends to visit for a Southern-style barbeque to meet Arthur?" Collier bellowed.

"I'm sure we can," Osmond replied, grinning at the prospect.

"That's a wonderful idea, Sonny. I want to invite Lisa, Phillip and the boys," Naomi chimed in.

"So be it. Osmond, get with Mamie and let us make plans," Collier instructed as he hugged both Peter and Naomi. Happy to see the return of the family lifestyle that once was, Osmond smiled, for he was already making plans in his mind for the barbeque.

www.ingramcontent.com/pod-product-compliance
Lightning Source LLC
Chambersburg PA
CBHW051148030726
47504CB00004B/1100